SHELTERING DUNES

Acclaim for Radclyffe's Fiction

2010 RWA/ FF&P Prism award winner *Secrets in the Stone* "is a strong, must read novel that will linger in the minds of readers long after the last page is turned."—*Just About Write*

Foreword Review Book of the Year finalist and IPPY silver medalist *Trauma Alert* "is hard to put down and it will sizzle in the reader's hands. The characters are hot, the sex scenes explicit and explosive, and the book is moved along by an interesting plot with well drawn secondary characters. The real star of this show is the attraction between the two characters, both of whom resist and then fall head over heels."—*Lambda Literary Reviews*

Lambda Literary Finalist *Best Lesbian Romance 2010* features "stories [that] are diverse in tone, style, and subject, making for more variety than in many, similar anthologies...well written, each containing a satisfying, surprising twist. Best Lesbian Romance series editor Radclyffe has assembled a respectable crop of 17 authors for this year's offering."—*Curve Magazine*

In **Benjamin Franklin Award finalist** *Desire by Starlight* "Radclyffe writes romance with such heart and her down-to-earth characters not only come to life but leap off the page until you feel like you know them. What Jenna and Gard feel for each other is not only a spark but an inferno and, as a reader, you will be washed away in this tumultuous romance until you can do nothing but succumb to it."—*Queer Magazine Online*

2010 Prism award winner and ForeWord Review Book of the Year Award finalist *Secrets in the Stone* is "so powerfully [written] that the worlds of these three women shimmer between reality and dreams...A strong, must read novel that will linger in the minds of readers long after the last page is turned."—*Just About Write*

Lambda Literary Award winner *Stolen Moments* "is a collection of steamy stories about women who just couldn't wait. It's sex when desire overrides reason, and it's incredibly hot!"—*On Our Backs*

Lambda Literary Award winner *Distant Shores, Silent Thunder* "weaves an intricate tapestry about passion and commitment between lovers. The story explores the fragile nature of trust and the sanctuary provided by loving relationships."—*Sapphic Reader*

By Radclyffe

Romances

Innocent Hearts

Promising Hearts

Love's Melody Lost

Love's Tender Warriors

Tomorrow's Promise

Love's Masquerade

shadowland

Passion's Bright Fury

Fated Love

Turn Back Time

When Dreams Tremble

The Lonely Hearts Club

Night Call

Secrets in the Stone

Desire by Starlight

Honor Series

Above All, Honor

Honor Bound

Love & Honor

Honor Guards

Honor Reclaimed

Honor Under Siege

Word of Honor

Justice Series

A Matter of Trust (prequel)

Shield of Justice

In Pursuit of Justice

Justice in the Shadows

Justice Served

Justice for All

The Provincetown Tales

Safe Harbor

Beyond the Breakwater

Distant Shores, Silent Thunder

Storms of Change

Winds of Fortune

Returning Tides

Sheltering Dunes

Visit us at www.boldstrokesbooks.com

SHELTERING DUNES

by

RADCLYﬀE

2011

This Trade Paperback Original Is Published By
Bold Strokes Books, Inc.
P.O. Box 249
Valley Falls, NY 12185

First Edition: November 2011

Credits
Editors: Ruth Sternglantz and Stacia Seaman
Production Design: Stacia Seaman
Cover Design by Sheri (graphicartist2020@hotmail.com)

Acknowledgments

Safe Harbor (the first in the Provincetown Tales) was one of the first books I wrote, and at the time, my intention was to write about a place I loved and populate it with characters I admired. I hoped to tell a love story filled with passion and healing. I wasn't thinking about archetypes, or the hero's journey, or any literary convention. I was thinking about what made a hero, and words like *honor*, *valor*, *bravery*, *dedication*, and *sacrifice* came to mind. I like to write lesbian heroes, because heroism is a daily part of queer life, whether we are serving our country and our fellow human beings, or living our lives, day by day, as honestly as we can, even as we demand our right to do so. Reese Conlon turned out to be an archetypal hero—the warrior chief whose attributes have not changed in centuries. She is not without weakness, or fear, or uncertainty, and she finds her strength as heroes often do, in a woman as strong as her.

When I wrote *Sheltering Dunes* (book seven), I wrote a different kind of hero than in many of my books. I usually write women of action because I believe women need to see themselves portrayed as being in charge, being leaders, being fearless, being capable and competent—because we are all those things. And of course, we are far more. In this book I had the opportunity to write a spiritual warrior, and Flynn Edwards has been one of my most satisfying characters to explore and develop. Like so many others in this series, Flynn came to Provincetown to leave her past behind and to search for her future. I hope you enjoy her journey and the unlikely love she finds, along with the return visits of other characters from the Provincetown and Justice series. Thank you all for continuing on the journey.

I'd like to thank my assistant, Sandy Lowe, for research support and the many ways she finds to free me to write; author Nell Stark for being an enthusiastic reader and a sensitive critic; Ruth Sternglantz for her tremendous job of editing this and all my novels; Stacia Seaman, who always brings a fresh eye and impeccable knowledge to the final edits; and my first readers Connie, Eva, Jenny, and Paula for support during the most difficult stage of all, the first draft.

And to Lee, who has weathered every storm, literally and figuratively, and still provides unwavering support—*Amo te.*

Radclyffe, 2011

To Lee
My shelter in a storm

CHAPTER ONE

Provincetown, MA

She couldn't be late on the third morning of a new job, not when the job was the only thing standing between her and everything she'd escaped. Pedaling the borrowed bicycle as fast as she could down the center of Commercial Street, weaving around parked delivery vans, early-morning coffee seekers, and dog walkers, she sped toward the restaurant at the far west end of town. Despite the chill coming off the harbor at six fifteen in the morning, sweat trickled down the center of her chest, dampening the pale blue tank top in a small circle directly between her breasts. Wisps of hair escaped the tie she'd carelessly wrapped around the thick waves at the back of her neck in her haste to leave the small, nearly airless room in the sprawling rooming house across the street from the harbor. One strand caught in the corner of her mouth, and she jerked her head, trying to dislodge it in the wind. Her heart beat a staccato rhythm against her rib cage. She couldn't lose this job. She had nowhere else to go. Here, she was safe, or as safe as she might ever be.

She glanced down at the thrift-shop watch, the hands moving far too quickly beneath the scratched crystal. Five minutes. She would make it just in time. Relief flooded through her like a tender word, unexpected and rare. She rocketed into the intersection of Standish and Commercial at the foot of MacMillan Wharf. A white van with black letters appeared like an apparition rising in a dream. She had one heart-stopping second to jerk the handlebars and swerve around the front grille, the screech of brakes and the blare of a horn piercing the early-morning stillness. The impact startled her more than anything else, and then she was airborne. The cool, damp air smelled of salt and seaweed, so different from the pungent odors of trash and broken dreams on the streets of the barrio.

❖

"Hey, Flynn," Dave called across the squad room, "are you going to play or not?"

Flynn closed her book, keeping her finger between the pages to hold her place, considering her answer. She'd been avoiding thinking about the Columbus Day weekend touch football fund-raiser for a week and a half. She ought to play. The game was a town tradition, the proceeds went to a number of community outreach programs, and she couldn't avoid seeing Allie in social situations forever. Other than brief encounters on the job, she hadn't seen Allie since the day Allie had been shot and Flynn had told Ash Walker that Allie needed her. Allie had needed Ash, not Flynn. No matter how much Flynn had wanted to be the one standing by Allie's bedside, had wanted to be the one Allie needed, she hadn't been Allie's choice. She'd never been Allie's choice. Allie had always been in love with Ash, and it hadn't taken Flynn more than seeing them together once to figure that out. So she'd walked away and Allie and Ash had worked out their issues, just like she'd known they would. She'd pretty much worked out her own too. She wasn't in love with Allie, not exactly. She might have been, if they'd seen each other a few more times. If they'd slept together, but they hadn't. Not quite. The spark had been there, the possibility had been there, but the timing had been wrong.

Flynn almost laughed. Timing seemed to be everything with her, and she had yet to get it right. She kept almost falling in love, only to discover she'd been too late or too love-struck to see there were problems, time after time. When she'd come here, changing the entire direction of her life, she'd hoped the pattern of her life would change as well. As if that were in her control. She knew it wasn't. Even if she hadn't believed that a greater plan, a greater power, was at work, she couldn't alter the road her life was destined to follow any more than she already had. She was done running. This was home and she was staying.

"I'll be there," Flynn called, because she couldn't change the facts. Not about Allie, not about herself, not about where she'd been or where she was going.

"Good." Dave tossed the damp rag he had used to polish the medic unit into a bucket. "I've seen you run and we need a fast cor—"

An alarm blared—the computerized dispatch system signaling a callout. Flynn dropped the book into the gear bag she carried everywhere when on duty, jumped up, and jogged into the vehicle bay. Dave was already climbing behind the wheel as she grabbed a radio. She dove into the passenger seat, stashed her bag on the floor, and buckled in as Dave roared out onto Shank Painter Road. He liked to drive, and she didn't mind riding shotgun. She slid the electronic tablet from the slot on the dash and pulled up the stats on the call. The details came up on her screen, relayed from the officer in the field to the emergency dispatcher who had entered the data into the system.

She read them out. "Standish and Commercial. Vehicle versus bicycle. Two injured. Police on scene."

"I still think the town oughtta close Commercial to vehicular traffic during the season," Dave muttered, swinging onto Bradford. "It's amazing we don't get more of these."

They were two minutes away, and Flynn quickly logged in the details on her tablet. "The next few weeks are going to be crazy, what with Women's Week coming up and then Fantasia right after that. Hopefully this isn't just the first of many."

Dave pulled in next to several police cruisers angled haphazardly across the four-way intersection, light bars strobing and radios squawking. Onlookers crowded the sidewalks and uniformed officers directed them back. One officer was taking a statement from the driver of a white catering van stalled in the center of the intersection, and two more flanked a person lying on the ground. Even from a distance, Allie was easily recognizable as one of the officers with the injured individual—her ebony hair, gathered in a twist at the back of her neck, and her statuesque body were impossible to miss.

"I'll check the pedestrian," Flynn said. "You clear the driver."

"Got it."

Flynn jumped down from the cab, unlocked the side compartment on the medic unit, and pulled out the red field-trauma kit. As she jogged over to the scene, Allie looked up, and the beauty of her dark soulful eyes was like a kick in the chest. Painful and exhilarating. Allie smiled and said hi with a hint of Southern drawl, and Flynn smiled back. No point in avoiding the truth. Allie was Allie, gorgeous and sexy without ever trying. Fate had made another decision for her, bringing her face-to-face with Allie's irresistible charm. Why fight it? Better just to let another piece of the past go, even if another part of her heart went with it.

"Hi, Allie." Flynn deposited her kit on the ground and squatted next to the victim, a young woman, who lay motionless on her back in the street. The woman, in jeans and a blue tank top, appeared to be in her early twenties, dark-haired, Hispanic maybe, with nutmeg skin, bold dark brows, a strong nose, and a wide, full-lipped mouth. Right now, her lips were pale and her coal-dark eyes unfocused and stunned. Flynn reached for her BP cuff and glanced at Allie. "What do we have?"

"She was on a bicycle," Allie said, "and she and the van over there met up in the middle of the intersection. According to the driver, he clipped the rear of the bike and she went over the handlebars. She was conscious when we arrived and moving all fours, but she's disoriented."

While Allie talked, Flynn wrapped the cuff around the young woman's right bicep, noting a tattoo of a heart with a knife thrust through it high up on her deltoid. She leaned over so the girl could see her face. "Hi. I'm Flynn, a paramedic. Can you tell me your name?"

The girl didn't answer.

Dave knelt down across from Flynn and smoothly slid a cervical collar around the young woman's neck, securing it with the Velcro tab. "Driver's okay. Shook up. How we doing over here?"

"Ninety over sixty," Flynn said as the digital readout on the blood pressure cuff settled. "Confused, but no apparent loss of consciousness." She tried again. "Hey, can you tell me your name? Do you remember what happened?"

The young woman muttered, "Mi—Mica. I'm Mica." She struggled, twisting from side to side, trying to get up. "I have to get to work. I'm going to be late."

"Don't try to move." Flynn rested her fingertips lightly against the girl's shoulder. Just that little bit of pressure was enough to keep her down. She set her stethoscope onto the bare skin of Mica's chest above the scooped neck of her tank top and listened to her heart and lungs. Everything sounded good, and she tossed the stethoscope back into her box. When she looked down, the girl's dark eyes were focused on her, clear but wary. "Can you tell me where you hurt?"

"Nowhere. I'm fine. I have to go." Mica looked past the blonde with the concerned gaze and gentle hands to the circle of uniformed officers surrounding her. A swell of panic flooded her throat. She couldn't afford to be hurt—she had no insurance and almost no money. Worse, she couldn't afford to be noticed, not by anyone, but especially not by the police. She needed to go to work. If she missed work, she could lose her job. Her boss hadn't wanted to hire anyone so late in the season, but she'd promised to stay all winter and work for partial wages if she had to. She needed the job. She needed to stay anonymous, unknown, unnoticed. She tried to pull the blood pressure cuff off her arm. "Please. I'm fine. I have to go."

"Whoa, take it easy." The paramedic—Flynn?—had a deep voice, calm but commanding. "You need to be checked out. We're going to transport you to the hospital in Hyannis."

"No!" The panic turned to terror. She'd worked so hard to disappear—she couldn't surface in the system now. "No! I'm fine. I don't want medical treatment."

"You've got a bump on your head," Flynn said, "and a scrape on your shoulder that need evaluation."

"I'm not going to any hospital." Details were coming back to her now—the wild bike ride, the white van in the intersection. The time. The time. She tried to turn her head to see what had happened to her landlady's bike. God, hopefully it wasn't trashed. She didn't have the money to replace it. "What time is it?"

Flynn frowned. "A little after six thirty."

"*Dios*, I have to go. I'm going to lose my job."

"You've been in an accident. It's not your fault. You're not going to lose your job because of it."

Anger replaced the terror. "You don't know that. You don't know anything about me." Mica pushed herself up. Her head swirled, and she swallowed back a wave of nausea. "You can't take me anywhere if I refuse."

"You're right," Flynn said, still sounding calm, still patient. "We can't. But you need to be examined." Her handsome face tightened in concentration. "How about if we take you to the local clinic. If the docs say you don't need to go to the hospital, we won't go."

"I can't," Mica exploded. "I'll lose my job."

"Okay, okay," Flynn said, gently squeezing Mica's arm. "How about this—tell me where you work. I'll call them myself and explain what happened. Will you come with us if I talk to your boss and make sure you're not going to lose your job?"

The other paramedic cleared his throat as if he was trying to interrupt or get Flynn's attention, but she ignored him, her eyes steady on Mica's. Something about the way she spoke, the way she looked, made Mica almost believe her, even though she knew better. People in authority said what they wanted you to believe and then did whatever they pleased. She knew better than to trust her. "Why should you care?"

"Why shouldn't I?" Flynn murmured softly.

Mica laughed, bitterness making her throat burn. "You don't know me. What do you want?"

"I want to be sure you're all right." Flynn's eyes, a crystalline blue, darkened like the storm clouds rolling in over the bay. "Look, I don't want to argue with you. I just want to take care of you. Let me and my partner take you to our unit and get you settled, and I'll stand right there and call your boss. You can listen to everything I'm saying."

One of the cops leaned down, a woman so beautiful she ought to be a model in some kind of magazine. "Flynn, we can take care of notifying her boss. Just get the information for us."

"No," Flynn said, still holding Mica's gaze. "I'll do it."

The cop sighed. "Ever the crusader." She squeezed Flynn's shoulder in a strangely intimate way, and Flynn's face changed for a second, as if the touch were painful.

"I want to talk to my boss," Mica said.

Flynn's mouth flickered and she smiled. "Are you always so stubborn?"

"None of your business."

"Fair enough. Dave, get the gurney." Flynn started to pack up her kit. "You got a deal. I'll call him, explain the situation. And you can talk to him after. Agreed?"

"Like I've got a choice?"

"You do have a choice," Flynn said seriously, as if she somehow knew that mattered. "I just want you to make a good one and not put yourself at risk, okay?"

Mica couldn't look into her eyes anymore. If she did, she might start believing this stranger really meant what she said, and she knew better. People didn't really care about each other, even when they were supposed to, but for sure not about an outsider. What did this stranger know about her, know about risk? She couldn't let herself be tricked into believing that anyone was going to care about her. It'd taken her long enough, but she'd learned. Now she knew better. The only person she was ever going to trust again was herself, even if it meant being alone for the rest of her life.

"Here we go," Dave said, positioning a backboard on the ground next to Mica.

Flynn said, "We're just going to slide you onto a backboard and then onto the stretcher so we can move you over to our unit. Let us do all the work. Just relax as much as you can."

"Just do it," Mica snapped.

"One, two, three," Flynn counted, and Mica felt herself being lifted with arms beneath her shoulders and legs. Then she was on the backboard and straps were tightened across her chest and pelvis, trapping her. She wanted to struggle. She wanted to tear the restraints away. She hated to be held down.

"Hey," Flynn said softly. "It's okay. We just don't want you to roll off. As soon as we get into the unit, I'll loosen the straps. Can you handle that?"

"Yeah, whatever." Mica struggled to calm her breathing, telling herself she wasn't a prisoner, these people weren't going to hurt her. Tears leaked from the corners of her eyes and she pretended they weren't there.

Then she was being rolled over the bumpy surface of the street to the yawning mouth of a medical van. Again she was lifted, and this time placed on a bench along one side of the van. She tried to raise her head again, wanting to find the blonde—Flynn. The panic wasn't so bad when she could see her.

Flynn pulled her cell phone from her belt. "Are you okay? I'm gonna climb out so I can get a good signal."

"Fine. Just get on with it already."

"What's the number?" After Mica reeled off a familiar-sounding number, Flynn hopped out of the unit and punched in the digits, trying to place the establishment. Ten seconds later, a man answered.

"Shoreline."

"This is Flynn Edwards, a paramedic here in town. One of your employees was in a traffic accident on her way to work. Mica." Flynn realized she didn't know the girl's last name.

"Christ," the guy said, "is she okay?"

"We're taking her to the clinic. She was worried about missing work. She doesn't want to go with us if she's going to lose her—"

"Tell her to get her butt over to the clinic and get checked out.

Have her call me later so I know when she'll be able to come back to work. I've gotta go call in a sub now—we're swamped. Big breakfast crowd."

"She wants to talk to you, but if there's no problem—"

The guy sighed. "Jesus. Just take her where you need to take her. Her job will be here when she gets back. I gotta go." And he hung up.

Flynn pocketed the phone and climbed into the back of the unit. She squatted down next to Mica. "He says your job is okay. He had to call someone in for you." She signaled Dave to go ahead and pulled the doors closed. "We'll be at the clinic in just a few minutes." She leaned forward into the front of the cab and grabbed her tablet. "What's your last name?"

The girl hesitated, and for a minute, Flynn thought she wasn't going to answer.

"Butler," the girl said finally.

Flynn filled it in. "Address?"

"606 Commercial."

"Is there someone you want me to call?"

When the silence grew heavy, Flynn shifted her gaze from the tablet to the girl on the stretcher. She was obviously in pain—her jaw was clenched and her eyes narrowed, as if holding back any sign of weakness. Her fingers were closed in tight fists. "Mica? Is there someone you want me to call for you?"

"No," Mica said in a flat, hollow voice. "No one."

CHAPTER TWO

Reese walked into the bathroom, a white fluffy towel in her hands, just as Tory stepped out of the shower.

"I thought you were feeding Reggie." Tory smiled, her eyes holding a question.

"I was." Reese pointed to the egg smear in the middle of her faded USMC T-shirt. "We finished everything, even the bananas, which we have suddenly decided are more fun to spit out than swallow."

Tory laughed. "Did *we* suddenly say why?"

"Oh yes." Reese nodded solemnly while holding up the bath sheet. "Yucky."

Still laughing, Tory turned so Reese could drape the towel around her shoulders. "Do I need to take over now and give her another bath?"

"Nope." Reese pulled Tory back against her chest. "Kate came early to get her. Reggie's off with Grandmoms and we're all alone."

"Really." Tory shivered slightly, pulling the towel more securely around her torso. "The shower's yours, then. I'll go get dressed."

"In a hurry to get rid of me?" Reese nuzzled Tory's damp auburn hair, inhaling the coconut vanilla scent that was so distinctly Tory. "When was the last time we were alone?"

"I don't remember," Tory murmured, arching her neck to give Reese better access. "But we have a plane to catch in an hour and a half."

"Mmm. Plenty of time."

"Darling, I'm going to get you all wet." Tory skimmed her mouth along the edge of Reese's jaw.

"I'm not complaining." Reese cradled Tory's breasts through the towel, gently caressing as she dried her. Tory tightened her butt into

Reese's crotch and Reese rumbled low in her throat. "That's no way to take my mind off how good you feel." She rubbed Tory's nipple through the soft cotton, her pulse soaring when the round peak hardened against her palm. She stroked lower over the damp bare skin of Tory's abdomen and feathered her fingers through the delta between Tory's thighs.

"Reese," Tory pressed her hand over Reese's, cupping herself with Reese's fingers, "the time. Our appointment with Wendy, remember?"

"I'm the sheriff. We won't get held up at the airport." Squeezing gently between Tory's legs, Reese nipped at Tory's earlobe. "We don't usually have morning time without the baby. I want to take advantage."

Tory spun in Reese's arms, wrapped an arm around Reese's neck, and let the towel fall to the floor. "I'd say you're taking advantage of me."

"Maybe so." Reese kissed Tory's throat and slid her fingers down Tory's belly and over the slick, hot folds between her thighs. "Maybe you should call a cop."

Tory opened her legs and tilted her hips, inviting Reese to enter. Her breath caught as Reese filled her. "I would," Tory gasped, slowly riding Reese's fingers up and down, "but I happen to know the sheriff is busy right now."

Reese pressed her cheek to Tory's, losing herself in the heat of Tory's body and the silken glide of skin over skin. Tory's quiet sighs of pleasure, the scratch of Tory's nails over the top of her hand as she thrust a little harder, a little deeper, eclipsed all concerns of planes, schedules, or any other obligation beyond making Tory come. This moment was everything. With Tory in her arms, with Tory holding her inside, she knew exactly who she was and where she belonged. "I love you."

"I love you," Tory said, her voice low and husky. "And you're going to make me come."

"I want you to. I need you to." Reese bit down gently at the base of Tory's neck, not hard enough to leave a mark, just hard enough to make Tory tighten around her inside.

"Oh God," Tory whispered, shuddering in Reese's arms.

Passion coated Reese's fingers. Firm hot muscles gripped, pulsing with life and power. Tory bucked in her arms, the thrust of her thigh stroking Reese's clitoris through the thin cotton of her boxers. Reese moaned against Tory's throat. "You make me so damn hot."

"Good." Tory jerked. "Oh damn, I'm going to come right now."

"You come for me, baby," Reese whispered. She backed up a step, pulling Tory with her, and leaned her ass against the counter so she wouldn't fall down. Nothing made her come harder or faster than Tory coming in her arms. Her hips spasmed. Close now. So damn close. She tried to keep her rhythm, wanting Tory to have everything she needed, but her mind was blurring, her control slipping. "I'm right with you."

Tory cried out, gripping Reese's wrist so hard she'd probably leave a bruise. Reese groaned, her thighs shaking, pleasure detonating in her depths.

"Oh my God," Tory murmured again, leaning bonelessly against Reese's chest. "I don't know how you do that to me."

"Do what?" Reese rested her chin on Tory's shoulder, breathing hard.

"Make me come like it's the first time, every time."

Reese chuckled. "Always feels like the best time, every time. Hell, my head is ringing."

"Darling," Tory muttered, dragging herself from Reese's embrace, "that's my phone."

"Any chance you can ignore it?" Reese grabbed a robe from the back of the door and handed it to Tory. "You're off today, remember?"

"I know, I know," Tory called as she rushed into the bedroom. "Hello? Dr. King."

Reese followed and leaned against the doorway. Across the room, Tory juggled her cell phone in one hand as she shrugged into the robe. Her hair was wet and tangled, her breasts flushed and still tight-nippled from her recent orgasm. Her shoulders and arms were muscled from her daily rowing, her toned abdomen slightly rounded, her thighs tight. She was beautiful. Looking at her made Reese's chest so full she could barely breathe.

"All right. I'll be right there." Tory tossed her phone onto the bed and gave Reese an apologetic smile. "I've got to make a stop at the clinic. Nita is busy with someone in heart failure and the paramedics are bringing in a trauma patient. I'm sorry. I'll be as quick as I can."

"That's okay. We'll catch a later flight." Reese strode to the closet and pulled out a button-down navy blue shirt. "We can call Wendy's office from the clinic."

"We could wait until next month," Tory said hesitantly.

"No, we can't." Reese stripped off her egg-stained T-shirt and tossed it toward the hamper on her way to Tory. She had been reluctant at first, worried and a lot scared. But Tory wanted this, and now, so did she. Grasping Tory's shoulders gently, she kissed her. "The thermometer says today is the day. We're going to Boston to make a baby."

Tory wrapped her arms around Reese's waist and pressed her face to Reese's chest. "Have I mentioned lately how much I love you?"

"I seem to recall something about that." Reese kissed the top of Tory's head. "I love you back. So, you ready to do this?"

"More than ready." Tory smiled. "Let's go take care of business."

❖

"You said you were going to take off the straps," Mica said, gripping the sides of the stretcher as the vehicle swayed around a corner and accelerated. She didn't really feel as if she was going to fly off the stretcher, but holding on to something made her feel more in control. Flynn squatted beside her, fiddling with the intravenous line she had inserted into Mica's right wrist. Her dark blond brows were drawn down in a frown, her lids—layered with long, thick blond lashes—curtained her eyes. She couldn't see Mica staring at her, so Mica stared. Flynn was good-looking in a crisp, Anglo kind of way—arched cheekbones, wide jaw, squarish chin with a tiny dent. Thin, narrow nose. She reminded Mica of the white girls who came from uptown to hang out in the rough bars of the barrio and flirt with dangerous boys. A couple of them had even flirted with dangerous girls. The first time a skinny redhead with perky breasts, bare midriff, and two-hundred-dollar jeans had flirted with her, offering to buy her a drink in exchange for a ride on Mica's motorcycle, Mica had laughed it off. She'd been afraid her homies would somehow sense the way her stomach twisted and she got all hot inside when the girl had smiled at her with just the tip of her soft pink tongue tracing over her full lower lip. Watching the redhead's tongue slide over the rosy surface, she'd gone liquid in places she never did when Hector touched her. She'd feared what Hector would do if he even suspected she enjoyed the Anglo girl's attention—less afraid for herself than for the girl. So she'd turned away, straddling Hector's lap at the bar instead, making a show of kissing him. But that night in the small alcove off the living room where she slept behind a blanket tacked to the archway, she'd thought about that redhead and her nipples had tingled and she'd gotten wet. When she woke in the morning, aroused and uncomfortable, she'd made herself come thinking about the redhead's tongue moving in slow motion over her pussy.

Flynn made her think of those rich girls with her clear, flawless skin and handsome face, but she was nothing like them, not really. Flynn looked at her with calm, certain eyes—eyes that asked for nothing. Those other girls had taunted and teased and flirted, all the while flaunting their privilege and fleeing back to their safe neighborhoods in their expensive cars as the night grew dark and perilous. She'd never slept with the redhead. She'd never slept with any of them. But she'd secretly wanted to.

"I never said I'd take the straps off, but I can loosen them," Flynn said, reaching for the buckle on the nylon belt across Mica's chest. She released that one, then the one across her hips. "Dave is a good driver, but I don't want you getting dumped on the floor. Is that better?"

Mica's tank had pulled up, and her bare stomach tingled where Flynn's fingers had brushed over her skin. No one had touched her in months, and those hands had been rough and hurried. Not careful and caring, like these.

Mica tried to turn her face away, afraid Flynn, with her piercing blue eyes, would see too much. "This thing on my neck is worse than the straps. Can you take it off?"

"I can't, I'm sorry. I think your neck is okay, but I don't want to take any chances until Dr. King clears you."

With every passing second, Mica's mind cleared and the churning in her midsection grew. She knew what these clinics were like—cold, impersonal, harried places where the sick and the injured were an inconvenience at best, targets for the frustrations and disappointments of others at worst. She would be sucked back in when she was so close to being free. What could she say to make Flynn let her go? "I can't pay."

"Do you have any insurance?"

Mica laughed mirthlessly. "Do I look like I have insurance? I can't pay for this. You're not helping me by forcing me to do this."

"I'm sorry. I don't want anything to happen to you. I'll talk to Dr. King. There are ways to—"

"No. I don't want you to talk to anybody. I'll take care of things," Mica snapped. The last thing she needed was someone else asking questions about her. "You've already made enough trouble."

"I'm sorry, you're right. I'm overstepping," Flynn said softly, and the concern in her voice softened the edges of Mica's anger.

"Never mind," Mica said. "You don't have to be sorry. I'll handle it."

"Okay. Whatever you want." Flynn squeezed her forearm lightly. "We'll get you checked out, you can call your boss, and Dr. King's office manager—Randy—can sort out the financial stuff."

Mica grimaced. As if anything could be that simple. "Sure. Whatever."

The ambulance slowed, made another turn, and crunched over gravel, finally stopping. The siren died with a lingering wail that echoed the ache in Mica's chest.

"We're here," Flynn said. "I'll stay as long as I can. If we get another call, I'll have to leave."

"I don't need you to stay. I'll be fine."

"I know you will," Flynn said.

The doors swung open, and bright sunlight streamed into the back of the ambulance. Mica blinked, tears blurred her vision, and a large dark shape loomed in the doorway. Hector! She jerked, her heart pounding erratically, and yanked at the straps imprisoning her. She must have made a sound, because Flynn gripped her shoulder.

"Hey, it's all right. Does something hurt?"

Mica wet her lips as the man climbed into the van. He might not hurt her right away, but if Flynn— His features became clearer. The other paramedic. Not Hector. Mica took a shuddering breath.

"Mica?" Flynn asked.

"Everything's fine."

Maybe if she said it enough times, it would one day be true.

CHAPTER THREE

The sky whirled dizzyingly over Mica's head as Flynn and the big man slid the stretcher out of the van. The collapsible legs clanked down with a jolt, and she bit her lip to keep from crying out. Her body shook as the paramedics maneuvered her across the uneven surface, stones crunching beneath the wheels with the snap of bones breaking. With her neck held immobilized by the wide stiff collar, her vision was limited, but if she tightened her belly and lifted her shoulders she could see a little bit in front of her. The first time she tried, the pounding in her head got worse but she felt less imprisoned, and that made the pain worth it. The second time, her stomach somersaulted. A police cruiser was parked next to the stone steps leading up to the door of a low-slung gray building that must be the clinic.

"Why are the cops here?" Mica wiggled her arm out from underneath the restraining straps and yanked on the buckle. "I didn't do anything. I'm not going in there."

"Hold up a second, Dave." Flynn hurriedly moved up the side of the stretcher until she was peering down at Mica. "What's wrong?"

"Nothing. Let me up."

"I'm going to release the straps," Flynn said, "but you have to promise—"

"Flynn," Dave said, his gravelly voice holding a warning.

"It's okay," Flynn said in his direction, her eyes asking for a promise Mica didn't want to make. "The straps are bothering her. She won't try to jump off."

Flynn said it as if she believed Mica wouldn't bolt. And Mica wasn't certain of that at all. Being questioned and probed by strange doctors was bad enough, but if the police were here, she'd have to run. Somehow.

"Don't make me do this," Mica whispered. She never asked anyone for anything, not even when silence only brought her more pain, but she asked Flynn. Maybe because Flynn let her search her eyes for a lie, a lie she couldn't find. The word was unfamiliar to her, but she said it anyhow. "Please. You don't know…"

Flynn leaned closer, so close a cool draft of mint and cedar drifted over Mica's face. "Whatever you're afraid is going to happen to you in there is not going to happen. No one is going to hurt you. I promise."

"You can't make that promise."

"Yes, I can. I know these people." Flynn lightly squeezed Mica's hand. "These doctors are great. You can trust them."

Mica tightened her lips, refusing to argue when the woman was obviously clueless. Flynn had no idea who she was or what she might have done. Why did Flynn just assume she was good, or innocent? What kind of person thought that way? "You're crazy."

Flynn smiled. "I've been told that before. But I'm harmless."

"Yeah, right." Mica tried to settle her breathing, tried to tamp down the panic. The more she protested, the more questions she was going to raise in people's minds. Maybe the best way not to draw attention to herself was just to go along with what had to be done. She could do this. She'd done harder things. She could lie her way through if she had to. She'd gotten away from tougher situations than this. One thing was for certain. She wasn't counting on Flynn or anyone else for help. And she didn't plan on trusting anyone. "Okay."

"No matter what happens," Flynn said, "it's going to be all right."

Mica didn't answer. She recognized a lie even if Flynn didn't.

❖

Philadelphia, PA

Hector Guzman stretched out his arm along the back of the sofa and punched in a number on his burn phone with his thumb while watching the girl kneeling between his legs suck on his cock. She was one of the new girls, paying her respects. She was fifteen, maybe sixteen, and as good with a knife as she was with her mouth, which was pretty damn good. She had all the moves—she knew what to do with her lips and her tongue and her hands—but his balls felt numb as ice. He ought to be feeling the tension about now, she'd been working him over for a good five minutes, but his hard dick might have been wood for real. He listened to the ringtone, frustration fueling his temper. He didn't need his cock to turn on him too. "Suck it, bitch."

"Yo, boss," his senior lieutenant Carmen said over the air.

Hector sighed inwardly. Maybe the diversion would get his cock back on track. "What's the word on the shipment?"

"Everything's set for the transfer tonight."

"Make sure we have plenty of backup. Tell them to get there early and hide well." He gripped the girl's black hair in his fist. Thick and long like Mia's, but not as soft. "I don't trust these Russians not to double-cross us."

"You got it, boss."

"What about the other thing?" As soon as Hector asked the question, Mia's face took shape in his mind. When he looked down, he didn't see the straining, tear-filled eyes of the young initiate, but the dark, fathomless eyes of the one woman he had never really owned. His ass tightened and pressure built in his balls. He gripped the back of the girl's head harder, forcing her mouth up and down his cock.

"Nothing for sure," Carmen said. "We'll find her, though. Our friends put out the word."

"Soon," Hector grunted, his hips rising and falling as he forced his cock in and out of the hot, wet throat. Mia. His woman. His. No one walked out on him. He twisted the silky hair in his fingers, felt his cock swell in Mia's mouth. She moaned, a desperate choking sound, and he came with a harsh groan. Pumping into the girl's throat, he growled, "Find her. The bitch is mine."

"Can you radio our twenty?" Flynn said as she and Dave maneuvered the stretcher into the empty clinic waiting room. Regular patient hours didn't start for another two hours. "I'll take her back."

"Got it," Dave said and went back outside.

Flynn braced her arms on either side of the stretcher and leaned over, looking down at Mica. "How are you feeling?"

"I've got a headache. A little one."

"Everything else feels okay?"

"It's kind of hard to tell, considering I can't move anything."

Flynn laughed softly as she guided the gurney down the hall on the far side of the vacant reception desk. "Good point."

The doors to the examining rooms on either side of the hall stood open, the tables covered with crisp white sheets, instrument trays gleaming. Flynn wheeled the stretcher into the treatment room and parked it next to the examining table in the middle of the bright, impersonal space. "I'll go find Dr. King."

"Wait." Mica grabbed Flynn's sleeve. "You're leaving?"

Flynn stopped, acutely aware of Mica's hand on her arm. Mica's tough façade had slipped a little bit, and a note of panic in her voice bled through her usual bravado. She was tough, defensive, obviously used to fending for herself and depending on no one, but she was also hurt and scared. Flynn was used to seeing people who were hurt and scared. Her job was about more than just rendering emergency care and transporting the sick and the injured. Part of what made the job satisfying for her was being able to ease some of that pain and suffering. All the same—her interactions with patients were limited, which was exactly what she wanted. She wasn't part of their lives. For a few critical moments in the midst of intense and often terrifying situations, she had the opportunity to make a difference, but there was very little chance for her to do any harm. And that mattered most of all. She'd found the distance she needed in this work, but she was having trouble maintaining the comfortable barriers with Mica. Mica's belligerent independence in the face of what had to be a frightening and painful experience tugged at Flynn's heart. She wanted to comfort her, despite all kinds of warning bells blaring in her head.

"I'm just going to find one of the docs," Flynn said. "I'll be right back."

Mica dropped Flynn's arm and her face took on a remote, shielded expression. "Whatever."

"I'll be right back." Flynn walked down the hall and glanced in the open door of Dr. King's office. Reese Conlon sat at the big oak desk, her feet propped on one corner, the chair tilted back, and her eyes closed. That explained the cruiser out front. The sheriff must've driven her wife to the clinic. Like all first responders, she could sleep anywhere. Flynn backed away.

"She's in with Nita in one."

"Thanks. Sorry to wake you."

Reese dropped her feet to the floor and sat forward, her blue eyes alert, as if she hadn't been asleep seconds before. "Anything I need to know?"

"I don't think so. Allie and Bri were on the scene." Flynn didn't see any need to tell her something felt off, not about the accident, but about Mica. Mica was scared out of proportion to what had happened. She was hiding something, but it was only a feeling. And for some reason, Flynn felt protective of her.

"Good enough." Reese leaned back and closed her eyes again.

Flynn walked back down the hall and tapped on the door to treatment room one. A few seconds later Tory King slipped out. Not that long ago, the doctor had been one of the patients Flynn had been called to see, and since then Flynn had regularly transported patients to the clinic. She liked and trusted both Tory King and Nita Burgoyne. "Hi, sorry to bother you, Doc. Just wanted to let you know I put the patient in two."

"What's the situation?" The dark green sweater Tory wore made her eyes even greener than usual, although right now they were dark with worry. The patient in one must be in trouble.

"She's stable." Flynn gave her a quick recap. "I can stay with her if you're busy right now."

Tory glanced at the closed door. "Nita is with Ned Framingham. Congestive heart failure—maybe secondary to an MI. He's going to need transport to Hyannis as soon as we get him stable. Can you take him or should we call for another unit?"

"I'll radio the base and tell them. We're already here."

"Great. Let me see to your patient, then."

"I told her I'd stick around," Flynn said, "if you don't mind."

Tory paused. "You know her?"

"No," Flynn said quickly. "She's just…She didn't want to come. I think she's kind of on her own. I sort of promised her…"

"Of course. As long as she's all right with you in the room, I'm fine with it." Tory smiled. "You're pretty good at this small-town stuff."

Flynn flushed. She didn't think anything was further from the truth. "Let me just advise dispatch of the pending transport and I'll be right in."

A few seconds later she slipped into the room and moved just close enough to the stretcher so Mica could see her. Tory bent over her, listening to her chest with her stethoscope. Mica was pale, her dark eyes wide, the pupils dilated. She looked like a frightened animal caught in a trap, and Flynn wanted to take her hand, to say something to soothe her. She put both hands in her pockets and smiled what she hoped was a confident smile. "How are you doing?"

"Just great," Mica muttered.

Tory straightened and gently removed the cervical collar. "Don't move your head. I'm just going to feel the back of your neck. Tell me if anything hurts."

"It doesn't," Mica said quickly.

"Good," Tory said mildly and continued her examination. "Any numbness or tingling in your arms or legs?"

"No."

"Vision problems?"

"No."

"Head hurt? And don't tell me no."

Mica sighed. "Some."

Tory smiled. "I'll bet. You've got a goose egg on your forehead, and you'll probably have a shiner by this afternoon."

"Yeah. Feels that way," Mica said, and Flynn had a feeling it wasn't the first black eye Mica had ever had. Her stomach tightened. She hated to see anyone in pain, psychic or physical, but Mica's pain and her obvious refusal to admit to it got to her more than usual. Maybe it was just Mica's stubborn insistence she was fine and could handle anything when she was so obviously hurt that touched her. Or maybe it was the way Mica had reached for her in an unguarded moment.

"Your shoulder is swollen," Tory said, "but I don't see any evidence of fracture. However, to be sure, I should x-ray you."

"No," Mica said quickly. "It's not broken. I know."

"You've had a fracture before?"

Mica averted her gaze. "A couple."

Flynn gritted her teeth. Mica was too familiar with trauma. The thought of someone hurting her made her insides burn. She stepped closer to the stretcher and gently clasped Mica's hand. "Maybe you should let the doctor check."

"Maybe you should lose your superhero cape too."

"And give up looking so cool?" Flynn smiled. "I don't think so."

"It's okay," Mica said, her face softening. "Really. I can tell."

Flynn rubbed her thumb over the top of Mica's hand. "Okay. You know best."

"I want to check your vital signs a few more times," Tory said. "If everything stays the same, you should be—"

"Tory!" Nita Burgoyne pushed open the door and called, "I need you. He's crashing."

"Damn," Tory murmured, and spun away.

Through the open door, Tory's and Nita's raised voices carried clearly. *Blood pressure's falling. Open the IV. Push the lidocaine...Is his wife here?...No. Charge the defibrillator...God, Tory, he asked me to call his minister. No time. Clear! No pulse.*

Flynn would've known what was happening in the other room even if she hadn't been a paramedic. But she was. That, and more. She crossed the hall and pushed open the door.

Tory glanced over at her, a question in her eyes.

"I'm a priest," Flynn said.

"Then come in," Tory said, starting chest compression. "We need you."

CHAPTER FOUR

S till no pulse." Nita Burgoyne, her eyes fixed on the EKG monitor, had her fingers over the femoral artery in the patient's groin. Her smooth mocha skin tightened at the corners of her mouth, drawing her lips into a narrow line, the only sign of strain in her elegant, composed features.

Flynn leaned over the head of the treatment table and looked down onto the face of the dying man. He might have been forty or eighty. Slight stubble darkened his slack jaw. Weather lines cratered his sunken cheeks. His skin was cool and gray, his eyelids closed and unmoving.

"Almighty God, look on this your servant, lying in great weakness…"

Tory pressed the heel of her hand to his sternum, delivering rapid compressions. "One, two, three, four…"

"…and comfort him with the promise of life everlasting…"

"Time?" Tory called.

"Four minutes," Nita replied. "You've got good perfusion here."

Though Flynn had no holy oil, the sacrament of Extreme Unction needed only her touch. She made the sign of the cross on the patient's forehead with her thumb.

"Nita?" Tory asked, her arms starting to tremble.

"From all evil, from all sin, from all tribulation…"

"Nothing," Nita said.

"…by the Coming of the Holy Spirit…"

Tory checked the clock. "Eight minutes. Come on, Ned."

"That it may please you to deliver the soul of your servant…" Flynn rested her fingertips on his hand and repeated the sign of the cross.

Reese said from the doorway, "Tory, you need me to take over?"

"...mercifully to pardon all his sins."

"Give us a second," Tory said, never breaking her motion. "Nita, anything?"

"Our Father who art..."

"Hold up," Nita said, "I think I've got something."

"...forgive us our trespasses..."

Tory leaned back and brushed her sleeve over her forehead. Sweat pooled in the hollow at the base of her throat.

"...lead us not into temptation..."

"Pulse is sixty. BP a hundred palp," Nita reported. "Nice going, Tor."

"...deliver us from Evil..."

"How's his rhythm?"

"...for Thine is the Kingdom..."

"Normal sinus. Occasional ectopy. His T-waves are flipped. Definitely an MI." Nita adjusted the IV drip. "He needs to be in a cardiac care unit."

"...and the glory, forever and ever..."

"Probably needs to be cathed and bypassed," Tory said. "Flynn?"

Flynn closed her eyes. *Amen.* She took a breath and keyed her radio. "Dave, we need a stretcher in here STAT."

Tory slowly climbed down from the stool she had been using to get proper leverage for chest compression. Her right leg seemed to fold and she lost her balance. Flynn reached to steady her, but Reese was there, unobtrusively cupping Tory's elbow.

"Got you," Reese said.

"Thanks," Tory murmured.

"All right?"

"Fine." Tory glanced at Reese. "Really."

The worry in Reese's eyes and the tender assurance from Tory stirred a bittersweet surge of longing in Flynn's chest. She averted her gaze, not wanting to intrude, needing to distance herself from desires that too often left her lonely and uncertain.

"Flynn," Reese said, "how about I get a cruiser over here to escort you up-Cape. Help clear traffic out."

"That would be great. Thanks."

The rattle of wheels and clank of metal signaled Dave's approach. Flynn detached the plastic IV bag from the metal pole at the end of the table, adjusted the drip to its lowest rate, and settled the bag on the sheet covering the patient's legs. Next she started transferring the EKG leads from the bedside monitor to the portable unit. "It will only take us a few minutes to get him ready."

Tory said, "Thanks, Flynn. For everything."

Heat suffused Flynn's face. She'd decided when she began her paramedic training program that the only skills she would use in the field were medical. Her job now wasn't to save souls, but to help save lives. Today had been an unexpected, unavoidable situation. She could no more *not* do what she had done than walk away from an accident victim in danger of dying for want of medical care. She appreciated that Tory didn't question her about anything. "You're welcome."

The patient opened his eyes, his pupils flickering unevenly, his gaze roving from face to face. With each second his expression became more confused and frightened. "What..."

"It's all right, Ned," Nita said quickly. "We're going to transfer you to the hospital in Hyannis. You may have had a heart attack, but you're doing okay now."

"Maggie?" he asked, his voice hoarse and uncertain.

"I tried to call your wife earlier and got her voice mail. I'll call her again," Nita said firmly. "Right now you just relax."

"What happened? I don't remember..."

"You had an irregular heartbeat, but we've got it under control."

"Am I going to die?"

"You had a rough patch, but you're very stable now." Nita smiled and squeezed his arm. "Dave and Flynn will take you to the hospital. They'll be in touch with us if there are any problems along the way."

"It's bad, isn't it?"

"It's serious," Nita said gently. "But I'm telling you the truth. You need to be in the hospital, but your chances of doing well are very good."

"I need to see my minister." Ned turned his head from side to side, looking anxiously from one face to another. "I need my phone. I need to call Father Williams."

Tory said, "I'll try to reach him and let him know where you are. But we can't really wait, Ned. I'm sorry. I want you in the hospital as quickly as possible."

"Please," Ned said, his voice rising. "I need—"

"Mr. Framingham," Flynn said, clasping his hand. His skin had warmed, and some of the color had returned to his face. The terrible stillness of almost-death had passed. "I'm a priest. I've given you last rites. Your minister will be able to see you later."

The shadows disappeared from Ned's eyes. "Thank you…do I call you Father?"

She smiled. "You can. Or Reverend. Or you can just call me Flynn."

"Father Flynn," he muttered and closed his eyes. "Thank you."

"Thank you, Flynn," Tory said again. "Now we really need to move him."

"We're on it." Flynn and Dave worked on opposite sides of the treatment table, silently performing their practiced routine of transferring patient, intravenous lines, catheters, and monitoring devices to the stretcher.

"I'll be across the hall," Tory said to Reese. "I have another patient to check, and then we can head to the airport."

"You're sure? Not too tired?"

Tory smiled. "Believe me, it will feel like a vacation."

"Can I come with you?" Flynn asked over her shoulder.

"Yes," Tory said.

"You got this, Dave?" Flynn asked. "I'll just be a second."

"Sure, go ahead. I'll finish up and give you a holler," Dave said.

Flynn followed Tory across the hall and into the treatment room where they'd left Mica. Stomach sinking, she stared at the empty treatment table.

"Maybe she went to the bathroom." Tory turned back to the hall.

"No," Flynn said, "she's gone."

"Well, damn it," Tory muttered, standing in the doorway of the treatment room with her hands on her hips.

"Trouble?" Reese joined them and slid her hand onto the back of Tory's neck.

"I don't know. My patient seems to have disappeared." Tory frowned and looked at Flynn. "Did you get the sense she was going to run?"

Flynn grimaced. "No, but I probably should have. She was reluctant to come at all, but I thought once she was here she'd be okay."

"Who was she?" Reese asked.

"A young girl who'd been knocked off her bicycle by a car," Tory said. "Did you check her ID, Flynn?"

"No. I just assumed the officers on scene did. She said her name was Mica Butler."

"Really? She didn't look like a Butler," Tory said.

Flynn grimaced. Mica's disappearance was accomplishing exactly what Mica seemed to want to avoid—attention. "Lots of reasons for that."

"You're right, of course," Tory said.

"And now she's just gone?" Reese scanned the hall. "Maybe she's still here somewhere."

"I don't think so," Tory said.

Dave pushed the gurney with Mr. Framingham out of the other treatment room. "Ready to roll, Flynn."

Flynn hesitated. "Will you let me know if you find her, Dr. King?"

Tory nodded. "I should probably check the bathroom, but I don't think she's in there."

"Thanks." Flynn grasped the end of the stretcher. "Okay, let's get Mr. Framingham to Hyannis."

Tory pushed open the door to the bathroom. "Empty."

"How much do you know about this girl?" Reese asked as she and Tory checked the other rooms. Mica was gone.

"Very little, really. I was just starting to evaluate her when Ned crashed." Tory collected her missing patient's chart and carried it back to her office. She sat behind her desk, and Reese settled on a chair in front of it. Tory scanned the intake sheets. "Flynn's field report doesn't indicate anything out of the ordinary. The girl was conscious upon initial evaluation. I don't have the first responder's report—that would've been filled out by your people."

"Let me find out who took the call." Reese pulled her cell from her front pocket. "Did you get the sense something else was going on with her, other than the accident itself?"

"As Flynn said, she seemed reluctant to be here. She wasn't very forthcoming with information, but that's not unusual with trauma patients. They're often confused or disoriented." Tory replayed the earlier scene in her mind. "There were a few things that bothered me. She seemed to be a little too familiar with physical injury. I didn't have a chance to talk to her about her past medical history."

"Domestic abuse?" Reese punched in a series of numbers. "Hey, Gladys. It's Reese. Can you run down who took the accident call a half hour ago and have them call me? Thanks."

"Abuse is certainly a possibility," Tory said. "But her reference to previous fractures and a black eye could have been due to an old trauma. I thought she was being uncommunicative as a result of today's accident. Obviously, I was wrong. What I took to be post-traumatic confusion was more…distrust."

"Or guilt?"

"Hmm. Maybe." Tory sighed. "If pushed, I'd say she was afraid of something. I wish I'd had more time to talk with her."

"Well, I trust your instincts. If you think something was off, then something was." Reese impatiently flipped her phone back and forth in her hand. "This town is a challenging place to keep safe. Most of the year keeping the peace is just a matter of dealing with medical emergencies, traffic accidents, missing kids, and the alcohol-related domestic problems that come with too few jobs and too much time. Then tourist season hits, the population swells by a magnitude of ten, and we've suddenly got a village crammed with itinerant workers, partying teenagers, and more sophisticated criminal types."

"You mean drugs and prostitution?"

Reese nodded. "And not just the homegrown back-room sex-for-sale variety either. Resort towns are starting to become targets for organized crime."

"I can't imagine this girl was involved in anything like that. She seemed more like a runaway, if I had to categorize her."

"Is she at risk physically as a result of the accident?"

"I don't think so—probably not. My initial exam didn't show anything of major concern. I wanted to observe her a while, and then Ned… I'm afraid I didn't do a very good job with her." Tory pushed the chart aside, checked her watch, and stood. "Damn it. We should go."

"Baby," Reese murmured, putting her arms around Tory's waist. "You had a guy dying across the hall. Cut yourself some slack here."

"I know." Tory leaned into Reese's embrace. "But just because someone isn't dying doesn't mean their need isn't just as great."

Reese kissed Tory and drew her closer. "Nobody in the world does this job better than you. Let me see what I can find out about her. Do you still want to go to Boston?"

Tory kissed Reese, absorbing the heat of her body and the surprising softness of her mouth compared to the hard strength of her arms. "Nothing is going to change the way I feel about having another baby with you. And I'm ready to get started."

❖

"You've been pretty quiet all shift," Dave said, stuffing his gear bag into his locker.

Flynn unbuttoned her uniform shirt, pulled it off, and folded it. She drew a plain white shirt from her locker, put it on over her navy T-shirt, and tucked it into her jeans. "Sorry. Not very good company, I guess."

Dave laughed. "Believe me, I'll take you over Barrymore any day. If I have to listen to him recite the latest baseball statistics for five more minutes, I might have to kill him."

"Yeah, and the World Series hasn't even started yet."

"Something's bugging you, though, right?"

"No." Flynn slammed her locker. She didn't want to talk about Mica.

"Uh—about the thing with Ned—what you did." He looked at her questioningly, his face creased with curiosity and maybe a little hurt.

Flynn held his gaze. "I'm a priest."

"Wow."

She smiled. "Not exactly."

He laughed and shook his head. "But you're not..." He looked uncertain. "Doing it...or whatever."

"No," Flynn said softly. "I'm not. I'll see you tomorrow, Dave."

His eyebrows rose, but he didn't ask anything else. "Sure thing."

Flynn headed outside and turned toward town, no destination in mind. She needed to walk off the agitation that had her nerves jangling all afternoon. She hadn't expected Mica to run. She'd misjudged her or underestimated what was really bothering her. Mica had been scared, she knew that, and worried about her job, but something more than that had made her run. But whatever trouble was chasing her wasn't Flynn's concern. She wasn't Mica's priest. She wasn't anyone's priest.

Chapter Five

Reese leaned both arms on the wooden deck railing behind the house and watched the Boston ferry skim into Provincetown Harbor, its running lights casting bright flickering tunnels across the inky surface of the water. A full moon rode high overhead, illuminating the beach with the brightness of daylight. In the swath of bushes that separated the house from the beach, silvery moonlight reflected off the eyes of some creature rummaging in the undergrowth for dinner. Damp night air thick with the sweet scent of kelp and the tang of sea life misted her cheeks. Her T-shirt stuck to her chest with a combination of salty air and sweat. Even though the night was humid, she didn't mind the dampness on her skin. After the desert, where the hot dry air evaporated every drop of moisture the instant it formed, leaving her eyes gritty and her skin sandpaper-parched, the dewy air was like a balm to burned flesh. She straightened at the sound of footsteps behind her.

"You've been awfully quiet tonight," Tory said, resting her hand in the center of Reese's back. She circled slowly, massaging the columns of muscles on either side of Reese's spine.

Reese turned away from the harbor, slid her arm around Tory's waist, and kissed her forehead. "Sorry."

"Don't be." Tory fiddled with a button on Reese's cotton shirt. "I'm not used to having you all to myself for a whole day. I'll get spoiled."

"Well, maybe we should try this again sometime, when we don't have to fly to Boston to be together."

Tory laughed and nipped at Reese's chin. "That's a novel suggestion."

"Do you think the little swimmers are ready yet?"

"Nicely thawed and ready for action."

Reese's breath caught in her chest. The thunder in her head was a mere fraction of the panic that had gripped her when she'd first contemplated another pregnancy. Since then she'd had time to think, time to be rational, time to appreciate what Tory needed. She steadied her breathing, quieted her pulse. Nothing should interfere with this moment, especially her fears. "I think we should head upstairs, then. We don't want to keep them waiting."

"In a minute." Tory settled into Reese's arms, looping her arms around Reese's hips and resting her chin on Reese's chest. "First, do you want to tell me what Wendy said this afternoon that's bothering you?"

Reese stroked Tory's hair. "What makes you think—"

"Don't even go there." Tory swayed, her hips notched comfortably into Reese's, their bodies fitting together seamlessly, as if they had always been two parts of one whole. "Ordinarily I'd wait, because I know you'll tell me when you're ready. But considering what's on the agenda for tonight, I think I'd better know first."

Reese sighed and rubbed her cheek on top of Tory's head. "Just now, I was thinking about the desert."

Tory stiffened infinitesimally and then relaxed again. "What about it?"

"I'm okay," Reese said, knowing Tory would immediately worry. She *was* okay. She'd been okay from the moment she'd climbed out of the transport that had brought her home and stepped into Tory's arms. Sure, she had nightmares, just like every other vet. She had regrets, guilt, and soul-deep remorse for the decisions she'd made that had led to the deaths of others. But she had been ready for the realities of war—she'd trained all her life for the sacrifice service demanded. She knew the price of war and that everyone—civilians and troops—paid, in one form or another. "Being here with you and Reggie is what gets me through every day."

Tory kissed her throat. "Me too. And I can't stand it when you're hurting."

"I'm not hurting." Reese stroked the thick silky tresses and absorbed the quiet strength she counted on every day. "Sometimes I try to imagine what my life would have been like if I'd never met you. If I didn't have you. If I didn't have Reggie."

Tory tightened her hold. "Why?"

"Maybe to figure out how I got so lucky. Maybe just to know what I need to do to be sure I never lose you."

"Oh, love," Tory murmured, pressing her mouth to the base of

Reese's throat. "I love you. You never need to worry about me not being here."

"You know what I see when I think about my life without you?"

Tory trembled. "What?"

"Nothing. Silent cold darkness."

"Darling, don't do this to yourself. If my having a baby is going to torture you this way—"

"No." Reese rubbed her hands up and down Tory's back. "It's not about another baby. It's about all the things I can't control. All the things that I can't guard against."

"You are a wonderful partner, an amazing mother, and a remarkable sheriff. You take care of all of us better than anyone I could ever imagine." Tory slid a hand between them and unbuttoned Reese's shirt. She parted the front, tugged Reese's T-shirt out of her pants, and pushed it up. She kissed Reese's chest in the valley between her breasts. "I love you. You're the most amazing, beautiful woman I've ever known."

Reese leaned back and gripped the railing with both hands. The cool night air teased across her nipples and they hardened. Her thighs trembled at the unexpected softness of Tory's mouth against her skin. "Tor. We're outside on the deck."

"It's dark and I don't care. You're mine, and I'll have you any way I want you, when I want you. And I want you right now."

Reese laughed. "You're not even pregnant yet. This is going to be fun."

Tory looked up, her eyes glittering. "You better believe it." She licked Reese's nipple until Reese groaned, toying with the opposite one at the same time.

"Tory." Reese's hips jerked, and she felt herself swell inside her jeans. "You know what you're doing to me, right?"

"Oh, I hope so."

Tory caressed Reese's belly and grasped the button on her jeans. "You didn't answer my question about what was bothering you."

"I don't like statistics. They don't mean anything when you're dealing with one person. Hearing there's a ninety percent chance you won't have the same problem you had the last time doesn't make me feel any better. Ten percent is way too high, Tor."

"I know. I agree." Tory rested her cheek on Reese's breast. "What else did you hear that's worrying you?"

"Women who have had preeclampsia are likely to have it a second time."

"That's true. But we're lucky—I work with a superb doctor every day. Nita will be watching me like a hawk over here, and I'll be seeing Wendy at least twice a month from the fourth month on. I promise." Tory popped the button on Reese's waistband and worked her way down to the next one. "And at the first sign of anything going wrong…" Tory dipped her fingers into Reese's briefs and pushed down, stopping just over her clitoris.

Reese sucked in a hard breath. "You can't promise—"

"Yes, I can. I know what I'm facing. I promise I won't let anything happen to me during this pregnancy. I won't put you through that again."

Reese held on to the railing so hard she was afraid she'd crack the boards. Her knees were wobbling. She was going to drop any second. "I need you."

Tory played her free hand up and down Reese's hard abdomen, then gripped the waistband of her jeans and tugged. "I know. I need you too. Right now I need you to be all mine."

"I'm always all yours." Reese grasped Tory's wrists before she lost all focus. "Let's go inside. Time to get the little swimmers on their way."

"Mmm." Tory leaned into Reese. "Rumor has it a well-timed orgasm will give them a running start."

"That can be arranged."

Tory laughed. Reese took her hand and walked out of the shadows into the safety of home.

❖

Flynn traveled west on Commercial, threading her way through the early-evening throngs. After Labor Day the tourist traffic cut down, but October was a popular month—the last gasp of Indian summer when the leaf peepers still flooded New England and the town geared up for Women's Week, one of the biggest events of the year. With Columbus Day weekend still a while away, most of the stores and restaurants were open and shoppers and sidewalk crawlers took advantage of the unseasonably warm early fall evening to stroll the streets. She slowed in front of the Shoreline restaurant. The plate glass windows were dark, and inside, chairs were piled on the small tables that filled the storefront. She knew Mica wouldn't be here—the restaurant, popular with locals and tourists alike, closed after a late lunch hour. Still, she had come to check, a bubble of expectation in her throat. And just as she had known, her anticipation was greeted with empty silence. The steeple clock at Town Hall chimed eight, and the unoccupied tables and chairs reminded her she hadn't eaten dinner. She didn't cook much, preferring to grab a sandwich or a piece of pizza after shift.

She turned and started back to the center of town. On impulse, she deviated down the board sidewalk to the Piper Bar. Midweek, off-season, the place was fairly deserted. A few locals sat at the bar, several couples swayed on the dance floor adjoining the rear deck, and a few others occupied tables around the edge of the room. One bartender worked the bar. Flynn slid onto a stool and waited.

"Help you?" A redhead in a tight black T-shirt with a sequined peacock over her breasts slapped a cocktail napkin in front of Flynn.

"A beer. Whatever dark you've got on draft."

"Sure thing."

The redhead turned away, and Flynn studied the napkin, remembering the last time she'd been here. She'd had a date with Allie. Their first date. They'd danced and walked home hand in hand. They'd kissed on her sofa, and the kisses had led to more. But Allie had stopped her when she might not have stopped herself, and that was unusual for her. She wasn't a go-all-the-way-on-the-first-date sort of person. But Allie had made it easy to forget who she was. Allie made it easy to forget a lot of things.

"Here you go. Three fifty." The bartender set a glass in the center of the white napkin, and a dark ring spread out around its base from water dripping down the sides of the glass. Flynn extracted a five from her wallet. "Keep the change."

"Thanks, hon." The bartender hesitated. "What's your name?"

"Flynn."

"I'm Marylou. You're new in town."

"Been here almost a month," Flynn said.

"Planning to stay?"

"Yes." Until she'd had the question put to her, Flynn had never actually considered her answer. But she was staying. Not because she had nowhere else to go, although her choices were somewhat limited. But this town beckoned to her. She felt at home here.

"Good to hear. I'll see you around, then."

"You will." Flynn pulled at her beer and watched the activity behind her reflected in the mirror over the bar. A door on the far side of the dance floor opened, and someone came through carrying a cardboard box of liquor. Flynn narrowed her eyes. She wasn't imagining things. Mica crossed to the bar and carried the box around behind it.

"Hey, Marylou," Mica said, "you want me to bring up a case of the Captain next? It looks like you're low."

"Why don't you just grab a couple of bottles," Marylou said as she pulled up a draft.

"Okay."

Mica set the box on the bar and started to stack the bottles into racks underneath. She worked quickly, as if she'd done the job before. Tory King had been right. Even in the dim, red-tinged light from the neon brewery signs hanging along the bar, the bruise around her left eye was apparent. She had the beginnings of a shiner that was probably going to be pretty dramatic in the morning.

Flynn slid down several bar stools, dragging her beer with her, until she was opposite Mica. "I would've thought you'd be too sore to work tonight."

Mica jumped, her eyes darting rapidly to Flynn before all expression fled her face. "I don't know what you're talking about."

"We met early this morning." Flynn lowered her voice. "When you had that accident on your bicycle."

"Yeah," Mica said, "I know who you are. Like I said then, I'm fine."

"Okay. I'm glad."

"I'll bet." Mica pulled the empty cardboard box off the bar and turned away, threading her way down to the opposite end, where she rapidly pushed her way through a door leading to the alley outside.

Flynn debated going after her and then decided whatever the reasons Mica had left the clinic, whatever demons chased her, were none of her business. She drained her beer and set it carefully onto the cocktail napkin.

"Buy you another?" Allie settled onto the stool next to Flynn. She wasn't in uniform now, and she looked young and fresh in a scooped-neck long-sleeved tee, hip-hugger jeans, and low-heeled boots. Her raven hair was loose around her shoulders.

"Hey," Flynn said, looking past Allie around the room. She didn't see Ash Walker anywhere. "How are you doing?"

"I'm good. What about you?"

"I'm good too. Shoulder okay?"

"It gets stiff now and then, but it's healed up."

"Good."

"So, how are *we* doing?"

Flynn smiled. "I think we're doing okay. How are things with Ash?"

Allie smiled, the kind of smile a woman in love smiles. "You know we had a past, right? Before I went out with you."

"Yeah, I figured that from some of the things Ash told me. And—well, the way you looked at her. You couldn't see anyone else."

Allie blushed, a rare sight. "Jeez—uncool of me. Okay, well, I'm sorry about the way things turned out with us—"

"No, there's nothing to be sorry for. We had a couple of really terrific dates. And I'm really glad for you."

"You're really scary nice, you know?"

"No, I'm not, but I can still be happy for you."

"Someday you'll have to tell me why you think you don't deserve it too."

Flynn frowned. "Deserve what?"

"Happiness."

CHAPTER SIX

Reese leaned on her elbow, slowly stroking Tory's abdomen. Tory's face glowed in the muted light, a softness about her eyes that pulled at Reese's heart. "You look beautiful right now. How do you feel?"

Tory turned on her side, keeping her hips slightly elevated on the pillow underneath her lower back, and kissed Reese. "I feel wonderful. How are you?"

"Sort of"—Reese lightly kissed Tory's breast above her heart and took a deep breath—"in awe, I guess. I like doing it this way, better than in the office." She rested her cheek between Tory's breasts and wrapped her arm around Tory's middle, melding the lengths of their bodies. "When I think about Reggie, and what a miracle she is, and that you did that—you created her for us." Reese's throat closed and she shut her eyes tightly, the surge of wonder warring with the rush of terror that always came over her when she thought about how precious Tory and Reggie were.

Tory's fingers came into her hair, gently stroking the back of her neck. "You know, none of this would be possible without you. You create the certainty in my life, the safety in our home, the promise of our future. You give me the strength to take this all on. I couldn't do this without you."

"I love you," Reese whispered.

"Oh, darling, I love you too." Tory nestled closer, grasping Reese's free hand and guiding it over her abdomen and between her legs. "Remember the part about giving the swimmers a helping hand?"

Reese's hips tightened and heat kindled in her belly. She raised her head and found herself in Tory's eyes. "Oh, I remember." Watching

Tory's face, she slowly stroked over the delicate folds and lightly caressed her clitoris.

"Mmm, that's good. You're so good." Tory wrapped her arm around Reese's shoulders and raised her hips further. Breathing more quickly, she pressed her hand over Reese's, guiding her fingers to the sensitive spot that always made her come. "As much as I love it when you tease me, I don't want to wait."

"You feel so soft, so warm," Reese murmured, continuing to tease, refusing to speed up and stroke harder where she knew Tory needed her. "Sure you can't wait?"

Tory nipped at Reese's chin. "Damn you. You know what I need. Right now." She skimmed down Reese's back and kneaded her ass. "I want you to come with me."

"Do you." Reese slid her legs over Tory's, pressing her center to Tory's smooth, firm thigh. She was throbbing, aching, her clitoris pulsating urgently. She almost always came when Tory did—she couldn't hold on when Tory was so totally hers. "I'm yours, you know. You'll make me come with you."

"Yes, yes, yes. Do it now. God, I love you."

Tory buried her face in the curve of Reese's shoulder as her hips rose and fell to the perfect cadence of Reese's strokes. "Now, you're making me come now. God. So good."

Reese tightened her grip and held Tory close, never letting up as Tory's hips bucked and she cried out, a breathtaking peal of joy and fulfillment. Shuddering on the edge, Reese struggled to keep her eyes open, wanting to see every second, wanting nothing in her mind, in her body, in her soul except Tory and the promise of life to come.

❖

Mica ripped the cardboard box apart, flattened it with her foot, and stacked it with the others next to the Dumpster in the alley. Ten thirty. She still had another half hour to work. Maybe when she went back inside, Flynn would be gone. She didn't want to see her questioning eyes or hear her soft, too-understanding voice. The quiet tenderness in her tone was too hard to ignore. Yeah, right—and too damn misleading. Mica grabbed another box and pulled it apart. Flynn had no reason to care about how she was feeling—even though it was a different kind of come-on than the girls who had tried to pick her up usually used. Pretty freakin' effective too. Maybe if they'd pretended to pay a little more attention to her, had looked at her like Flynn did—like she was really *there*—and spent less time being worried about how sexy they were, she might have tumbled to one of their invitations. She was glad she hadn't. She'd made enough mistakes getting hooked up with Hector, but what choice had she had back then, anyhow? Just sixteen, needing to fit in, needing some protection from the men and boys in the neighborhood who were eyeing her like prime territory to be claimed, needing the support of the girls who were so different from her but the only friends she had. And later she had family to think of—family to protect. She had to join the 13, and the way to join was by hooking up with a guy. Lucky for her, Hector had claimed her right away, and she hadn't had to be passed around from guy to guy the way a lot of the new girls were. Lucky for her too that Hector had other women, had kids with other women, and he hadn't pushed her to have one for him. Lucky, yeah right. That was her—lucky, all right. The weight of Hector's body pressing down on her, smothering her, drove her breath from her chest and she gasped. The relentless choking pressure of him driving into her throat made her gag. Her head spun, and she grabbed the side of the metal bin for support. Not now, God, not now. Her heart galloped and spots danced before her eyes, even in the dark.

A crunching sound at the mouth of the alley grated over her skin, and she jumped, sucking in air, her chest heaving. Someone approached in the shadows, slow heavy footsteps, cautious, searching. Searching for her maybe? She expected them to come, even though with each passing day she started to hope they wouldn't. She'd seen what happened to other girls who tried to get out of the life. They always came back, either on their own or on the end of someone's chain. Hard to break free when all you'd ever known was the gang, when the only ones who'd ever taken care of you—even though you paid a price—were others just like you. Others who understood the laws of the street—you paid in flesh to survive, whether you were a woman or a man. The men paid with blood, the women paid with their bodies. Everyone paid with their souls. She'd run when she had nothing left to give and she couldn't pretend anymore not to see what Hector was doing. She'd waited too long, and now she knew too much.

Easing back toward the closed door of the club, Mica kept to the shadows, willing herself to be swallowed by the dark. Reaching behind her, she felt along the cold steel door for the handle, desperate to be quiet, desperate to disappear. Sweat broke out on her forehead and ran down her face. Her stomach curdled and fear settled deep in her pelvis. She wouldn't let them take her. She'd rather die than go back. She gripped the slick knob and turned it. The metallic click ricocheted around the narrow alley, louder than a gunshot. She froze.

A deep male voice grunted, "Hey. Where you going, baby?"

She shoved the door open with her shoulder and practically fell into the haven of the bar. She slammed the door, spun around, and scanned for an escape route. The red lights over the bar, glaring like the light bars on cop cars, hit her in the face and blinded her. Unable to focus, she scrubbed at her eyes. Which way to run? Out the back, onto the deck, and down to the beach? She might be able to hide under the piers or make it to a dark alley. Or across the dance floor and out the front door? Still plenty of people around this time of night—maybe she could hide in plain sight. She couldn't stay here—if that was Hector's man out there he wouldn't care who got in his way. You didn't run from Hector and you didn't return empty-handed. She raced around the end of the bar and skirted across the nearly empty dance floor toward the exit. If she got out to the street before he did, she might just be able to blend into the crowd.

"Hey!" Marylou called. "Hey, Mica? Where you—"

Flynn stepped into her path. "Mica? What's the matter?" Flynn extended a hand as if to touch her, but dropped it and fell in next to her, hurrying to keep up. "Are you all right?"

"Go away," Mica said. "Don't touch me."

"I won't. I promise. Just tell me—what's wrong?"

Mica looked back over her shoulder. The door to the alley remained closed. There was no lock on it. If he'd wanted her, he would've come in. Maybe she was safer inside. Maybe he was just waiting for her to come out. She stopped just inside the door, next to the stool where the bouncer sat on the weekends. She peered through the open door and didn't see anyone on the sidewalk outside. Panting, she pushed her hair out of her face. "Nothing. Nothing is wrong. Go away."

"Look, you don't have to tell me anything, okay? I'm not asking any questions." Flynn backed up a step, as if knowing Mica needed space. "Just tell me one thing. Are you safe?"

Mica stared. She was so used to being physically dominated, the small gesture calmed her, but she wouldn't be fooled by kindness. "What the hell are you talking about?"

"I know something's wrong. You wouldn't have run out of the clinic this morning otherwise."

"I already told you." Mica pulled her defenses back around her.

With every second that passed and no one came for her, the panic subsided. "I don't have any money, I didn't want to go there in the first place. It's as simple as that."

Flynn nodded. "Okay."

Mica narrowed her eyes. "Just like that?"

"Why not?"

Maybe because you don't look stupid, and you should know everybody lies? Mica put her hands on her hips. "What planet do you come from?"

Flynn smiled. "New Hampshire?"

Mica laughed. "Maybe that explains it."

"Explains what?"

"Never mind. I have to get back to work."

"I thought you worked at Shoreline."

"I do. In the morning. I work here at night." Mica headed back to the bar and Flynn followed. The brunette who had joined Flynn earlier was still sitting at the bar, watching them. Mica hated being watched. She stopped and glared at Flynn. "What do you want now?"

"Another beer?"

Flynn smiled, and man, she was beautiful when she did. Even in the partial light, her eyes were unbelievably blue. Deep and dark and really sexy. Mica remembered watching her that morning, leaning over the man on the table in the room across the hall. Flynn's face had been so intense, as if what she was doing was the only thing that mattered in the world. As if that man was the only person who mattered. The way she'd touched him had been so gentle, but so powerful. Mica heard the words again—*Our Father who art in heaven*—remembered them from long ago, the sound echoing in the silent vastness of the church. Words that she learned meant nothing, maybe even worse than nothing. Lies, about tenderness and love and salvation. Watching Flynn with that dying man made her wonder for one fractured second if there wasn't some tiny flicker of good that still flared somewhere in the world. She snorted at her own stupidity. Start thinking that way and you'd end up under someone's boot. Or worse.

"Who are you, exactly?"

"My name is Flynn."

"Yeah, I remember you telling me. But that's not what I meant. I saw you this morning, with the guy across the hall." Mica scowled. "What are you?"

Flynn's jaw tightened. "I'm a priest."

"Yeah? You can be one? When you're a woman, I mean?"

"Yes."

"So how come you're riding around on an ambulance?"

"That's a long story."

"Huh. A priest with secrets?"

"Something like that," Flynn said.

"So you ought to know questions can be dangerous."

"Silence can be worse."

"Sounds like a line."

"It's not a line. I don't want anything from you."

Mica stopped, searched Flynn's face. "That's bull. Everyone wants something."

"Do you?"

Mica thought about the long walk home. About the man in the alley. About Hector's long reach. Maybe being alone wasn't so smart—at least tonight. If the crazy priest or whatever she really was wanted to stick around, having someone to walk her home might be a good idea. "Yeah. Yeah, I do."

"What?"

"I want you to have another beer, and then maybe I'll let you walk me home."

Flynn hesitated, then nodded. "I can do that."

Flynn's gaze never moved from Mica's eyes, but Mica felt as if a hand swept over her body, caressing her. That was nuts, but her nipples tightened and her pussy clenched all the same. Flynn might be harder to string along than the girls she'd learned to play for the money they'd spend on her while trying to get into her pants, but she knew how to keep her secrets safe. She was good at that.

CHAPTER SEVEN

Flynn settled back onto the bar stool and pushed her half-finished beer away. The dark brew looked flat and empty.

"Want another one?" Allie asked.

"No. I think I'm done for the night."

"Some kind of problem there?" Allie asked quietly, tilting her chin slightly toward Mica, who was sliding glasses onto narrow racks above the far end of the bar.

"No," Flynn said, "no problem." It seemed like she was saying that to a lot of people where Mica was concerned. A niggling sensation in the back of her mind warned her she was making a mistake, but she pushed the kernel of foreboding away. She didn't know anything about Mica—good or bad. All she knew was Mica was running from something—ghosts, maybe, and there was no crime in that. She should know. Her own ghosts were only a few footsteps behind her.

"She's cute," Allie observed.

Flynn grinned. Allie was one of those gorgeous women who exuded sex, drew other women's attention like a magnet, and lustily appreciated the sexual allure of females. Apparently being in a relationship didn't squelch her natural instincts, and no reason that it should. "She is."

"Why does she look familiar?"

Flynn hesitated. She didn't want to hurt Mica, and as fun and casual as Allie seemed in her off-duty hours, there was much more to her than her sexy, playgirl side. She was a smart and serious cop. On the other hand, Flynn had no reason to protect Mica. As far as she knew, Mica didn't need protection and the urge to offer it was only her own issues at work. "She's the girl on the bicycle who was hit by that van this morning."

"Right," Allie said, her gaze following Mica as she worked. "I really thought she was hurt. I'm glad to see she's all right."

"Yeah, me too."

"I should tell her we've got her bike at the station. It's pretty banged up. I don't think she's going to be able to ride it until she gets a new wheel and the frame straightened out."

"She's lucky," Flynn said, thinking how easily the broken and twisted frame could have been Mica's body. The image, one she'd seen over and over again on calls, brought a wave of acid rolling through her stomach. She didn't want to think of Mica as one of those victims. As any kind of victim. "I'm sure she'll be glad to get it back."

"I'll go tell her."

Allie sauntered the length of the bar, and Flynn watched Mica as Allie approached. Her shoulders tightened, she put down the glass she'd been holding, and she flicked a rapid glance at the door behind her. She was ready to run if she had to. The evidence was unmistakable if you knew what to look for. And if Flynn could see it, so could Allie.

Flynn couldn't hear the conversation, but when Allie turned away and headed back, a fleeting look of relief passed over Mica's face. Mica glanced down the bar, and when she saw Flynn watching, her expression became stony and her eyes defiant. Daring Flynn to read her. Maybe daring Flynn to care.

She shouldn't care. She should know better. Mica was nothing like Debbie. Debbie had been lost, desperately seeking solid ground, searching for direction, and Flynn had been there to guide her. That's what she'd thought she was doing—giving support and guidance. Exactly as she had been led to believe was her mission. Somewhere she'd failed to hear the true story behind Debbie's fears. Failed to recognize the terror that plagued her. Failed Debbie. And now, was she simply seeking redemption with a woman who didn't need saving and who would never give her absolution?

"You know her very well?" Allie leaned against the bar, her thigh just touching Flynn's, her body blocking Flynn's view of Mica.

"Not really," Flynn said, easing away from the contact. At the end of the bar, Mica continued to work.

"Huh. Looked like you did—when you were talking earlier."

"Just met her this morning."

"Okay. Well, have you decided to play ball for the fund-raiser?" Allie asked.

Happy for the reprieve, Flynn turned partway on the stool and focused on Allie. Her eyes were beautiful, and sharply appraising. Flynn wondered what she saw. "Yes, I'll be there."

"Good. I'm captaining the red team. I could use a good running back."

"That's what Dave said. What makes you think I can run?"

Allie grinned. "Baby, you're built for it."

Flynn laughed. She loved that Allie could always make her laugh. "So you say. I'll be proud to wear the red, Captain."

Ali squeezed Flynn's shoulder. "Good. I'm going to head home. Ash is supposed to call."

"Tell her I said hi," Flynn said, finding it hurt less to say this time.

Allie smiled. "Thanks. I will."

Flynn turned back to the bar and Mica stepped in front of her.

"Girlfriend?" Mica asked, a note of disdain in her voice.

"No. Friend."

"I thought priests weren't supposed to lie?"

"I'm not. She's got a girlfriend."

"You're pretty good at sliding around a question, aren't you." Mica grabbed a wet rag and started wiping down the bar. "Since when did having *one* girlfriend mean you can't have another one?"

"Doesn't work that way for me," Flynn said, having no idea why she was explaining. "I went out with Allie a few times, but she was still in love with someone else. That someone else showed up."

Mica stopped, the white terrycloth balled in her fist. "You still have a thing for her."

Flynn stopped herself before she could give the automatic response. A lie would destroy whatever chance she had of ever gaining Mica's trust. "I think I still have a thing for what might have been. We didn't go out that long—never got to the point of having anything serious."

"Is there a time limit or something?" Mica snorted. "Sometimes things happen fast. Somebody gets their hooks into you and you can't shake loose."

"You sound like you know." Flynn didn't like the idea, which made no sense at all.

Mica shrugged. "No. Not me." She started rubbing out the water rings on the bar again. "Besides, we were talking about you."

"I'm not hung up, but I still have some feelings."

"Yeah. I can see how that would happen." Mica grinned, a wholly natural and captivating grin. "She's really hot."

Flynn laughed. "Yeah, you got that right."

Mica paused, leaned toward Flynn. "But then, so are you."

Flynn's thighs tightened and a drumbeat started in the pit of her stomach. "That's some line."

"It's not a line," Mica said, leaning over a little more. Her gaze did a slow crawl down Flynn's body. "I'll be done in a few minutes."

Flynn ignored the voice warning her to be careful. "I'll be waiting."

❖

Outside Atlantic City, NJ

Hector climbed out of the rear of the Hummer and waited while his lieutenants piled out of all four doors and surrounded him, shielding him from any potential ambush. He slid his hand under his oversized Eagles jersey and felt for the Glock in his right front pocket. He brushed his fingers past the cold steel and onto his cock, taking courage from the dual symbols of his power. "Stay tight. Be ready."

"Yo," came a series of gruff replies. They moved forward as a phalanx toward the three men in suits and overcoats standing next to the idling limousine. The big guy in the front, Leo, watched them approach impassively. His white-blond hair was cut close to his scalp, making his massive head and neck appear even larger. His shoulders strained the seams of the expensive cashmere coat and his thighs bulged beneath his blended wool trousers. He dressed like a businessman but he looked like a thug. Hector wasn't intimidated by the clothes. A bullet would pierce silk as easy as polyester.

"You bring the product?" Leo asked.

"In the car." Hector hunched his shoulder toward the limo. "You have the goods?"

"Two cases. AK-47s."

"Twenty kilos," Hector said, "prime Colombian white."

"Good."

"What about the girls?" Hector asked.

Leo's granite jaw became even stonier. "Not part of the bargain."

"Remy said we'd get three."

"Remy doesn't make deals."

Hector cupped his crotch, squeezed his balls, and brushed his hand over the Glock in his pants. "No girls, no coke."

"No coke, no guns."

Hector shrugged. "We can get guns from the Bloods."

"Not like these."

Hector shrugged again and made like he was turning away.

"Two," Leo said. "But they been used already."

"Done." Virgins were nice, but after the first time, they were just like all the others anyhow. The girls the Russians supplied were worth compromising on that score—always well-trained, usually healthy, and obedient.

"Someone will drop them off tomorrow night."

Hector signaled to Carmen. "Make the exchange." He backed away, keeping his eye on the muscle who flanked Leo. When he was far enough away to feel comfortable, he turned his back and walked back to the Hummer. He climbed into the rear and wiped sweat from his face.

Carmen hopped in five minutes later. "All taken care of, boss."

"Any word on Mia?"

"Ramirez got a cousin of hers to talk. She says Mia headed north. On the train, maybe."

"Where north?"

Carmen shook his head. "She still won't say, and Ramirez was persuasive. Could be she doesn't know."

"Get her cell. Mia would've called her. We'll find someone who can trace the calls."

"What you going to do when you find her?"

"Nothing," Hector said, rubbing his palm over his dick. He was getting hard thinking about Mia and the lesson he'd need to teach her. "Just want my homegirl back home."

❖

Reese's cell phone rang and she snatched it off the bedside table. Rolling out of bed, she padded naked out into the hall. "Conlon."

"I'm sorry to wake you up, Sheriff," Allie said, "but I didn't think I ought to wait till tomorrow…"

"No problem." Reese eased the bedroom door closed. From the

amount of moonlight slanting through the skylight in the hall, she figured it was still early. She couldn't remember the last time she'd fallen asleep so early or so deeply. "What have you got?"

"Remember you called me this morning to ask me about the girl who was hit by the van?"

"The one who left the clinic before Tory finished her evaluation. Yeah, I remember."

"I ran her ID this afternoon, and I just checked back tonight because I was waiting on a few things. The computer system hasn't been—"

"Yeah, I know. I'm trying to get more money in the budget to replace the whole system." Ever since Nelson Parker had gone out on medical leave, she'd taken over as acting sheriff and, come election time, figured it would be permanent. She liked everything about the job except the politics. "You find something?"

"No," Allie said. "That's just the thing. I didn't find anything at all."

"So she's clean."

"No, I mean I didn't find anything on her in the system. No credit cards, no driver's license, no previous addresses, no Social Security number."

Reese walked into the baby's room out of habit. The crib was empty, and for a fraction of a second, her guts seized. Then she remembered. Reggie was with her grandmothers. Reggie was fine. Tory was asleep across the hall. Her family was safe. Her stomach settled. "So she's either off the grid, or she's not who she wants us to think she is."

"That's my take on it."

"There's no law against flying under the radar. Of course, if she's working, she ought to be paying taxes."

"She's working, all right. I just saw her in the Piper." Allie drew in a deep breath that made Reese think she wasn't happy about what she was going to say. "You think we should bring her in?"

"We don't have any real reason to do that." Reese walked into the guest room where she kept extra clothes so she could dress in the middle of the night without waking Tory. She opened the closet door and pulled a khaki uniform shirt off the hanger. "I can meet you at the station and we can talk about it."

"Oh hell, no. I don't want to drag you out tonight. I just have this feeling—"

"Tremont," Reese said, "if you've got a feeling, don't ignore it. You've got good instincts."

"Thank you, ma'am."

Reese smiled. "We need to do a lot more digging before we draw any conclusions."

"I can widen the computer searches."

"Absolutely, that's a place to start. We ought to send her picture around and see if that pops anything for us." Reese shrugged into the shirt but left it unbuttoned. "I'll come in early tomorrow morning and we can get started. Good enough?"

"I, uh, thought maybe I'd just keep an eye on her tonight."

"A stakeout? What else is going on that makes you think there's something there?"

"I talked to her tonight. She looked like she was a second away from running."

"Again," Reese said softly. The girl was clearly afraid of the authorities. That could mean anything—she could be a victim just as easily as she could be a problem. "If she goes straight home, I want you to do the same. I don't want you running any kind of surveillance by yourself. If you have the slightest suspicion of anything off, I want you to call me. I'll be your backup."

"Yes ma'am," Allie snapped, and Reese could almost see the salute.

"Well done, Tremont." Reese started back to the bedroom. "Remember, you even get a twinge that something is off, I want a call."

"You got it, Sheriff."

Reese disconnected and slipped back into the bedroom, making her way to the bed in the dark.

"You have to go?" Tory asked.

Reese sat on the side of the bed and set the phone on the bedside table. "No. That was Allie, calling about the girl you had in your clinic this morning. She doesn't seem to have any verifiable identity."

Tory slid her hand under Reese's shirt and rubbed her back. "What do you think that means?"

"Almost anything." Reese shrugged out of the shirt, tossed it onto a nearby chair, and got back under the covers. She pulled Tory into her arms and kissed her. "Sorry I woke you."

"That's okay. I think just to be extra sure, we should try that helping-hand thing again."

Reese chuckled. "Does just thinking about getting pregnant make you horny?"

"Darling, you make me horny." Tory pulled Reese on top of her. "You're not tired, are you?"

"Not even a little. I'm all yours."

"Of course you are. And right now, I have work for you."

Reese kissed her. Allie would call if she needed her. Right now, Tory was all that mattered.

CHAPTER EIGHT

Flynn finished her Diet Coke and turned the empty glass between her hands, watching the last of the ice melt. Mica had signaled she was finishing up and would be ready to leave soon. Mica worked quickly and efficiently, clearing glasses and empty bottles from tables around the room, emptying ashtrays on the open deck that extended over the beach, restocking the bar. She didn't seem to notice the appreciative glances from the women, mostly singles now, occupying stools at the bar or leaning on the deck in casual poses, appraising their chances of company for the night. Flynn didn't want to be one of the women staring at Mica, tossing out a flirtatious remark as she passed, hoping to draw her attention. She tried not to watch her, but Mica was the most attractive woman in the room—her tight faded jeans hugged her curvaceous butt, and her sleeveless T-shirt with a washed-out Harley-Davidson logo stretched tightly across her full breasts showed off her lithe, muscular arms. When she bent over, the shirt slid up her back and a bit of ink showed above the waistband of her hip-huggers. The tat was big, and with a twinge in her belly that ought to have been a warning but just felt good, Flynn wondered how low it went. In a word, Mica was built, and combined with the strong, broad planes of her face, her luminous dark eyes, and full lips, that spelled downright gorgeous. Who wouldn't want to look at her?

So Flynn looked, and occasionally when Mica glanced her way, Flynn thought she caught a flicker of a pleased smile. Maybe Mica really had been flirting with her earlier. She wasn't entirely certain she read signals from women accurately. When she'd first gone out with Allie, she'd told Allie she wasn't a virgin, which was true, but she still didn't have a lot of experience. Celibacy wasn't a requirement in the seminary, but she'd been far too busy at first with her studies, and then too busy falling in love with the wrong woman, to get much practice. After she'd left, she'd dated, but she still felt like she was learning the rules. Not that the rules mattered right at the moment. She wasn't dating Mica.

Just that morning, Mica had been her patient, and Flynn wasn't the kind of paramedic who followed up with patients for any reason—social or medical. She didn't track down ER staff to find out what happened to the injured she'd delivered to the hospital or to discover the fate of the babies she'd transported in the back of the medic unit on a wild ride through dark streets at night. She was happier walking away, doing what she could in the moment and then letting go. She didn't need to know. She couldn't change the outcome. She needed a clear beginning and a definite end that had nothing to do with her, except for those few critical moments when she was certain she was doing the right thing. In this one area, emergency care, she trusted her instincts. She trusted herself.

Unlike a few of the others, she'd never once tried to date anyone she'd met on a call, even when their injuries had been minor or nonexistent and the call had turned out to be more social than medical. She'd vowed never to let her personal and professional lives bleed into each other again. Walking Mica home was almost an exception to her rule, but as long as she was only being friendly... She caught herself up short, wondering if she was lying to herself the same way she had lied to herself about Evelyn.

At first she'd denied her attraction, then called her growing desire friendship, and only when she'd confessed her feelings had she been abruptly reminded she'd willingly misread everything. If she hadn't been so involved with her own personal anguish over Evelyn, maybe she would have seen Debbie's pain more clearly. Maybe everything would have been different. If Evelyn had been her only mistake, she might have been able to forgive herself.

Flynn closed her eyes and let the pain wash through her on the familiar crest of guilt and remorse.

"You ready?" Mica asked, sliding up next to her.

Flynn hadn't seen Mica come around the end of the bar. She hadn't seen anything as she'd looked inward and backward, replaying what she hadn't said—what she should have done—and how the outcome might have been different if she'd had better instincts. If she'd had the instincts she'd needed and once believed she'd had. If she'd been a better priest.

"Yeah, sure." Flynn stood.

"You okay?" Mica didn't move and Flynn ended up standing very close to her. So close the scent of dark spices and a hint of chocolate surrounded her. Mica's eyes were soft and warm, as open and welcoming as Flynn had ever seen them. Mica's fingers trailed lightly down Flynn's arm. "You looked like something was...bothering you."

Flynn flushed. She didn't confide in people easily, but the unexpected tenderness in Mica's gaze made her want to confess. She almost laughed. How had the tables turned so completely, and when did she start believing absolution might be found on earth? "I'm fine."

Mica shrugged and stepped back, the sliver of warmth in her eyes chilling. "Suit yourself."

"Sorry."

"For what?"

Flynn shoved her hands in her pockets. They walked side by side to the door in silence and the gulf between them widened. Every step made Flynn panic just a little, as if she needed to get back to solid ground before she sank beneath the weight of her own memories. "I'm not usually moody."

"No?" Mica kept walking and didn't look at her. "What are you usually?"

"You ask hard questions."

"You like bullshit better?" Mica slowed on the narrow wooden sidewalk that led from the club to the street. She seemed to be looking around, but the dim, narrow alleyway leading to the street was empty. At the far end, people strolled by on Commercial even though it was close to midnight.

Mica waited, her silence a challenge.

"I don't know what I am anymore," Flynn said. "I like my job. Keeps me busy. I don't think about much of anything else." Even as she said it, Flynn saw her life for what it was—a highway to nowhere, and she was taking it as fast as she could. She was running away every bit as much as Mica seemed to be. "And no, I can do without the bullshit. I'm sorry I can't—"

"Look," Mica said sharply, "forget I asked. Your business."

Flynn nodded. The walls were up again. Just as well. She needed the walls too. "Have you had anything to eat tonight?"

"I've been busy too, you probably noticed." Mica headed toward the street.

"I noticed." Flynn caught up to her. "How's the headache?"

"Can we leave off talking about my head and my stomach and any other part of me," Mica grumbled. "I took a spill, I didn't get hit by a subway train. I've had worse injuries dropping my bike."

"Harley?" Flynn pointed to Mica's T-shirt.

Mica grinned, pure pleasure lighting up her face. "Yeah. A sweet little classic Softail."

"So why were you on a bicycle this morning?"

"I sold it."

Flynn heard the message in Mica's clipped words. An off-limits topic—at least for right now. "Look, I could use something to eat. Want to stop at the Post Office and grab a sandwich?"

"No."

"My treat."

Mica stopped in the middle of the street across from Town Hall. "Message time, Flynn. I asked you to walk me home, and if you get lucky, maybe I'll ask you up to my room. But if I do, it'll be on my terms because I want to get laid, not because I owe you anything."

"Mica," Flynn said quietly, "you don't owe me anything and you never will. If I offer something, it's because I want to do it. Maybe because I'm hungry, maybe because I'd like your company."

"Yeah, sure. Why would you like my company?" Mica ran her hand over her chest, slowly tracing the outline of her breast until her fingers trailed down her belly and angled across her crotch. "This kind of company, I get that. But like I said, that's not for sale."

Flynn blew out a breath. "Okay. We have a little problem here."

"No, we don't. See you around."

Mica moved so fast she was halfway up the block before Flynn got her ass in gear and jogged after her. When she caught up, she said, "I don't pay girls for sex, cash or otherwise. I don't take girls out to dinner and expect them to sleep with me afterward. I don't even expect a good-night kiss after taking a girl to a really good movie."

"Then you're a loser," Mica muttered.

"Yeah," Flynn sighed. "That might be why I never get laid."

Mica laughed. "You are some kind of weird chick."

"I think you told me that already."

"So you're not looking to get laid?" Mica cut Flynn a disbelieving look.

"No, I'm not."

"So what do you really want?"

There it was, the question she'd been trying to answer ever since she'd left the seminary. What did she really want? Some things she knew for certain. She needed to feel useful. She needed to know that her life meant something. The best, the finest way she knew of doing that, was to make someone else's life a little better. She'd grown up believing from as far back as she could remember that the way for her to serve was to minister—to provide a safe place to speak, to listen without prejudice, to guide without judgment—that had been her goal. She had never felt the need to convert others. She believed people came to God in their own way, in their own time. Her mission was to help, and if she was truly lucky, to heal. In the months since she'd left the seminary, she'd cared for the body instead of the soul. She should have felt more satisfied. She should have felt if not peace, at least solace. But she didn't.

They'd slowed until they were barely moving. People streamed around them, laughing, talking, making plans, living. Irrepressible humanity. Flynn tried to remember the last time she'd felt like she was living, and she remembered Allie in her arms. She took a deep breath.

"I'd like some company," Flynn said. "I don't feel like being alone right now."

"Wow, your lines really do need a little work. That doesn't exactly make me want to let you jump my bones."

Flynn laughed. "I was thinking we'd have a late dinner and then I'd walk you home. Like we agreed."

Mica chewed her lip, glanced behind them, and lifted her shoulder. "Sure. Why not?"

Why not? Strangely lighthearted, Flynn decided not every question needed an answer.

❖

Allie leaned against the corner of Vorelli's restaurant, shielded by passersby, and watched Flynn and Mica carry on a conversation in the middle of the street as if nothing else was going on around them. Flynn had a way of doing that—zeroing in on you until you felt like the entire world disappeared and all that mattered was what was happening in that instant between the two of you. Allie couldn't remember the last time she'd been to church, but she remembered what it felt like to confide in Flynn, to expose herself. To let herself be comforted. She'd felt safe. Flynn must have been an amazing priest.

Flynn had given her shelter. No one had ever made her feel quite that safe, not personally, not in her heart—except Ash. Allie could easily have given her heart to Flynn if Ash hadn't already owned her, body and soul. Still, a little bit of her heart tugged every time she saw Flynn. She didn't want to sleep with her, she didn't want to claim even a little bit of Flynn's heart, but she wanted to see her happy. She loved Flynn like she loved Bri—like she loved few people—all the way deep down inside.

Every time she saw Flynn, she wondered what could have possibly made Flynn give up being what she must have been so good at. That was a question she was going to get answered one day soon. But right now, she wondered what the hell Flynn was doing. They bumped into each other regularly on shift and off, and she'd never seen Flynn pick up anyone before. She'd had to make the moves the few times they'd gone out. And now Flynn was getting all tangled up with exactly the wrong kind of girl.

Even if she hadn't known Mica was hiding something, she wouldn't have wanted Flynn to hook up with her. Girls like that played girls like Flynn—teasing them, stringing them along, using them. That little dark-haired cutie was a hardcore badass, and if she wasn't in trouble with the law already, she was headed that way. She would probably use anybody and anything to get what she needed. And Flynn was such a goddamn sucker. So sweet. So kind.

Damn it, Flynn, what are you doing?

Flynn and Mica started off again, cutting through the crowd, and Allie fell in behind them. She wouldn't have called Reese if she hadn't been certain something was off with Mica, and talking to her for a few minutes in the Piper had made her even more certain. The girl had been skittish, more than skittish—she'd looked like the hounds of hell were after her. That would've tripped her trigger even if Mica hadn't been hanging around Flynn. She wasn't about to stand around doing nothing and watch Flynn get dragged into something that might get nasty. If she had to traipse around town in the middle of the night, every night, to find out what the hell was going on, she would.

And first thing in the morning, if the computers didn't give her a lead as to the girl's identity, she'd have to go at it the old-fashioned way. She'd convince Reese to let her bring the girl in for questioning. Reese had said to trust her instincts, and her instincts were telling her trouble, big trouble, was waiting right around the corner.

CHAPTER NINE

"So," Mica said, "this is it."

She slowed in front of a ramshackle building that once must have been an elegant captain's house. Now, even in the weak light cast by the moon ducking in and out of the clouds, the shabbiness was hard to miss. Peeling paint, sagging porch, shutters hanging askew. She'd been lucky to get the apartment—more like a big room, really, with the bonus of having a private bathroom, and she'd used the last of her money paying the first month in advance.

"Thanks for dinner," Flynn said.

Mica shook her head. "You paid, remember? So that's my line."

"Tell you what," Flynn said. "Let's make a deal—no lines. I won't if you won't."

"What does that leave us with?" Mica asked, looking for the con.

"The truth."

"Yeah, right. But why not?" She tossed the ball back to Flynn. Her play. Let's see what she called truth. "So why the dinner?"

"Like I said before, I enjoy your company." And she sounded like she meant it. Looked it too—her eyes glinting in the moonlight, an easy smile making her look sexy and sleek.

For a crazy nanosecond, Mica contemplated asking Flynn upstairs with her. She'd had a good time at dinner—a really good time. Flynn was easy on the eyes, easy to talk to, easy to be with. Too easy. She made Mica forget for minutes at a time to be careful, to be wary. Flynn even made her forget now and then to pay attention to who walked by, who followed in the near darkness, who might be waiting up ahead. Dangerous. Stupid and dangerous, all because Flynn made her forget her own rules. And now she was thinking about asking Flynn upstairs? Yeah, right.

"Are you working tomorrow?" Flynn asked.

"I work every day, if I can," Mica said.

"Then you probably have to get up early. I should let you go."

Flynn didn't move away, and neither did Mica. Nothing waited for her upstairs. A silent room, an empty bed, another night when she kept the loneliness at bay by replaying the alternatives in her mind. Hector's mocking laugh, his rough hands, the wild, crazy gleam in his eyes.

"You want to come up?" Mica blurted. When she looked into Flynn's eyes, she couldn't see Hector's.

"I think we should stick to the original plan," Flynn said seriously. She cupped Mica's chin and kissed her on the cheek before Mica could jerk her head away. "Thanks for tonight."

Mica stiffened. Flynn's lips were soft and warm. She smelled like autumn in the park, with just a hint of sweetness beneath the rich scent of burning leaves. Mica hadn't walked in the park since she was ten and her mother took her and her brother and sister to the playground on the rare Saturday or Sunday she wasn't working. Then her mother had lost her job and gotten hooked up with a man who'd put his hands on Mica's ass one too many times, and she'd found a new family. After she'd joined MS-13, there were no more late-afternoon walks in the park, not even the little scraggly one along the waterfront across the highway from the high-rise where she lived. Mica pulled away from the kiss before her body asked for more. "What the hell was that? If you don't want anything—"

"I don't." Flynn backed up. Her blond hair silvered in the moonlight. Her lanky body, all dangerous edges and teasing curves, shimmered like a blade. "You're beautiful, you know."

Mica's breath snagged on a lump in the middle of her chest. "Flynn—"

"Night, Mica."

Her name whispered on the wind and Flynn was gone.

Mica waited, holding her breath, her belly tight and aching, anticipating the instant when Flynn would reappear. She touched her fingertips to her middle, felt her muscles clench—an unfamiliar longing swirled in her chest. Flynn didn't come back, and after a minute, Mica sucked in a breath, spun around, and climbed the porch. She let herself in and hurried up the dark stairs to the second-floor rear apartment. The room smelled musty and abandoned, but underneath the heavy scent of loss, she detected a hint of the sea, and hope. Leaning back against the closed door, she shut her eyes. Her face tingled from the touch of Flynn's lips. That ache in her belly was bigger, part loneliness—that she was used to—and another part so unusual she hadn't recognized it at first. The slow burn of desire flickered and flared. Her breasts tightened, her nipples pebbled underneath her T-shirt. Her belly quivered.

None of the girls she'd played with, not even the ones she'd kissed in the shadows when the loneliness got too big, had made her want so much. She'd been crazy to ask Flynn to come upstairs. She couldn't afford to let anyone inside her defenses. Especially not someone who made her forget for minutes at a time that her life was not her own.

❖

Allie let herself into her garden apartment between Commercial and Bradford a little after one. Her cell phone finally caught a signal and she saw she had voice mail. She dropped her keys onto the table that doubled as a dining table and desk and scrolled through the short list, her heart kicking up when she spotted Ash's number. She slid her thumb over the Listen icon.

Hi, babe, I guess you must be asleep. Sorry I didn't call sooner— I'm in some kind of a dead zone and can't get a signal half the time. Talk to you in the morning. I love you.

Allie replayed the message. Ash's husky voice cut through her as if she hadn't heard it hundreds of times before, leaving her awash with joy and desire and old fears. Ever since Ash had come back into her life a few weeks ago, the old wounds had started to heal, but she still had moments when she walked into the empty apartment and nearly drowned under the crushing memory of the long, lonely months after Ash left her. God, she'd been miserable. She'd very nearly slept with Flynn to push the pain away. She didn't regret having met Flynn, having gotten close to her, but a small part of her worried she might have been using Flynn, and the guilt burned. She hit Call and waited, her stomach jittery with anticipation.

"Hi, baby." Ash sounded wide-awake.

"Hey," Allie said, moving through the living room to her bedroom without turning on a light. "Sorry, did I wake you up?"

"No, I'm watching TV," Ash said. "I've been in the car so much I needed to unwind a little bit before trying to sleep."

"How's it going?" Allie pushed the speaker button, set the cell phone on the dresser, and pulled off her T-shirt. "Are you almost done?"

"Getting there. I've got a couple of sites to visit tomorrow morning and then I'll hit the last ones on my return leg. I ought to be back soon."

Dancing from foot to foot, Allie pushed out of her jeans and the rest of her clothes until she was naked. She grabbed the phone, carried it to the bed, and slid under the covers. The sheets were crisp and cool, too cool without Ash. "That's good."

"What are you doing up so late? Didn't you have the day shift?"

"Yeah." Allie absently brushed her fingers over her chest, her fingertips grazing her nipples. They hardened instantly. She smiled, feeling herself get wet, thinking how easily Ash could turn her on. Just thinking about her was enough to do that—add her voice, and she was in trouble. "Something came up and I ended up working some tonight."

"Trouble?"

"I'm not sure. Maybe." Ash's work as an insurance investigator specializing in high-risk or suspicious claims made her an excellent investigator, and Allie respected her opinions. Sometimes it was hard having an older girlfriend with more experience in just about everything, but she was learning to hold her own. Where work was concerned, she wasn't too proud to accept input from another professional. "There was an incident this morning where a girl on a bicycle got hit by a van. Seemed pretty routine, but then she skipped out of the clinic before Tory could examine her. Reese asked me to follow up. The thing is, I can't find anything on her."

"You run all the databases?"

"I sent her name, DOB, and description out everywhere—DMV, IRS, missing persons—but the results are slow coming in. So far, though, nothing."

"Might not mean anything. Might not be anything to find."

Allie smiled. Sometimes Ash and Reese were hard to tell apart. "I know. The thing is…"

"What, baby?"

"Flynn caught the call this morning and transported the girl to the clinic. And now it looks like…Well, it looks like she might be getting involved."

Silence on the line. Ash knew Allie and Flynn had dated. Ash knew Allie had called it off too. Allie waited.

"Did Flynn tell you that?" Ash's voice was neutral, casual.

"No. I bumped into her at the Piper and this girl was working there. I talked to her and she just didn't feel right. I ran it by Reese, and she said to hold off until all the computer searches came in. I asked Reese if I could keep an eye on things, just to get a sense of what was going on."

"Wait a minute. You just got home because, what? You were doing surveillance? With who?"

"Nobody. I was just kind of keeping an eye on them."

"Jesus, baby," Ash said sharply. "What the hell is Reese thinking, letting you do that solo? You're barely healed from the last gunshot wound."

The hairs on the back of Allie's neck stood up. If she'd been a dog, she would've growled. She took a long breath. Fighting over the phone was stupid. "Ash, I'm a cop, remember?"

More silence.

"Ash?"

"Yes, I remember," Ash said. "Sorry. I love you. I worry."

"I worry about you too." Allie smiled and circled her fingertips over the warmth in the center of her belly. "Well, there was nothing to worry about, because nothing happened."

"And if there's any more surveillance to be done, you'll do it with backup?"

"Promise."

"You know," Ash said, "I miss you."

"I miss you too."

"Oh yeah? How much?"

Allie laughed. "If I tell you, you'll just get a big head."

"Probably. But tell me anyway."

"A lot. The bed is too big without you. And I'm horny."

Ash chuckled. "Baby, you're always horny."

"Just hurry home."

"I will."

A rustling noise came over the phone. "What are you doing?"

"Getting into bed," Ash said.

"Oh yeah? What are you wearing?"

"Besides a smile and a hard-on?"

Allie's belly tightened. "That's nice."

"Speak for yourself. And I'm not wearing anything."

Allie cupped her breasts, squeezing gently. Her nipples were hard, aching. She rubbed them and her clit stiffened. "I don't think it's fair that just talking to you gets me so horny."

"Fair doesn't enter into it. Have you been thinking about me all night?"

"Mmm-hmm."

"How about I snuggle in next to you and warm you up?" Ash's voice turned silky and hot.

"I'd like that." Allie closed her eyes and tucked the phone close to her face on the pillow. She often woke up in the morning with Ash curled around her, sheltering her in the curve of her body the way the village, on its thin finger of sand, curved around the harbor, keeping everyone within safe. With Ash holding her tight, she was protected. Ash kept her safe—not just her body while she slept, but her heart with every breath. "I love your hands on me."

"Baby," Ash whispered, "I love touching you. Do you want me to touch you now?"

Allie cradled one breast in her palm and rolled the nipple lightly between her fingers. She pressed the pads of the first two fingers of her other hand against the base of her clitoris, feeling it beat in time to her racing heart. "I want you to do a lot more than touch me. So hurry up home."

"We don't have to wait, you know."

"I know. I could come listening to the sound of your voice, but I think I'll wait."

Ash chuckled. "Really?"

"Yeah. It's not like me, I know." Allie dipped one finger lower, into the satiny heat, and moaned at the ripple of excitement.

"It doesn't sound like you're waiting. And if you don't stop, there's no way I'm going to hold out."

"I love wanting you as much as I love coming."

"Aren't we lucky we can have both."

Allie thought about the endless nights after Ash left, of the women she'd dated, trying to forget, and then, discovering she couldn't forget, the weeks when no one touched her. She hadn't even wanted to come by her own hand, because the orgasm was a lonely mockery of what she really wanted. The single bright memory in all those weeks was Flynn. "I don't ever want to be without you again."

"I'm so sorry, baby," Ash murmured.

"No, you don't have to be. That's behind us now."

"But you still remember, I can tell."

"I remember being without you." Allie cupped herself, desire making her swell, making her ache. The wanting was all the sweeter for knowing Ash was hers. "I have you now. I'm not letting you go. You're mine."

"Completely."

"That's all that matters."

"Close your eyes and let me hold you while you sleep, baby," Ash said.

"I love you. See you soon."

"I love you too."

Allie ended the call and closed her eyes. Ash was everywhere, in her heart and her soul, and she would be there the next day, and the day after that. That certainty was everything she needed.

❖

Flynn rolled over and watched the moon track across the sky through her bedroom window. She'd left it open even though the breeze bordered on cold so she could hear the foghorn toll from the lighthouse on Long Point. The smell of the sea reminded her of how insignificant she was in the vast ocean of time, smaller than a speck of sand on the shores of an endless universe. She would crumble under the weight of her own inconsequentiality if she didn't have some way to contribute to that wonder.

Almost three a.m. Mica was probably asleep. Or perhaps she was lying awake watching the same moon move across the cloud-strewn sky, wondering, like Flynn, how the night might have been if Flynn had accepted Mica's invitation and gone upstairs with her. Flynn hadn't anticipated the invitation, even though Mica radiated loneliness. Flynn recognized the shadows in Mica's eyes and the sadness Mica tried to hide. Mica was too strong and too stubborn to admit it, but some things were impossible to hide. Flynn recognized a soul on the run.

Flynn laced her fingers behind her head and watched the shadows flicker on her ceiling. Mica. What ghosts haunted her? What demons chased her? And why shouldn't two people help each other through the night when they shared the same pain?

Chapter Ten

R eese," Tory murmured sleepily, "where are you going?"
"To get the baby." Reese leaned down and kissed Tory. "Go back to sleep."

"What time is it?"

"About five."

Tory pushed up in bed. "You're dressed for work. What's wrong?"

"Nothing. I just thought I'd go get her. You know she's always up early, and so is my mother."

Tory shifted over and patted the bed next to her. "Sit down for a minute."

Reese sat. She knew what was coming, and like most times, she'd have no answer. Before Tory could ask, she said, "Nothing's wrong. Really. I just couldn't sleep."

"Were you having nightmares?"

Reese took Tory's hand, threaded her fingers through Tory's, and kissed Tory's knuckles. The dreams of running through the desert at night, heart pounding and ears ringing, the sky overhead alight with fireworks that might've been beautiful if they hadn't been so deadly, didn't really count as nightmares, did they? How could something she'd lived through really be a nightmare and not just a memory? "No. I'm fine."

"I have no doubt of that." Tory rubbed her thumb over the top of Reese's hand. "But you don't usually leave while I'm sleeping. I don't like waking up and finding you gone."

Reese fished the piece of paper from the breast pocket of her uniform shirt and held it up between two fingers. "I already had the note written to put on my pillow where you'd see it. And besides, I was coming back and Reggie and I were going to make breakfast. Really, I just wanted you to sleep longer." Reese hitched the sheet down until she'd exposed a few inches of bare skin below Tory's sleep shirt and kissed her stomach. "After all, you've got a job to do and you need your rest."

Tory laughed. "I don't think there's anything I can do to make things happen any faster at this point, including sleep."

"Excited?"

Tory's eyes sparkled. "I am. I want this."

"I know. So do I." Reese didn't feel the slightest uncertainty when she said it. She *did* want another baby. She just didn't want Tory endangered.

"Will it help if I tell you everything's going to be all right?"

"Baby," Reese murmured. "It always helps."

"Well, if you're up and breakfast is in the offing, I might as well get up too." Tory pushed the sheet the rest of the way off. "I'll make coffee and feed Jed while you collect our offspring."

"Deal." Reese got up, found Tory's robe, and handed it to her. "You know, part of the reason I like being a cop in the town where I live is I feel like I can keep you safe by keeping everyone else safe. Does that make sense?"

"Of course it does. Especially for you. You were raised to protect and serve." Tory wrapped her arms around Reese's shoulders and pressed against her, the robe on the bed, forgotten. "I love you for that. And I love you because you're getting up at the crack of dawn to get our daughter and bring her home. I love you because tonight, when I'm tired and wondering if I'm making any kind of difference at all, I'll be able to look at you and Reggie and know that I am. That I matter because I'm in your life."

Reese held Tory tightly against her chest and rubbed her cheek in Tory's hair. "You don't just matter. You're everything."

"Like you are for me." Tory kissed her jaw. "Go on now, Sheriff. Important duty calls."

❖

Even after picking up Reggie, fixing pancakes with Reggie's help, and giving her a bath to repair the damage, Reese still got to the department before seven. Other than the night deputy handling phones, the place was empty. She pushed through the swinging gate that separated the small seating area just inside the door from the rest of the room where the desks for the patrol officers were located. She poured herself a cup of coffee and walked into her office, a small cubicle with big windows tucked into the back of the main room. She had a half hour or so before roll call to review the reports from the night shift. While not quite the off-season, the early fall was less busy in town than the summer. The stack of reports was half the size it would have been during the height of the tourist season. All the same, there'd been plenty of activity—several traffic accidents, a handful of brawls, a lost child thankfully recovered within a few minutes, and the random domestic disturbance. She didn't see anything from Allie, and she hadn't expected to. She'd given Allie an order to call her if she suspected any kind of trouble, and Allie wouldn't disobey. If anything had happened in the unofficial surveillance Allie had been running on the girl with the questionable identity, Allie would've called her.

Someone tapped on her open office door and she glanced up. She expected to see Gladys, the dispatcher who seconded as a secretary, civilian liaison, and just about anything else they needed in the department by way of support staff. Allie Tremont, in uniform, waited in the doorway instead.

"Come on in," Reese said.

"Morning, Sheriff." Allie carried a chipped white porcelain mug with steam rising from the top. She had circles under her normally vibrant deep brown eyes. This morning, their luster was dulled with fatigue.

"Long night?" Reese asked.

"No, not really." Allie dosed her coffee liberally with Splenda and tossed the paper pack into the trash. "I got in about one or so, but I couldn't sleep. Ash is out of town—" She colored. "Sorry. Not relevant."

"That's okay. I don't sleep very well when Tory's away either."

Allie's eyes widened. "Uh yeah."

Reese guessed Allie's surprise was because she didn't usually talk about anything personal while on the job, especially not with younger officers who were barely more than rookies. Then again, Allie wasn't a rookie any longer. Allie had taken a bullet just a few weeks before and had handled it like a veteran. She'd trust Allie at her back any day.

"I guess you get used to it," Allie finally said. "Coming home to an empty place, I mean."

"I don't know," Reese said. "I haven't."

Allie shot her a look of appreciation. "I don't think I will either. And she travels a lot."

Reese nodded and sipped her coffee. "I take it nothing turned up last night on your surveillance."

Bri Parker appeared in the doorway. "What surveillance?"

"What is this, a party?" Reese asked. "Why are you both early?"

"No reason." Bri looked sharp and alert, her khaki uniform pressed within an inch of its life, razor-sharp creases in her pants and shirtsleeves. Her boots were black mirrors. Her thick black hair was trimmed just at her collar in the back and shorter along the sides. Even though Bri was in her early twenties, Reese thought she might've grown another inch or so in the last year. She had to be close to six feet now and starting to fill out a little bit. She'd always been lanky, but now she was beginning to muscle up.

"Sorry," Bri said, shooting Allie a penetrating look. "I thought I heard something about surveillance."

"It's nothing," Allie said.

Bri's brows drew down and she glanced from Reese to Allie. Her jaw tightened. "Okay." She spun on her heel and disappeared into the squad room.

Allie sighed. "Any reason I can't brief her?"

"None that I can see." Reese smiled. "In fact, I'd recommend it. Catch me up later if anything turns up on the girl."

"Yes ma'am." Allie jogged between the desks and plunked her butt down on Bri's desk. "Do you always have to be such a horse's ass?"

Bri shuffled papers on her desk, not looking up. "I don't know what you're talking about."

"You damn well do. You're upset because you think something happened that you don't know about. And you're probably jealous that I was talking to Reese—"

"Whoa, whoa," Bri protested. "I'm not jealous of Reese."

"Me then?"

Bri grinned and quickly smothered it. "Jesus, no. I haven't lusted after you for...a long time."

"I'm broken-hearted."

"You're full of it too." Bri glanced toward Reese's office, but she'd closed the door. "So what's going on? If you were doing surveillance, it must be something good."

"Maybe, I don't know." Allie told Bri about her suspicions about

Mica, and her phone call to Reese. "There's nothing solid at this point. So you didn't miss anything."

"I don't know, Al. I'd go with your gut. You need some help running down the computer traces?"

"No, but thanks. At the rate they're coming in, I'm not going to get overwhelmed."

"So you want to swing through town, see what's cooking? We got a few minutes before roll call."

"I guess you'll be riding with Carter again," Allie said quietly.

"Now who's jealous?"

"You wish." Allie grabbed her uniform hat and settled it over her brow. "Come on. Let's see what's shakin'."

CHAPTER ELEVEN

Flynn ran along the harbor's edge, skirting along the crescent shoreline that extended from Long Point through the center of town to the East End. The tide was on its way out, and the moist sand left in its wake was dark and firm beneath her feet. Her footsteps filled with water almost as soon as she made them, obliterating her path within a few seconds, as if she had never been there at all.

The still air smelled of seaweed and brine. The sun blazed brightly but the intense heat of summer was tempered by the first breath of fall. Beneath a crystal-blue sky dotted with billowing white clouds, the harbor glinted like a steel-gray mirror. Higher up the beach, early risers walked barefoot, carrying their shoes in one hand and coffee cups in the other; gulls circled and swooped, looking for scraps; and dog owners tossed balls and sticks out into the water where sleek canine heads broke the surface like schools of porpoises in pursuit. The day was as beautiful as any she'd ever seen. As she ran, the shroud of a sleepless night fell away and she breathed deeply, the excitement of a new day, ripe with possibility, buoying her. Mornings were her favorite time—when the defeats and disappointments of the day before had been distanced by the dark, and dawn promised another chance.

Slowing, she checked the big black clock with gold hands on the tower at Town Hall. Seven fifteen. She angled up the beach, sinking into the soft dry sand with every step. The muscles in her calves ached pleasantly, and a light sheen of sweat coated her bare arms and the triangle of skin where the vee of her T-shirt exposed her chest. When she reached the street, she thumped her running shoes against the edge of the wooden sidewalk to shake loose the clumps of moist sand, giving herself another few seconds to change her mind. When she couldn't delay without examining exactly why she was hesitating, she strode down Commercial toward the West End where Mica worked. She'd been thinking about seeing Mica again ever since she'd left her standing outside her rooming house earlier in the week. When she'd gotten up that morning, she'd told herself she was going for a run, but in the back of her mind, her destination had always been the Shoreline.

The restaurant fronted the harbor, and once inside, she skirted the tables in the main room and found a deuce near the railing on the open-air deck that extended over the beach. While she was perusing the menu, Mica appeared carrying a huge round tray laden with plates to a table occupied by a party of six—two women, one Caucasian and the other African American, and four children. Mica was as fast and efficient serving food as she had been working the bar, but today, she smiled at the kids and appeared to be making small talk. Her white short-sleeved shirt was tucked into tapered black jeans that emphasized her narrow waist and curvaceous hips. A tattoo, indistinct from so far away, adorned her right upper arm. Her hair was down, the heavy black waves blowing in the harbor breeze. Flynn's mouth went dry. Mica was all kinds of sexy.

Mica looked over, her lips pursing as her smile disappeared. Flynn nodded and Mica set the tray on one of the empty tables and threaded her way between the chairs over to Flynn. "What gives?"

Flynn smiled. "I was hoping for breakfast?"

"That's what we do here." Mica crossed her arms. The top two buttons of her shirt were undone, and her bronze skin glistened. Her jeans were cut so low the arch of each hipbone slanted beneath the waistband, bold curves inviting the caress of hands.

Flynn almost told Mica she looked amazing, but caught herself just in time. Mica had made it very clear that she didn't trust compliments. Flynn couldn't ask her how she was feeling, even though she wanted to know. Mica didn't like to reveal personal information and didn't like being asked. Short of commenting on the weather, Flynn couldn't think of anything else to say except the truth. "I was thinking about you this morning and I ended up here."

"Yeah, right. Your breakfast order?"

"Poached eggs, wheat toast, chicken sausage."

"Got it. You want juice?"

"Orange would be good."

"Be a few minutes."

"That's okay. I don't start my shift until nine."

Mica turned away and Flynn settled back in her chair to watch the boats. She had nothing on her mind, and the pressure she always felt to be doing, moving, was strangely absent. Strange but not unpleasant. She was waiting for Mica, nothing else, and that was okay.

❖

While Mica waited for her orders to come up, she leaned against a post in the main section of the restaurant and watched Flynn. She'd pushed her chair back from the small table, extended her legs underneath, and tilted her head against the back of the chair. Couldn't be a very comfortable position, but she looked good all the same. She must've been out running. Her navy blue T-shirt with the paramedic emblem on the chest had a dark diamond-shaped pattern down the center of her chest. Sweat. Her hair lay in damp tendrils on her neck. Her bare arms, still holding a summer tan, were sleek and lined with prominent veins coursing over her wrists and the tops of her hands. She looked strong. She looked damn good.

"Orders up," the fry cook called and Mica went to fill her tray. She served everyone else before Flynn, and by the time she reached her, it looked like Flynn was asleep.

She almost didn't want to disturb her. The tightness around Flynn's eyes and mouth, that she hadn't realized was there until now, had disappeared. Her face had relaxed, and she looked…younger. She was always hot-looking, but now she was just beautiful.

"Hey," Mica murmured close to Flynn's ear, "wake up, your breakfast is ready."

Flynn shot upright, her eyes scanning rapidly. "What?"

"Yo," Mica said. "Take it easy."

Flynn scrubbed her face. "Sorry. I can't believe I fell asleep."

"Late-night action?" Mica grinned.

"Not exactly. I just didn't sleep much."

Mica almost said she hadn't either. She rarely slept a night through—waking up, heart racing, wondering if every sound in the hall was someone on their way to her door. No way was she sharing that, but she almost wanted to. Flynn had a way of catching her off guard, simply because Flynn was never on guard herself. If Mica didn't know better, she'd think Flynn always told the truth. But that couldn't possibly be, because no one ever did. She slid the plate onto the table in front of Flynn and set down her orange juice. She placed a cup of coffee next to it. "Thought you could use this."

Flynn grasped the mug, raised it up, and breathed deeply. "You are so right. Thanks."

"Well," Mica said, remembering how they'd sat over sandwiches the night Flynn walked her home, not talking much, just watching foot traffic on Commercial and occasionally commenting on the sports channel. She'd almost forgotten La Mara, and right now, she wished she could pull out the chair opposite Flynn and sit down. Maybe ask her what her day would be like. How she'd ended up in this town. Why she wasn't wearing a collar. She couldn't remember the last time she wanted to know anything about anyone in her life. What was even scarier, she almost…almost…wanted to tell Flynn about hers. She backed away from the table. "Enjoy it."

"I will." Flynn turned in her chair. "Mica?"

Mica hesitated. "Yeah?"

"You working tonight?"

"Every night, remember?"

"So maybe I'll see you."

Mica shrugged, ignoring the quick jump of her pulse. "Whatever."

Flynn smiled. "Yeah, whatever sounds good."

Shaking her head, Mica beat a retreat. She didn't understand Flynn at all, and that couldn't be a good thing. Could it?

Philadelphia

Detective Dellon Mitchell leaned down and kissed her girlfriend on the mouth. "See you later, babe."

Sandy Sullivan rolled over and grabbed Dell's wrist, yanking her down. She shoved the covers aside, exposing her warm nude body, and kept pulling until Dell tumbled on top of her.

"Hey," Dell said, laughing. "I'm geared up here, babe."

"Yeah?" Sandy slid her hand up the inside of Dell's thigh and cupped her crotch. "I'm not feeling the love, baby."

Dell reached under her black T-shirt, pulled her holster from the waistband of her jeans, and dropped it onto the bedside table by feel. Sliding her thigh between Sandy's, she covered Sandy's smaller body easily and kissed her hard, slipping her tongue into Sandy's mouth, tasting her heat and the leftover remnants of the peppermint toothpaste she'd used at bedtime. "Not that kind of gear."

"No problem." Sandy wrapped her legs around Dell's hips and squirmed underneath her. "You always feel good, no matter what kind of gear you're packing."

"Well, I'm glad you think so." Dell nibbled on Sandy's lower lip, thinking if Sandy kept it up she'd have to change her pants, because one of them was gonna leave a wet spot somewhere. But what the hell, she had plenty of jeans. Sandy arched her back and stretched under her like a cat. A big, tempting cat.

"Mmm," Sandy murmured, "isn't it too early to be going to work?"

Dell kissed Sandy's nose. "For rookie patrol officers, maybe, but not for us big bad detectives."

"Oh, kiss my ass too." Sandy shoved at Dell's chest, but Dell didn't budge. Instead, she nuzzled Sandy's neck and bit lightly at the soft, fragrant skin above her collarbone. Sandy was still soft in all the right places, but the police academy training had given her muscles where she didn't used to have them. Dell had always loved how girly Sandy could be while she was smiling sweetly and busting your balls. She was still girly, still as sexy as she had been the first time Dell had seen her in a micro miniskirt and a skimpy top that barely covered her breasts, and what was even better now—Sandy was all hers. Dell sucked at the spot she'd just bitten.

Sandy slapped Dell on the shoulder. "Cut that out. I can't go to work with a hickey. I'll never hear the end of it."

"Hey, babe, everyone knows you're mine. So they all know what a stud you're married t—" Dell laughed harder when Sandy punched her in the arm. Damn it, that was going to leave a bruise. "Ow. Hey!"

Sandy grabbed a handful of Dell's hair and tugged her head back. Sandy's eyes were a brilliant blazing blue, her blond hair still short and spiky. Everything about her was hot, hot, hot. "You better not be talking about your studly activities around the squad. It's enough I have to live down the fact I'm a hooker—"

"*Were* a hooker." Dell kissed Sandy again, slower and softer. "Were, baby, and you've always been a lot more than that."

Sandy had just finished the police academy, and though she never complained, she'd had a hard time with some of her classmates who didn't think she belonged there. Dell would've kicked some ass over the subtle harassment, but she knew that wouldn't help Sandy's case. Sandy wouldn't want her to get in the middle, either, but Sandy never wanted anyone to stand up for her. Sandy was too used to going it alone after years on the street, and as much as Dell wanted to protect her, she respected Sandy too much to smother her. But she wouldn't stand by and let anyone hurt her either. So maybe she had mentioned here or there that Sandy had a rabbi. That just maybe that rabbi was Detective Lieutenant Rebecca Frye. Everyone knew, from a wet-behind-the-ears rookie to a seasoned detective, that if you had Frye behind you, you'd earned it, and then some. Because Rebecca Frye didn't give an inch for anyone. So when word had gotten around that Frye had sponsored Sandy's admission to the academy, the grumbling stopped. And then Sandy had taken care of the rest. She'd proven herself in the field and in the classroom.

"You finished at the top of your class, babe," Dell said. "You earned respect."

"I know." Sandy eased out from under Dell until they were lying face-to-face on the pillow, arms and legs entwined. She stroked Dell's cheek. "Most of the time it doesn't bother me. But I don't want people thinking less of you because of me."

Dell sucked in a breath and leaned her forehead against Sandy's. Could her girlfriend be any crazier? Didn't Sandy know by now she was the best thing to ever come into her life? "You know that's a load of crap, right? Because I get so many points for having a blazing girlfriend like you, my rep is untouchable. Believe me, I want everyone to know you're my girl."

"Yeah, yeah, Rookie," Sandy said, still calling Dell by the nickname she'd used since the first time she'd seen her. "You'll say anything to get in my pants."

"True." Dell kissed the tip of Sandy's chin and pulled her closer until their breasts and bellies and thighs melded. "But I love you like crazy too. I'd be so screwed without you."

"Not happening," Sandy whispered.

There'd been a time when Sandy would've looked away, disbelieving her. Or worse, walked away. A time when Sandy hadn't believed anyone could love her. Hadn't believed anyone could want her for more than a quick fuck in a dark alley. Even now, sometimes, Dell could see the flicker of uncertainty in her eyes, when the memories came back too hard. But most of the time, Dell succeeded in making Sandy believe how special she was, and how much she needed her. If it took her a hundred years, she was going to make sure Sandy believed all the way through how special she was. Besides, telling Sandy she loved her made her feel good too.

"You're it for me, babe."

"You're awfully smooth, you know." Sandy tucked her head in the bend of Dell's shoulder and rubbed her bare breasts over Dell's chest. "I don't suppose you have time to fuck me, do you?"

Sandy's breath was fire against Dell's throat, and her clit shot up hard. "Oh man, that's it. I wish I could, babe, but the Loo called for an early briefing this morning, and you know I can't be late."

"Sometimes I wish you were just a regular detective and not on Frye's super-duper elite HPC squad. Then you could blow off the schedule once in a while like everybody else I see is doing down at Police Plaza."

"You're kidding, right?"

"Yeah. You wouldn't fit in down there any better than I do. If you weren't working high-profile crimes, you'd be so miserable I'd probably never get laid." Sandy grinned. "So what will you be doing all day while I'm riding around in a patrol car with my training officer, being lectured to and treated like I don't have two brain cells to rub together?"

Dell stifled a laugh. Being a trainee sucked, but everyone had to do it, and part of the TO's job was to bust on the trainees to make sure they didn't get themselves or someone else killed the first time they went out on their own. Still, it was tough on the ego, and for someone as independent as Sandy, even harder. "After the briefing? The same thing I've been doing for the last six months—working the streets, talking up the CIs, trying to find a way back into Zamora's operation. Ever since we took down their Eastern European pipeline, everything has gone dead quiet. We can't get a handle on anything—girls, dope, guns. The lieutenant thinks there's been a power shift, maybe with the Colombians or Salvadorans moving in. But if anybody knows, they're not talking."

"Something will break," Sandy said. "The streets never stay quiet for long."

Slowly running her fingers down Sandy's back, Dell settled back for another minute of peace. Sandy was right. Something would pop, soon, and when it did, things would get real hot, real fast. She couldn't wait.

CHAPTER TWELVE

Philadelphia

"Fuck!" Hector rolled off the girl whimpering underneath him and pulled the cell phone from the back pocket of his pants. His jeans were halfway down his thighs, and he grabbed the bitch's hand and wrapped it around his still-hard dick. He pressed the phone to his ear. "Yeah, what?"

"We got a lead off the cousin's cell log," Carmen said.

"Tell me you know where she is." Hector squeezed the girl's hand around his cock and dragged her fist up and down, showing her how he liked it.

"Not yet, but we got a good idea of where she was headed."

"Where?" Hector pushed up in bed, slapped the girl's hand off his softening cock, and shoved his junk into his jeans. Some girls you just couldn't teach. They acted like they'd never seen a stiff cock before. He made a mental note to hand this bitch off to one of his lieutenants. She was a lousy fuck.

"Somewhere in Massachusetts."

"What the fuck is she doing there? You sure?"

"She called her cousin a few times right after she took off. First time was New York City—maybe she took a bus or something. Then a couple more times, once in Connecticut and another time in Massachusetts. The last time pretty close to Cape Cod."

"What the fuck is out there?"

"I don't know. I've never been anywhere except to Jersey City on a run."

"You got a town name or something?"

"Not yet—our guy at the phone company can tell general area, you know like area codes or some shit like that—but with cell phones, not cities necessarily."

"How does that help us?"

Carmen grunted. "We know where to look, we reached out to a few friends up there. She can't hide forever. She's got no money, no friends, no family. We ask around, we'll find her."

"We need to get to her before she does something stupid and the cops pick her up. Besides, rules are rules." The MS-13 had one fundamental rule, and everyone knew it—once in, you never left. Not unless you were dead. If you tried, you would be dead.

"Yo, boss, I hear you."

"Good. We don't want the members to think anybody can walk away from us, no matter who they are." He didn't want to do it, but the stupid bitch wasn't leaving him any choice. Mia had been gone too long for him to keep it from the higher-ups, and he couldn't have his troops thinking he couldn't control his own woman. She needed to come back, one way or the other. And soon. "Find her. I don't care who you have to hurt."

❖

Provincetown

"You care if I put on the ballgame?" Dave asked.

Flynn looked over from where she sat on the threadbare mustard-colored sofa in the squad ready room, reading a history of gravestone carvings in New England cemeteries. Old churches fascinated her. Her father and his father and his before him, as far back as the family tree could be traced, had been clergymen. She and her twin had grown up immersed in symbolism and lore. She'd spent hours in the myriad small cemeteries tucked away in wooded groves on country roads, behind abandoned gas stations, or nestled in the bends of meandering creeks— reading names, tracing family lineages, imagining the lives that had passed over the same ground she had just walked. Continuity, the connections between things past, present, and to come, gave her a sense of purpose and rendered some meaning to the enormity of existence. She tossed the book aside. She hadn't really been concentrating well enough to read it anyhow. "Who's playing?"

"The Sox and—"

"That's enough for me. Sure." Flynn welcomed the diversion.

Usually she could lose herself in a book, and when history failed, the Scriptures usually provided enough questions to keep her mind focused. But not this afternoon. She kept thinking back to breakfast, and Mica. Mysteries intrigued her as much as history, and Mica was nothing if not a mystery. If Flynn judged by their conversations alone, she'd have to conclude Mica didn't want anything to do with her. Mica sent out clear stay-away vibes, at least verbally, and Flynn wasn't one to push where she wasn't wanted. She had the feeling Mica had been pushed plenty in her life. No one ran away from a happy existence.

But people gave off other signals besides verbal, silent messages Flynn often paid more attention to than what was said. Too often, people said what they *thought* they should say, or hid their feelings behind anger or gallows humor or sexual innuendo. But people were often unaware of their body language, which made their feelings harder to hide.

Mica wasn't an easy read. She was good at hiding what she felt, physically and in conversation, but Flynn was very good at discerning the little signs that others might miss. Her ability to hear the unspoken had been honed in a family where preserving the peace had been more important than dealing with hard truths, and those skills had been refined in the seminary. Other than administering the sacraments, a priest didn't have a much more important function than to recognize the truth. If one couldn't, how could one possibly preach? So she'd watched Mica while she was eating breakfast, when Mica wasn't watching her. Mica had been constantly busy, serving tables that had filled rapidly after eight when tourists and townspeople alike began to venture out. Flynn took her time over her meal. She enjoyed watching Mica thread her way between tables, talking and occasionally laughing with customers. She moved quickly, confidently, sensuously. And every now and then when Mica had finished taking an order or while she was clearing a table, she'd glance in Flynn's direction. Mica'd been aware of her, and that meant something.

When Flynn had gone to the register to pay her bill, Mica had passed by carrying a tray laden with dishes and glasses to be washed.

"I'll see you later," Flynn said.

Mica shot her a glance, as if she hadn't expected her to be there, but she'd smiled, and the smile had been warm with a whisper of pleasure along the edges.

Yes, Mica had noticed her. And from a woman like Mica, that counted a lot.

"You okay?" Dave asked.

"Sure. Just got a lot on my mind."

"Okay. You want to drive tonight?"

Flynn smiled at the ultimate gesture of friendship. "No, you go ahead. I'm good riding shotgun."

Dave smiled, looking relieved. "Okay, then."

"Go ahead and turn on the—"

The siren blared and a second later Flynn's radio sounded a callout. She and Dave jogged to the garage and clambered into their unit. Flynn strapped in and logged on to the mobile computer terminal to read out the details from dispatch. "Female assaulted at Commercial and Dyer. Police on scene." Flynn's chest seized. That was half a block from Mica's apartment. "Let's go."

Dave took them out with a screech of tires as Flynn flipped on the siren and started her incident report. Lots of other houses in that area. Lots of street traffic. The victim could be anyone. Besides, Mica was working.

Flynn glanced at her watch. Two in the afternoon. She counted backward in her head. Yesterday Mica had said she started at six thirty. She was probably off now, and if she'd walked home, she'd be right about at the location of the presumed assault. Flynn hissed in a breath, a hard lump forming into the pit of her stomach. She keyed the dispatcher on the dashboard microphone. "Name or description?"

"Don't have anything yet, hon. All I know is it's a woman and she's apparently pretty banged up."

"Okay, thanks." Flynn vibrated with the warning bells clanging in her head. She didn't believe in coincidence. She had never believed in an elaborate grand plan where humans were only fixtures, destined to play out some unknown pageant decided upon by a higher power. But she did believe in fate. She believed some events were destined, but humans had free will. Sometimes life-changing circumstances arose that challenged and tested, and the decisions people made altered the shape of their destiny. Just as she had faith in the amazing capacity of humans to change, to grow, and to impact their destinies through their own actions, she also knew there were mysteries in the universe that defied explanation—mysteries and wonders that spoke of more than the finite universe of humanity.

Her instinct was to reach out to those who crossed her path, those whose lives touched hers. To fulfill her mission, she'd learned to keep herself apart, and when she'd failed, she'd abandoned her calling for a new life. But she couldn't change who she was. Mica touched her, and she could no more deny that than she could deny her faith. She feared another test was coming, and Mica was part of it.

Flynn pointed to a side street blocked by a police cruiser. "There."

"I see it," Dave said. "I'm gonna have to get up on the sidewalk to get the unit in there."

"Let me out here." Flynn popped the seat belt and pushed her door open.

"Hold on! Let me stop before you fall out and I have to put you on a gurney."

Flynn jumped down, keyed the equipment compartment on the side of the unit, and pulled out her FAT box. "I'll meet you there."

Running ahead, she shouldered through the crowd of onlookers and made her way down a narrow alley between a bed-and-breakfast and an art gallery. Allie knelt on the uneven stones next to someone with long dark hair. A dark wet stain spread out from beneath the victim's head. Flynn's stomach clenched. A second later her training took over, and her mind cleared. She squatted next to Allie and opened the trauma kit.

Allie gave her a quick glance. "Late twenties, unconscious when we arrived. We're not sure when the incident occurred."

The woman's face was swollen with purplish bruises and scattered lacerations. Dried blood caked her mouth and her left eye. Rust-colored specks scattered her white shirt—more blood, almost certainly hers. Her stomach was exposed where her blouse had been pulled from her jeans, but her pants were still buttoned and zipped. Flynn's breathing slowed. This wasn't Mica.

"My name is Flynn," she said, beginning the introduction she always used whether the victim appeared to be unconscious or not. The human mind registered all kinds of stimuli even when an individual appeared to be comatose. While she talked, she checked that the woman's airway was clear and inserted a short plastic airway to keep her tongue from sliding back and blocking her trachea; she listened for breath sounds on both sides, checked vital signs, and did a quick cursory exam.

Dave arrived, took in the scene, and set about starting an IV.

"I'll call Tory," Flynn said, "but I think we'll need to transport right to Hyannis. She's going to need a CAT scan and observation."

"I'll call her," Allie said, her face tight with suppressed anger. "I'm going with you. We're going to need her statement as soon as possible. Latimer is already canvassing the neighbors."

"Thanks," Flynn said.

Allie walked away and Dave said, "I'll get the gurney."

Flynn secured the victim's neck with a cervical collar, and she and Dave rolled her onto a backboard and transported her to the gurney. They pushed the gurney up the steep uneven path to the road and toward the unit. The crowd had grown in the few minutes she'd been there, and she spied a familiar face.

Mica stood on the sidewalk, her face pale. Flynn climbed into the unit, secured the gurney, and leaned out to close the rear doors while Dave headed for the cab. She motioned Mica over, and after a second's hesitation Mica slipped between the onlookers and appeared beside the open doors.

"Are you okay?" Flynn asked.

"Yeah," Mica said quietly, without her usual comeback. "Is she okay?"

"I don't know yet." Flynn grabbed the handles on the doors. "I have to go now. I'll talk to you later."

"Okay. Sure." Mica stepped back as Flynn pulled the doors closed.

"Be careful, okay?" Flynn said.

As the unit pulled away and Mica disappeared from view, her voice carried to Flynn. "You too."

Flynn settled next to the patient for the ride up-Cape. She wished she didn't have to leave right now. Mica had looked scared, and she wanted to know why. Even more, she wanted to be sure no one hurt her.

CHAPTER THIRTEEN

Hyannis, MA

Allie paced outside the closed curtain of the emergency room cubicle, waiting for the green light from the emergency room doctors to interview the victim. Flynn had stopped for a second to brief her when they'd all arrived. The girl had regained consciousness in the medic unit during transport and was talking a little bit, but not very much and not very coherently.

Allie's anger simmered just beneath the surface, a scalding tide that burned through her, a fury she couldn't walk off and she needed to. She had a job to do; she couldn't let her outrage distract her. She hated seeing anyone get hurt under any circumstances, but when women were assaulted, she could barely keep her fury under control. Someone had done that to Bri once, and every time she saw a woman lying battered and bruised and bloody, she imagined what it must have been like for Bri, only a teenager at the time. Imagining how Bri must have suffered, how terrified Caroline must have been, made Allie half-crazy. As much as she missed being partnered with Bri, she was glad Bri hadn't been riding with her today. Even though she knew Bri could handle it, probably better than she could, Bri couldn't possibly be unaffected by what had been done to that girl.

Allie ached to find the animal who had done this. She wanted him on the ground on his belly, with her knee in his back and her cuffs clamped down around his wrists. She wanted him to feel helpless, the way this girl must have felt helpless, and she wanted justice. Not for some ideological principle of right and wrong, but for something very, very practical. She wanted the girl bleeding behind that curtain to have the satisfaction of seeing whoever did this to her pay. Her job was to find him and to deliver him for judgment.

The curtain twitched and Flynn stepped out. "It'll be another few minutes."

"How is she doing?"

"Concussion, probably a fractured orbit. They don't think her jaw's broken, though, and there isn't any sign of internal injury."

"That's good, then," Allie said, thinking nothing about this could be good.

Flynn leaned against the wall, her hands in the pockets of her navy blue uniform pants. She looked tired and worn.

"You okay?" Allie asked.

"Yeah," Flynn said. "I just really hate this, you know?"

Allie suppressed the urge to touch her. Flynn stirred something in her, the desire to comfort and protect. But there was just enough tension still humming between them for her to know that trying to be the person to ease Flynn's pain was a bad idea. She didn't want Flynn, not the way Flynn needed, and they both knew it. But she couldn't turn her thoughts and feelings off like a water faucet either. She knew where she belonged. She belonged with Ash, had loved Ash from the first moment she'd seen her, and would always love her. But Flynn was special, and Allie ached to see the unhappiness in her eyes. "How've you been really?"

Flynn smiled, that slow, tender smile that was so damn sexy. "I'm tougher than you think."

"Oh, believe me, I know." Allie remembered the night they'd almost made love in Flynn's apartment. Flynn had moved over her with power and certainty. Flynn had been intense, passionate, in charge. Flynn might be one of the gentlest women Allie had ever met, but that gentleness covered a core of steel.

"So don't worry, okay?" Flynn said. "I'm good. We're good."

"I'm glad. Really glad. So what about you and your new friend?" Allie asked, knowing that was a lame-ass way to go about things but not knowing any better way to do it.

"My friend?" Flynn pushed hard away from the wall. "You mean Mica?"

"Mica. Right. How much do you know about her?"

"Why are you asking?" Flynn had an edge in her voice.

"I was following up after the vehicular incident, and I can't seem to find her in the databases."

"Following up."

"It's my job, Flynn."

"Maybe there's nothing to find."

"Yeah, that seems to be everyone's opinion," Allie said.

"But not yours?"

"Come on, Flynn." Allie lowered her voice. "You have to admit her behavior is suspicious."

"Other than skipping out on a medical exam, I can't see that she's done anything wrong. She doesn't have insurance. She wouldn't be the first person to avoid medical care because they can't afford it."

"If that's all it was, I'd agree with you. But she's evasive, she looks like she's hiding something, and when you put that together with the fact that her ID is probably fake—you have to come up with the same answer I did. She's either in trouble or she *is* trouble."

"Sometimes, Allie," Flynn said tightly, "people are just scared. Sometimes they have a really good reason to be."

"Do you think I've never been scared, Flynn? Do you think I wasn't scared when I thought Ash might have died? When I was facing down a gun in the street?"

Flynn winced. "Hey, I'm sorry, okay? I know you're doing your job. Just don't jump to any conclusions."

"I won't. I promise. But you need to promise me something too," Allie said. "Just be careful. You're too damn trusting, Flynn. You're too kind."

"You're wrong, Allie. You don't know me as well as you think." Flynn sighed. "I have to get back. Call me if you find out anything from the patient?"

"I will." Allie noticed Flynn had not answered her question. Whatever she knew about Mica, she wasn't telling.

❖

Provincetown

Mica emptied a bucket of ice into the sink underneath the bar, one eye on the front door. She felt stupid watching for Flynn to come in, and even dumber when she acknowledged the fluttery feeling in her stomach that had been there since she got to work at six thirty. She'd never gotten excited about seeing anyone before. She hadn't really dated anyone except a couple of boys when she was eleven or twelve, and she'd figured out really quickly that they didn't do anything for her. She'd never really thought about dating girls, even though there was a group of chicks, a girl gang, who hung out together and fucked each other and everybody knew it. Those girls had to fight a lot to keep together, but that wasn't why she stayed away from them. She wasn't afraid of a fight—she just hadn't seen herself as one of them. Some of them were Hispanic, a bunch were white, some were African American, but their identity was different than hers. They were together because they were queer. She hung with her people, the ones who spoke her language—the language of the streets. She sided with the ones who understood what it was like to live where she lived, speak as she spoke, fight the same enemies. She went with the ones who just might be able to protect her. And then when she was inside, she didn't have any choice. There were girls in MS-13 who liked other girls—she knew from the whispered hook-ups she overheard when the guys weren't around, but they didn't get it on openly. The girls were there to serve the men, and those who wouldn't didn't last very long.

And now here she was, running from the life, running *for* her life, and getting all worked up about some girl she didn't even know. Not just any girl either. A freakin' priest. What did that mean, exactly? How did that work? She had no reason to care that Flynn said she was coming by, but she did. Like she said, stupid.

"Hi, Mica," Flynn said as she slid onto a bar stool.

Mica straightened, swinging the empty white plastic bucket in her right hand. She'd been watching for Flynn all night and then missed her entrance while she was daydreaming. What if Flynn had been someone else? What if she'd been one of Hector's scouts? She was going to get herself killed. "Hey."

"How's it going?"

"Same as any other night." Mica glanced down the bar. The crowd was light and the bartender was chatting with a regular. She needed an excuse to keep working and ignore Flynn, but she wasn't really pressed to do anything right then. And she didn't really want to ignore her. Flynn looked good. Black sweater, blue jeans, boots. Nice tight, lean body. Nice face. Really, really nice face. "You don't look like the bar type to me."

Flynn laughed. "I'm not sure what that is, but I mostly come in here to relax."

"Is that what you call it?"

"Most nights. But that's not why I'm here tonight."

Lightning sizzled through Mica's blood. "Oh yeah? Why are you here?"

"To see you."

Mica drew a blank. She didn't have a comeback. She couldn't get used to Flynn always answering a question with what sounded like simple truth. But then, how would she know what simple truth sounded like? She'd learned pretty early that what should have been simple truths never were—I love you meant I want to own you, you're beautiful meant I want to fuck you, I'll always be here for you meant I'll be around as long as I get something out of it. She shivered.

"Are you okay?" Flynn asked.

Mica shrugged angrily, as if she could shake off the past. "I meant, why are you here in this town? Shouldn't you be in a parish somewhere?"

"Could I have a beer?"

"I'm not a bartender."

"Okay. Then how about I get a beer when the bartender is ready, and I drink it while you work. Then later, when you're not working, I'll tell you what you want to know."

"Why?"

"Because you asked. And because I want to tell you." Flynn reached across the bar and touched Mica's arm. Her fingertips were warm, soft. Like her lips had been. Mica's skin tingled all over, as if electricity were shooting out from the small spots where Flynn touched, heating her body like an electric coil on a stove. "I don't have anyone else I want to tell, Mica."

"I don't understand you," Mica said.

"I'm not complicated. When I look at you, I feel things."

Mica swallowed. This was crazy. She shouldn't be here like this. She shouldn't care what Flynn said next, but she did. "What things?"

Flynn smiled. "Are you sure you want to know? Some of them might be X-rated."

"Just some of them?" Mica tried to sound dismissive, but she wanted to laugh too. Flynn made her want to laugh. No one ever had before. "Spill."

"I think you're beautiful. You make a spot inside my chest glow, like sunlight on my skin, only inside. I think you're tough and strong, and that makes my heart race a little bit. Sometimes I think you're sad, and I want to make you smile. You make me feel all kinds of things, and when I think about you, I want more."

"If I thought you really meant all of that—"

"I do. Someday I hope you'll believe me."

Mica almost believed her now. Flynn was easy to believe. Flynn was going to make her weak, make her vulnerable, and if that happened, Flynn was going to get her dead.

"You don't want to get involved with me, Flynn," Mica said softly.

"How do you know?"

"Because I know you don't know me."

"Then let me. I'll talk to you and you can talk to me. That's how it works."

"You don't know how anything works in my world."

Flynn slid her fingers down Mica's arm and grasped her fingers. Flynn's hold was gentle, but firm. Certain. And the heat shot lower, into Mica's depths.

"Then teach me. Let me learn you."

Mica trembled. Her belly flared and for a second, her head grew as light as her heart. "And then what do I do when you walk away?"

"Why isn't it easier to start out thinking I won't?"

Mica shook her head vehemently. "I can't."

"Give me a chance, Mica. Please."

How could she say no? No one had ever given her a choice before. They'd taken or commanded or threatened. But they'd never stood before her completely open and vulnerable and given her the choice to stay or walk away. She threaded her fingers through Flynn's and the connection felt right. Scary, but right.

"I'm on a short shift tonight. Ten o'clock?"

"I'll wait."

"I'll get you that beer—draft, right?"

"You remembered." Flynn smiled, and a blaze ignited in Mica as if Flynn had poured gas on kindling. Mica didn't run. She was going to burn for this, but she couldn't run from the promise in Flynn's eyes.

CHAPTER FOURTEEN

Allie awakened to the sound of the lock on the front door sliding home and footsteps crossing the living room toward the open bedroom door. She didn't turn on the bedside light. She liked waiting in the dark for Ash. One or the other of them so often returned during the middle of the night after a late shift or an out-of-town job, they'd gotten used to moving around the bedroom by memory. She liked lying under the covers, absorbing the small sounds of Ash emptying her pockets, piling change and keys and her wallet on the dresser, taking off her clothes. Those small familiar tasks of Ash coming home to her made Allie think of permanence, of an endless tomorrow. The safety and certainty of that future warmed her as much as knowing in another minute Ash's hard, strong body would slide next to hers. Ash approached the bed, and Allie pulled the sheets back.

Ash lay down with a sigh. "Hi, babe."

"Hi, baby," Allie whispered.

"Sorry to wake you. I didn't think you'd be in bed."

"I didn't sleep much last night, so I turned in early tonight. It isn't late, is it?"

"Just a little after ten." Ash turned on her side and drew Allie against her.

When Ash kissed her, the last shadows of worry and longing disappeared from Allie's mind. Right at that moment, all she knew was Ash was here, and hers. "I love you."

Ash stroked her back and kissed her throat. "I love you too. You okay?"

"Mmm-hmm." Allie pulled Ash on top of her, opening her legs so Ash could settle between her thighs. She stretched beneath Ash, fitting her breasts and her belly into the solid planes of Ash's body. "I'm really, really good right now. I bet in a few minutes, I could be even better."

Chuckling at the not-so-subtle message, Ash braced herself on her elbows and skated her mouth over Allie's. The feel of Allie's warm pliant flesh, the scent of her—light and sweet with an undertone of dark orchids—went through her like a knife. Wanting her was a sweet agony she would gladly bleed for. "Jesus, I missed you so much."

"Do you think you always will?"

"Babe, I'm sure of it." Ash skimmed her open mouth over Allie's breast, scraping her teeth lightly over Allie's nipple.

Allie made a soft purring sound in her throat, the kind of sound she made when she was happy and turned on. Ash loved pulling that moan from her, almost as much she loved Allie's cries of pleasure when she came. She rocked her hips between Allie's, slipping her tongue deeper into her mouth, stroking slowly in all the places she knew got Allie even hotter. When she'd been away for a few days, Allie was always on edge when she got home. Allie was going to need a lot more reassurance to convince her she wasn't walking out on her again. A lot more time, a lot more reassurance, and a lot more moments like this. Sex was more than just physical pleasure for Allie. For her too, but Allie was one of the most passionate women she'd ever met. Allie connected with others in a lot of different ways, but sex was definitely one of her most intense forms of expression. Allie absorbed sensation with every glance, pulled in emotion through her fingertips with every touch. Making love to Allie was just one way to prove she was staying—and definitely no hardship.

"I've been thinking about this since we talked last night." Ash wanted to be the one to fill her, to satisfy her, to convince her she'd be there every single day from now on. She caressed Allie's belly, stroking softly until Allie's hips lifted and her legs went tight.

"Ash," Allie murmured, half warning, half plea, "I've been ready since last night. If you're not careful—"

"Don't worry. I'm going to be very, very careful." Ash slid her fingers between Allie's legs, finding the silken path that took her home. She entered Allie in a long smooth thrust, and Allie gasped. Sometimes she took Allie slow, sometimes she liked to tease her until she begged, but after she'd been away a while, she took her fast the first time, reminding Allie of what was theirs alone. She kissed her mouth, pushed deeper, filled her until there was no space between them. "I love you."

"I love you," Allie murmured, her fingers digging into Ash's shoulders. "More than I ever...thought...oh God, Ash, I'm going to come."

"That's right, babe, that's right." Ash clenched her teeth, her clit pounding, the urgency in her loins painting her vision red. She wanted to own her, down to her last fiber, she wanted to move her the way no one else ever would or ever could, the possessive passion driving her nearly insane. She picked up her pace and Allie came, squeezing down around her fingers, twisting and whimpering.

"Don't stop, don't stop," Allie cried. "I'm going to come again, baby. Don't stop."

"I know, I know," Ash whispered. She slowed, but didn't stop—moving deeper with each tight stroke. The tide of Allie's pleasure caught her by surprise, and before she could get control, she went under. "I can't...I'm coming. God Allie, touch me—hurry."

Ash lifted her hips and Allie scissored her fingers around Ash's clit. Allie squeezed erratically, her attention fractured by the orgasm breaking inside her.

"Harder," Ash groaned. "I'm almost there. Harder, please. Please, oh fuck."

"Ash!" Allie bucked under her and Ash exploded, coming hard in Allie's hand. Her mind gave way, her breath gave out, and she crumpled, helpless and drained. Allie wrapped her up in her arms, and Ash closed her eyes. She'd wanted to comfort Allie and found peace instead.

❖

"All set." Mica grabbed her denim jacket from a peg on the wall behind the bar and swung around the end to join Flynn.

Flynn pushed her half-finished beer aside and they walked outside. The streets had come alive and were filled with couples strolling hand in hand, groups of boisterous club crawlers, families with tired children in tow. Despite the still-warm days, the nights were cool, and Flynn put her hands in her pants pockets.

"Cold?" Mica asked.

Flynn smiled. "A little bit."

"You want my jacket?"

"Then you'll be cold."

Mica hunched a shoulder. "I don't get cold that easily." She looked Flynn up and down. "Except I don't think it'll fit you."

"I appreciate you offering. I'll warm up in a few minutes." Flynn hesitated. "Although I suppose you could put your arm around me and get me warmer all that much faster."

Mica laughed. "You are so obvious."

"I need practice."

"Seriously." Mica slowed, seemed to study Flynn's face. She wrapped her arm around Flynn's waist. "Better?"

Flynn's pulse jumped into the stratosphere. Mica was smaller than her, an inch or two shorter, more delicate appearing, but the arm around her waist was firm and strong and she liked the way it felt. "Much, much better."

"You sound surprised."

"Maybe a little."

"Why? You think I need taking care of and you don't?" Mica didn't let go of her, but she sounded angry.

"It's not that," Flynn said. "I'm just not used to it."

"Not used to what?"

Flynn sighed. "Being taken care of, I guess." She'd never really been with a woman she could lean on. No one's fault, but that hadn't been her role. With her parishioners, she'd had to be strong. With Evelyn she'd had to be the voice of reason, although she'd failed at that pretty miserably. She and Allie had come together as two bruised souls, seeking solace in one another. They both had been a little too hurt to do more than hold on.

Mica's arm tightened around her waist. "So enjoy it."

"I will." Flynn slid her arm around Mica's shoulders, lightly cupping her upper arm. The position was intimate, more intimate than anything she could remember. The time she and Allie had walked home holding hands came close, but she hadn't had any expectations that night.

She felt differently now. Even though she knew nothing was going to happen between them, a frisson of excitement stirred in her belly, and she let the thrill spread through her. Mica was incredibly beautiful.

"Something wrong?" Mica asked.

"No, why?"

"Because you're shaking all over."

"I'm really bad at this. I'm sorry."

"At what?"

"Dating, I guess."

"Oh man, don't tell me you're a—"

"No, I'm not." Flynn laughed. "Everyone's always asking me that.

I just…haven't had all that much practice either. And it's kind of been a while."

"Are we dating?"

"I'd like to."

Mica gripped the waistband of Flynn's jeans, as if she thought Flynn might go somewhere. "I don't know how to do that."

"That's good, because neither do I."

"Maybe it would be better if we just fucked."

"I'm sure that would be great," Flynn said, proceeding by feel as if she were in a blacked-out room without the slightest glimmer of light. She didn't doubt for a second if she said the wrong thing, made the wrong move, Mica would flee like a skittish animal. She didn't have a roadmap. She had no game plan. She had instincts that could barely be called instincts, based on nothing except the fear she'd seen in Mica's eyes and the uncertainty she'd heard in her voice. "I think going to bed with you would be fabulous. But I'd sort of like to work up to it, so when we get there, we can do it more than once."

"You mean in a row?"

Flynn laughed again, feeling as if she'd dodged one landmine only to face another one. "Well yeah, that too, but I was sort of thinking that I didn't want it to be a one-time thing."

"So what if that's all I want—one time?"

"Then that would be good to know up front." Flynn stroked up Mica's arm, over the crest of her shoulder, and lightly clasped the back of her neck, letting her fingers rest against the side of Mica's throat. She was so warm. So soft. "It's your call, Mica. But I have to warn you, I have a feeling that one time is going to leave me awfully hungry. So I'd rather we wait and find out if we maybe could do it differently."

"I don't know if I want to wait." Mica threaded her fingers through Flynn's and pulled Flynn's hand away from her neck and down inside her jean jacket.

Flynn's palm rested just at the top of Mica's breast. If she moved her fingers an inch lower, she'd be caressing the hard point of Mica's nipple. The cauldron of excitement in Flynn's stomach exploded and shot down her legs, through her chest, and out her fingertips. "Oh man, I don't want to wait now either. You're driving me crazy."

"Yeah? I like that." Mica rubbed her hip against Flynn's as they walked, dragging Flynn's hand down and molding it to her breast.

"No fair," Flynn muttered. She tugged Mica into the shadows under the awning of a closed clothing store, tilted Mica's face up with her free hand, and kissed her. Mica tasted sweet with a little bit of a tangy bite. Flynn had seen Mica take a shot of bourbon right before they'd left the bar, the only drink Mica had had all night. The whisper of whiskey tingled on Flynn's tongue. She wanted to keep kissing her, but if she did she'd have to touch her, and she couldn't do that here. "Sorry, I just needed—"

"Me too." Mica wrapped her arms around Flynn's shoulders and pressed against her, tilting her head back and giving Flynn her mouth.

Flynn kissed her again, deeper and more thoroughly. When she lifted her head she was gasping for breath. "Mica, we can't—I'm sorry. I should've waited."

"I think you should shut up and kiss me again."

Flynn looped her arms around Mica's waist and swayed with her in her embrace. "I want to. I really, really want to. But I'd rather be alone with you, somewhere private. Just in case."

Mica grabbed Flynn's hand and tugged her back onto the street. "Then you better hurry up. You already got me hot. Now you better deliver."

Flynn practically had to run to keep up. She was getting dizzy, not from the pace, but from a lighthearted excitement she'd never known before. "Me? *Me?* It's all you, Mica. You're amazing."

"Like I said, you're crazy." Mica smiled up at her, a blazing smile that made her look so young and so free, Flynn's heart wept.

"No argument. I told you I'd be hungry."

"It's okay," Mica said. "I like you that way."

They passed through the center of town and into the East End, where the crowds thinned rapidly. Storefronts gave way to bed-and-breakfasts. The galleries along the way were all closed and dark. Soon they were alone. A block from Mica's, Flynn noticed Mica glancing over her shoulder for the third time. "Something wrong?"

"No," Mica said, but she sounded distracted and her expression was tight.

"You sure?"

"Yeah." Mica's smile was forced, all joy gone from it. "Come on, we're almost there."

They'd almost reached the alley where Flynn had tended to the woman who'd been assaulted when running footsteps bore down on them from behind.

Mica cried, "Flynn, run—"

Flynn didn't have time. A heavy blow landed in the middle of her back, throwing her off balance. She stumbled forward into the darkened alley and crashed against the side of the building. She almost fell, caught herself with a hand against the building, and swung around, desperately searching for Mica. A man, judging by the size of the attacker, had Mica around the waist and was dragging her farther down the alley, into the dark.

"Let her go! Let her go! Help! Someone call the police!" Flynn charged, still yelling at the top of her lungs. She took a running leap and grabbed the guy around the neck, hoping the weight of her body would knock him down. He was twice her size and she didn't have a prayer of taking him one-on-one. He grunted when she hit him, and the three of them landed in a heap in the sand and stones.

"Flynn," Mica gasped. "Get out of—"

Mica's voice ended in a strangled gasp. Flynn grabbed the arm circling Mica's neck and yanked. A fist caught her just under the diaphragm and the air exploded from her chest. She couldn't suck in a breath and curled into a ball, gasping and writhing. Her lungs were on fire. All she could think of was Mica. He had Mica.

CHAPTER FIFTEEN

Philadelphia

Dell rode the elevator to the third floor of the renovated warehouse in Old City where JT Sloan lived and, along with her business partner Jason, ran a cyber-security firm. Since the High Profile Crimes Unit had merged with Sloan's civilian operation, the warehouse had become their headquarters. Dell liked that a lot better than a few desks shoved together in some corner at One Police Plaza. Here, she felt like they were in their own world, where Rebecca Frye led the team and they all contributed, regardless of rank or experience. She was still a rookie detective, but she felt as if she'd earned her stripes and the Loo treated her that way. Everyone did.

So it especially sucked when she wasn't contributing. She hadn't accomplished anything all day. She'd hit all her usual places, hunting up confidential informants, talking to the street girls, even spending a few hours at the Trocadero after dark, hoping someone had heard something about where all the action had gone. None of the drag queens, transvestites, or drag kings who frequented the Troc, and whose affiliations often crossed ethnic and cultural divides, had any intel.

Ever since the HPC unit had busted the human trafficking ring smuggling young girls from Eastern Europe into the country to fuel the porn and prostitution business for the Zamora family, crime had gone underground. None of the team believed they'd stopped the Hydra-like organization, even though they'd cut off one of its main heads. Kratos Zamora, one of the two brothers in charge of running everything from guns to crack cocaine to girls for hire, had been shanked in his jail cell before he even went to trial. His brother Gregor was suspected of having orchestrated Kratos's assassination. Whatever information

Kratos might have traded in a plea bargain to reduce his prison time had died with him. Gregor, so far, was untouchable. For all intents and purposes, he was an upstanding businessman.

The only rumor Dell had been able to pick up after pounding the streets for twelve hours was the same one she'd been hearing for the last six months—vague rumbles that new blood was moving in from Central America by way of the West Coast and challenging the long-established crime hierarchy on the East Coast. MS-13 and its offshoots were organizing, merging disparate cliques into cohesive gangs with solid leadership and better communication. Unlike traditional crime families that tended to specialize in one type of crime, La Mara would take on anything to turn a profit—drugs, guns, prostitution, pornography—and their currency was violence and intimidation.

The police were scrambling for leads—they had faces, they even had some names, but what they didn't have was evidence. The OC guys were running wiretaps wherever they could, shooting thousands of surveillance photos, trying to put undercover officers into the gangs, but infiltrating well-organized groups took years. And every day that passed, more girls died in the service of masters who only saw them as commodities to be sold, bartered, bargained for, and discarded when their use was over. Every day more schoolkids became addicted to the drugs that flowed freely, every day young men died in gang wars fought not with fists and chains, but with automatic weapons. The battle was unending; only the colors of the uniforms and the symbols tattooed on faces, arms, and torsos changed.

Dell stepped off the elevator and the doors slid silently closed behind her. She threaded her way through the desks, computer workstations, monitoring equipment, file cabinets, and other workaday equipment that filled the huge loft. Ten thirty at night. Most of the lights were off, but she wasn't surprised to see one monitor glowing. Sloan leaned back in her swivel chair, her hands flying over the keyboard as data streamed across the thirty-inch screen. From across the room she looked relaxed, sleepy even, but Dell knew better. She'd looked into Sloan's face enough times to know her sharp indigo eyes would be intensely focused and her scarily quick mind assessing, collating, and discarding facts as rapidly as they appeared.

Dell pulled out a nearby chair and dropped into it. Sloan glanced over, brushing her hand through her jet black hair. The platinum wedding band glinted on her left hand. She wore her usual jeans and tight white T-shirt. She looked nothing like the Justice agent she'd once been, or the current civilian liaison to the police department. "What are you doing here?"

"I don't know." Dell stretched out her legs, clasped her hands behind her head, and stared at the ceiling. "Sandy's got swing shift and won't be home for a while. I'm getting nowhere. I think I must be missing something. Have you got anything?"

"Not yet. But there's encouraging chatter."

"Chatter." Dell sat up straight. "Meaning?"

"Jason and I have been working on this new algorithm to track low-level street activity that ordinarily would get written off as too minor to mean anything—drive-bys, bar fights, domestic disturbances, drug busts. Minor street activity that usually flies under the radar."

"Yeah? Why?"

"Because when you can't see the big picture, you need to start looking at the small pieces. Remember, maybe once or twice a year we'll take down a huge shipment of cocaine or find a container full of girls, but those big hits never stop the crime machine from running. Business as usual is mostly small deals—selling a trunk full of guns, street soldiers peddling a dime bag here, a vial of crank there, some sleaze shooting a thirty minute porn flick on dirty sheets with his iPhone in the back of some warehouse. Your scumbag pedophile uploading a handful of blurry photos to his friends for a small charge."

"How does tracking all that help us?"

"I'm pulling data from the central system downtown and mapping geographical profiles of where crimes are occurring, which gangs are involved or suspected to be involved, assigning territories, looking at shifting borders."

"Does the brass know?"

Sloan grinned, a feral smile that would have made Dell's blood run a little colder if she hadn't known her. Sloan had been betrayed by the very system she'd fought for, and she had no respect for organized law enforcement. She followed no one's lead, other than Frye's. "They're not using it, so I might as well."

That figured. Dell leaned forward, clasping her hands between her knees. "What does all that tell you?"

"The old territories are in flux—boundaries are changing."

Excitement shot through Dell's chest. "Like we thought, new regimes."

"Definitely. By cross-referencing crimes with the new geography along with what little intel we're getting from vice, organized crime, and homicide, we can start placing people inside the high-activity zones, which means we can start building profiles of leadership."

"Yeah, I got it." Dell glanced across the room to the huge whiteboard where they posted photographs and other data on the hierarchy of the various crime families. What had once been a simple genealogy with one dominant ruling crime faction now looked like an array of stars circling a sun. The smaller constellations weren't splinter groups, but new gangs moving in. La Mara was one, but only a few photos with names underneath were arranged in that constellation. No clear leader had been identified.

"So how do we figure who's who?"

"You tell me." Sloan's eyes glinted.

"We need someone inside, but infiltrating a gang takes a long time."

"Or?"

"We turn someone already inside."

Sloan nodded. "Exactly. I've set up a capture net to monitor any busts involving anyone from the hot zones, anyone *associated* with anyone from those areas, anyone who we might be able to leverage into giving us intelligence."

"You know," Dell said, "if we could get to someone like that, we could use them to get one of our people inside. Save us a lot of time."

"You got anybody in mind?" Sloan grinned.

Dell ran her hand over her chest and rested her fingertips just above her belt line. She hadn't been undercover for a while. After things got really hot with the Zamoras, Mitch had to disappear for a while. She missed him. "Yeah. I know just the guy."

❖

Provincetown

Flynn retched, her stomach empty, nausea rolling through her like an oily tide. Gravel bit into her cheek, burning the abraded skin. She blinked dirt from her eyes and rolled onto her belly, trying to get her hands and knees underneath her. She was so weak she couldn't push herself up. If she could just get a breath, just one short breath, she could get to her feet, she could find Mica, she could tear that bastard apart for putting his hands on her.

Screams filled the alley.

Oh God, not Mica. Please, please don't let her be hurt.

The screaming trailed off into a steady wail, reverberating inside her head. Her lungs expanded sharply and cool salty air burst down her throat. She sucked in a lungful, coughed, sucked in more, and managed to push to her knees.

Siren. Not screaming. A siren.

"Mica?" Her voice was barely a croak.

A bright light hit her in the face and she raised her arm, trying to shield her tearing eyes.

"Hands in the air," someone shouted.

Flynn raised her other arm. "Mica," she gasped. "A guy…took Mica."

"Flynn?"

Flynn couldn't see through the glare, but she recognized Bri's voice. Dark shapes raced by at the edges of Flynn's vision. "Bri, somebody's got Mica." Fear gripped her throat so hard she couldn't get the rest of the words out. She shoved upright and staggered, nearly going down again. "He's got—"

"Hey, take it easy." Bri's arm came around Flynn's waist. "Let's get you over here where you can sit down."

"No." Flynn tried to pull away. "Mica." She scrubbed her eyes and saw swaths of light cutting through the dark near the beach. Flashlights.

"Got something," someone yelled.

Flynn's heart stilled in her chest and she managed to break Bri's grip.

"Stay here, Flynn," Bri ordered, a command edge in her voice. "More backup's on the way."

"I need to find her. If she's hurt—"

"If she's hurt, we'll take care of her."

Flynn couldn't just wait. Mica was out there in the dark, maybe hurt, maybe dying. Life ended so quickly, without warning, without rhyme or reason or logic. Life's plan wasn't meant to be understood. Flynn knew that, but she'd never been able to accept it. She couldn't accept it when Debbie had done the unthinkable, and she couldn't accept it now. If she could have found peace with God's wisdom, she'd still be wearing her collar. She yanked away from Bri. "I'm not leaving her out there alone."

"Sorry, Flynn, but you need to stay out of the way." Bri waved to a sandy-haired officer. "Smith, keep an eye on her until the EMTs come."

Two figures stumbled out of the darkness into the flickering blue light that bathed the alley.

A uniformed officer called, "Need a medic."

A second, raspy voice cut through the jumble of voices. "Get your hands off me. Where's Flynn?"

Mica. The fist of terror crushing Flynn's chest eased. Mica sounded royally pissed off. She'd never heard anything sweeter. "Mica? Mica!"

"Flynn!"

Flynn ran toward the sound and Mica broke free, stumbling toward her. Flynn braced herself and Mica crashed into her arms. Pain raged through her chest, but she wrapped her arms around Mica and held her close. "Are you hurt?"

"No." Mica's hands flew over Flynn, tracing her shoulders, her chest, her sides. "Did that motherfucker stick you?"

"I'm okay." Flynn winced when Mica squeezed her right side.

"Like hell you are." Mica searched the faces of the officers milling about, her arm around Flynn's waist. "Yo, you guys! Over here. She's the one who needs a medic. I think her ribs are broken."

Bri stepped out of the crowd. "You're both going to the clinic. Once you've been seen to, I'll get your statements."

Another cruiser screeched to a halt in the street, a door slammed, and Reese Conlon strode down the alley. She took one look at Flynn and Mica, then turned to Bri. "Do we have the assailant?"

"Negative," Bri said. "We were here maybe a minute or two tops after this all went down. A civilian walking by heard someone yell for police and hit nine-one-one. We were ten-seven at the Wired Puppy. Two seconds sooner and we would've had him."

Reese's cool gaze slid over Mica and Flynn. "Looks like you got here in time."

More sirens, the crackle of radios, and the alley quickly filled with paramedics and more officers. EMTs from the night crew pushed a gurney toward Flynn and Mica.

"Who's first?" a short muscular blonde asked, staring at Flynn in concern. "God, Flynn, are you all right?"

"Yeah. I'll walk, Chris," Flynn said.

"Like hell you will." Mica pointed at the EMT. "Her ribs are broken. She needs to ride."

"You heard the lady, Flynn," Chris said, taking Flynn's arm and leading her to the stretcher. "No use fighting us all."

Flynn gave in. Her legs were about to give out. When she tried to lie back, pain shot through her chest and she felt something pop. She groaned.

"What is it?" Mica said sharply. "Where are you hurting?"

"I think the cartilage is separated," Flynn said, gritting her teeth. "It hurts like hell but the ribs aren't broken." She raised her hand and Mica took it. Mica's knuckles were scraped and bloody. "You sure you're okay?"

"Yeah," Mica said her expression closing down. "I'm just great."

"You've got blood on your shirt," Flynn said gently, her stomach twisting.

"Yeah." Mica glanced down as she walked along beside the stretcher. "It's not mine, though. Asshole had a switch. Now he doesn't."

CHAPTER SIXTEEN

Allie awoke disoriented, unsure if it was morning or night. The buzz of her cell phone vibrating on the bedside table reminded her of a swarm of angry wasps, and she resisted the urge to slap at the air. She searched in the dark for a touchstone and found it in Ash's warm body pressed against her back. In an instant she remembered climaxing with Ash inside her, falling asleep with Ash in her arms. She knew where she was, who she was, and she groped for her phone. "Tremont."

"Hey," Bri said. "Sorry to get you up, but I thought you'd want to know someone jumped Flynn and another girl tonight."

"Is Flynn all right?" Allie pushed up in bed and Ash, waking instantly, wrapped an arm around her waist. "What happened?"

"Not sure yet. We're on the way to the clinic right now."

"The girl…Hispanic, early twenties, about five-seven, black hair, brown eyes?"

"Sounds right. That the one?"

"Yeah. I'll be there in ten."

"Roger that."

Allie disconnected and shoved the covers aside. "I have to go in. Sorry."

Ash clicked on the lamp on her side of the bed. "What's going on?"

"That was Bri. Flynn and Mica—the woman I told you about— were assaulted. That's all I know." Allie grabbed a pair of jeans off the shelf in the closet. Her hands were shaking.

"How bad?"

"I don't know. Damn it. I knew something was going on. Tell me this is a coincidence." Allie yanked a shirt off a hanger. "If I'd questioned her the way I wanted to instead of waiting for the damn computer checks, I might have—"

"Hey." Ash's hands came down on Allie's shoulders, and she drew Allie back against her chest. Ash kissed her temple. "Facts first, right?"

Allie took a breath and gave herself a second to let Ash's calm strength settle her. She didn't usually get emotional where work was concerned. If Ash was hurt, yeah, her world tilted. Flynn was a friend—okay, a little more than a friend; the exact definition escaped her—but that still didn't explain why she felt so guilty. "I feel like this is my fault, somehow. Like I should know what's going on and I don't."

"Babe," Ash murmured, turning Allie to face her. "You're doing all you can do. Go find out what's going on and take it from there. You're a good cop. Better than you should be for someone your age."

Allie laughed and slugged Ash softly in the shoulder with her fist. "Don't go pulling that older and wiser crap on me."

Ash grinned. "Well, as soon as you get your temper up, you start thinking more clearly."

Allie kissed Ash hard on the mouth. First she'd make sure Flynn was all right, then she'd find out who Mica really was, and she wouldn't stop digging until she had the answers she wanted. "I love you."

"Same here. Take it easy out there, okay?"

"I always do."

❖

The back doors of the medic unit opened, and Mica looked out on the same parking lot she'd seen before. The same clinic, only lit tonight by floods at the corners of the roof and over the door. She was strapped to the same stretcher, but this time she was awake and Flynn was on a stretcher across from her. A lot more police cars pulled in around them than the first time too.

Her chest seized. This was bad. She'd gotten away the last time before she'd been asked questions she couldn't answer, but she wasn't so sure she could do that again. Too many cops and a lot more questions. Then there was Flynn. She turned her head, peering around the blond EMT who was bent over Flynn in the tight space, organizing the lines and tubes and monitors attached to her. Flynn had a plastic collar Velcroed around her neck, an IV in her arm, and a bunch of wires attached to her chest. Her eyes were open, but in the flat yellow light of the ceiling dome, she looked dead. Dead people got this look about them—their eyes stopped shining the second their soul, or whatever it was inside them, disappeared.

Mica's heart hammered hard against the inside of her ribs.

"Flynn?" Mica wet her dry lips. "Flynn, are you okay?"

Flynn's eyelids flickered and she turned her head a tiny bit until the collar stopped her. "Yeah. You?"

"Good. I'm good." Mica got her breath back and the pain around her heart lessened. "I'm sorry."

"Why? Did you kick me?" Flynn's voice was hoarse, lower than it usually was.

"You know what I mean."

"I do, and there's no reason for you to be sorry." Flynn raised the hand that wasn't strapped down and tugged at the collar on her neck. "Come on, Chris, I don't need this. It's driving me crazy."

"Sorry, Flynn," Chris said. "You know the drill. It looks like somebody played soccer with your head. The immobilizer stays on until Tory says it can come off."

The male paramedic who'd been driving climbed into the back, and Mica gripped the stretcher for the trip into the clinic. The medics took Flynn out first.

"I want to go with her," Mica called. "Let me out. I don't need to be—"

Chris knelt by her side. "You'll be inside in just a second. She's in good hands. Nobody's going to let anything happen to Flynn."

"Yeah, sure." Mica knew better. No one was ever safe. Anything could happen to Flynn, and no one would tell her.

❖

Tory heard familiar footsteps coming down the hall outside her office. She didn't have to see Reese's face to know that was her. Reese might be a cop now, but she walked like a marine. Sharp, steady, perfectly even steps, as if she always knew her destination and never wavered. Warm heat flooded through Tory's chest. The thing she loved best about Reese was how steady she always was. How sure and strong. Even when she was hurt and frightened, Reese never wavered.

"Incoming," Reese said from the doorway.

"I heard the sirens. How bad?"

"Both walking wounded. I'll leave the rest up to you." Reese leaned against the doorway, her brow faintly furrowed. "You didn't get much sleep. How are you feeling?"

Tory smiled. "Is this the first of the million times you plan to ask me that in the next nine months?"

Reese's brows drew down further. "Try two million."

Tory laughed. "I'm fine. If you'll remember the last time, I—"

"I remember, Tor," Reese said darkly.

Tory came around her desk and motioned Reese in. "Close the door."

Reese pulled the door closed, and when she met Tory in the middle of the room, Tory pressed her palms to Reese's chest and kissed her. "I've only got a second. I know you remember the last time. You remember how it ended. Try to remember how exciting it was, how miraculous, to feel the baby kick the first time, and think about Reggie and all she's given us. I'm going to be fine. Promise me you'll try not to worry."

Reese slid her hand around the back of Tory's neck and tugged her closer. "I can't promise that. But I can promise I'll enjoy every second of this pregnancy."

"Well, maybe not the morning sickness part. I won't ask that of you." Tory kissed her again and stepped away. "I've got to go."

"I'll wait. I'll need statements from them."

"I'll let you know as soon as you can see them." Tory went into the hall and met Chris Connelly, one of the local EMTs, outside treatment room one. Another EMT was assisting a patient in treatment room two. "Which one first?"

"This one," Chris said, indicating the room behind her. "The patient in two is stable—a few lacerations and abrasions, some blunt force trauma to her neck, but none of it looks too serious. Her vital signs are stable, no loss of consciousness." She grimaced. "Flynn, on the other hand, took a beating. She was disoriented at the scene, but no documented loss of consciousness. She's got a significant contusion on her right temple and localized right rib tenderness. Possibly fractures."

"All right, I'll start with her. Can one of you stay with the other patient just to be sure she remains stable?"

"Yeah, I'll radio base we're not available for calls until you give us the go-ahead."

"Thanks, I appreciate it. I can wake Nita up, but by the time she gets here, I'll probably have a chance to look at both of them."

"No problem," Chris said.

Tory walked over to Flynn and picked up the clipboard on the bottom of the bed. She scanned it quickly. Vital signs were all normal, although her pulse was rapid and her blood pressure high. An area over her right temple and cheekbone was swollen and discolored. She leaned down and squinted at the area. Not a fist. A shoe, most likely. Anger simmered but she pushed the distracting fury aside and rested her hand on Flynn's wrist. Her pulse was bounding. Stress, fear, pain. "How are you feeling?"

"Not bad." Flynn's voice was reedy and thin.

"Show me where your chest hurts," Tory said as she fit her stethoscope to her ears. Flynn covered an area on her lower right side, and Tory avoided the spot as she moved her stethoscope over Flynn's lung fields. Breath sounds were present, but depressed. Flynn obviously wasn't taking a deep breath. She set her stethoscope aside and pushed Flynn's shirt up. A five- by eight-inch area over her right lower rib cage was mottled purple. She gently palpated the area, and Flynn stiffened, trying unsuccessfully to hide a wince. Tory didn't feel any crepitus from air in the tissue or grating from shattered bone ends grinding together, but the degree of Flynn's pain suggested a fracture. "We'll need to X-ray you."

"Have you seen Mica yet?"

"The other patient?"

"Yes."

"Not yet. Mica. Wait a minute. The girl who was hit while riding her bicycle?"

"Yes, that's the one."

Tory made a few notes on the clipboard. Red flags were waving from every corner. "That's a pretty unlucky coincidence."

"The driver of the van was from up-Cape," Flynn said slowly. "This guy wasn't from around here. Not related, I don't think."

"Well, you don't need to figure it out for me. Reese will be talking to you in a little while. What we need to do now is get you X-rayed."

"Can I talk to Mica first?"

"If it will keep her from running out again, yes. But she'll have to come to you. I don't want you moving around until I've seen your X-rays."

"Okay. Whatever you say."

"Let me finish looking at you, and then I'll get her. Where else do you hurt?"

Flynn closed her eyes. "I think that's about it."

"That's enough."

Flynn nodded, saving her breath. Every inhalation was like swallowing fire, and her stomach, even though it was empty, was still in revolt. She did not want to vomit. All she wanted was to see Mica, but she knew that wasn't going to happen unless she cooperated. The sooner she got her X-rays, the sooner she'd be able to see her. She needed to make sure Mica was all right, and she needed to make sure she didn't disappear.

The trip to and from X-ray was an exercise in torture—every movement incited another surge of stabbing pain. Tory gave her some Percocet, and after a few minutes that started to help. Flynn concentrated on keeping her breathing even and her heart rate quiet. Prayer was like meditation for her, and after so many years, she could easily slip into that self-contained zone where mind and body existed on separate planes. The meditation helped dull the burning pain, but knowing she'd see Mica after the procedure helped even more.

Chris, who had volunteered to transport her to the X-ray bay, wheeled her back to the treatment room just as Tory came out of the room opposite.

"Mica?" Flynn asked.

"She'll be over in a minute. I'm going to go read your films." Tory nodded to Chris. "Thanks. I think you and Vince can take off."

"Sure thing, Doc." Chris leaned over the stretcher to Flynn. "You take it easy, you hear? I don't want to see your face at work for a few days."

"I'll call the captain in the morning," Flynn said.

"I'll take care of it." Chris squeezed Flynn's shoulder. "Just get some rest."

"Hey," Mica said, sidling up to the stretcher. A red, angry swath of bruises encircled her neck. Fingerprints.

Flynn pictured the shadowy figure clamping an arm across Mica's throat and dragging her away. She reached for Mica's hand and when Mica immediately took hers, Flynn's pounding pulse settled. "Did he hurt you?"

"Nah," Mica said with a shrug. "He was too busy whaling on you."

Flynn smiled. "I'm glad I could offer a diversion."

Mica stroked Flynn's arm, her dark eyes wide and worried. "He really did a number on you. I'm so sorry."

"Hey. Not your fault."

Mica bit her lip, looking as if she wanted to say something, but she remained quiet.

"When we get out of here," Flynn said, "will you tell me what's going on?"

Mica flicked her gaze to the door as if worried someone might overhear. "You don't want to know. There's nothing you can do and—well, you see what kind of trouble you can get into just being around me."

Flynn gripped her fingers more firmly, sensing her wanting to withdraw. "You weren't the one making the trouble. Don't run out on me."

"You ask a lot."

"Do I? Do you mind?"

"I don't know." Mica frowned. "I just don't want you getting hurt anymore."

"Why don't you let me worry about that."

"Because you don't seem to have much sense."

Flynn smiled and tried not to laugh. She couldn't breathe enough to laugh. "You know, you really make me feel special."

Mica grinned. "Good." She blushed. "'Cause, you know, you are."

"Mica," Flynn said seriously, "the police will want to talk to us. Can you do that?"

"Sure," Mica said quickly. "Why not."

Flynn recognized the bravado for what it was, an attempt to cover up her uncertainty. "I know these people. You can trust them."

"You think so?"

"I know so."

"I wish..."

"What?"

"Never mind."

"Look, when this is over, I want you to come home with me."

"Um, I think your timing needs a little work."

"Not that way," Flynn said. "I don't think you ought to be alone. And besides, I'm not going to be very functional and I could use the company."

Mica narrowed her eyes. "I think you're playing me now."

"Maybe. Is it working?"

"Maybe." Mica ran her fingers through Flynn's hair. "Maybe I feel a little bit sorry for you."

"Thanks." Flynn leaned her cheek against Mica's palm, relieved that Mica had agreed to stay with her. Whoever the guy was, he was still out there, and Mica was vulnerable. She wasn't going to let anyone hurt her.

Allie strode through the door. "Hey, Flynn. Are you okay?"

"I'm okay." Flynn tugged Mica a little closer, afraid she would bolt. "A few bumps and bruises is all."

"Uh-huh." Allie didn't look like she believed her, her cool gaze assessing Mica. "Dr. King said it would be okay if we got your statements now. I'll take you," she said to Mica, "first. Come with me."

Mica glanced at Flynn, and Flynn nodded. "I'll be here when you're done."

Wordlessly, Mica followed Allie from the room. Flynn fought down a wave of fear that she wouldn't see Mica again. She tried telling herself she was overreacting, but she knew better. Sometimes people walked out the door and never came back.

CHAPTER SEVENTEEN

Tory sat at her desk finishing her notes. She looked up when Reese appeared in the doorway, talking on her phone.

"Hold on a second," Reese said to whoever she had on the line and looked at Tory. "Status report?"

"I'll fill you in when you're done." Tory gathered the files and moved over to the sofa in the small sitting area across from her desk. A minute later, Reese joined her.

"Problem?" Reese asked.

"No. They're both stable and capable of speaking with you."

"Allie said you gave her the green light. She's going to talk to the girl first. I was on my way to talk to Flynn." Reese crossed her ankle over her knee and leaned back, stretching out one arm along the back of the sofa until her fingertips touched Tory's shoulder. "Something's bothering you."

Tory grasped Reese's hand and threaded her fingers through Reese's. "Are you thinking one of them might have been targeted?"

"It's certainly possible. Going by the statistics, though, a random assault—possible robbery, even gay bashing—would be more likely."

Tory stroked Reese's palm, thinking about Mica. The girl hadn't run away this time, but everything about her screamed that she wanted to. She rarely made eye contact, her answers were short and uninformative, and her manner belligerent—at least on the surface. She had an edge of anger, all right, but her attitude seemed fueled more by fear than anything else, and that bothered Tory. Her instinct was always to heal, and while she was able to tend to Mica's body, she hadn't been able to help her escape whatever monster was chasing her. "My ethical responsibilities are getting a little tangled here. You know, patient confidentiality."

"This is an official police investigation," Reese said. "We need to know what's going on, especially if one of them is a target. This could've been a homicide investigation. They were lucky."

"I know that. But I'm also their doctor, and our conversations are confidential."

"True." Reese's tone was casual. She wasn't pushing, but she wouldn't. Not just because she was Tory's partner, but because Reese believed in the fundamental merit of rules and regulations. She would entrust her life to the hierarchy that created order and safety out of chaos. "You'll have to decide how much is confidential and what is essential for us to know in order to see that this doesn't happen again."

"I'm sorry," Tory said. "I wish I *did* have something substantial to point you toward, but I don't. I'm just really worried that the next time one of them shows up here, they're going to be a lot more seriously injured."

"I intend to see that doesn't happen," Reese said. "I appreciate your impressions. Tell me what you can, I'll ask what more I need to know, and you answer whatever is appropriate. You've got good judgment. I trust you."

"Thank you." Tory collected her charts and sat back down. "I can give you a physical update. They were both viciously assaulted, although Flynn was the more seriously injured." She ran through her physical findings for each patient. "On the basis of this, if one of them is a target, I think it's Mica."

"Why, if Flynn took the brunt of the beating?"

"From what I've put together from the two of them, it sounded as if the assailant was focused on Mica, and Flynn got in the way. She was…"

"Collateral damage." Reese's expression never changed, but she had to be thinking about the troops she had lost.

"I hate that term," Tory said.

"So do I. What you've told me is very helpful. What else?"

"Mica's ID says she's from New York City, but when I mentioned a few places, she didn't seem to be very familiar with any of them. Doesn't necessarily mean that she's not being truthful, but I suspect both her name and her address are false."

"That jibes with what we've found out so far." Reese regarded Tory steadily. "Any distinguishing marks or characteristics?"

Tory hesitated. "She has scars indicative of knife wounds—one on her lower abdomen, several on her arms, one on her back. I can't really tell now how serious they might have been, but she's no stranger to violence. She has a number of tattoos, most of which are actually very well done. The large one on her back says…" She looked at her notes. "La Mara. Someone's name, I imagine. The others—"

"Wait a minute," Reese cut in. "Two words…La Mara?"

"Yes."

"Is there a number?"

"Huh." Tory pictured the design in her mind. "I didn't see it initially, but yes, the scroll after the words that I thought was decorative is actually a fairly complex and quite beautiful thirteen."

"Thanks. I appreciate the information." Reese stood up, her face settling into the stark lines Tory recognized as ultimate focus. Reese was now on a mission.

"This is serious, isn't it," Tory said, rising with her.

"It could be." Reese brushed the backs of her fingers over Tory's cheek. "Wait here until I can have someone take you home. I'm going to go into the office in a few minutes and make a few calls."

"All right. I've got plenty to do until you have an officer who's free." Tory slid her arms around Reese's waist and kissed her quickly. "Can you make it home for breakfast? Pick up the baby on the way? We might as well let her sleep the rest of the night with Kate and Jean."

"I'll be there." Reese looked at her watch and frowned. "Why don't you catch some sleep while you're waiting for a ride? The paperwork can keep."

Tory smiled. "Spoken like a true cop who I happen to know hates paperwork. If I get tired, I'll nap. Be careful."

"I will." Reese kissed her. "I love you."

Tory waited until the sound of Reese's footsteps ended with the opening and closing of one of the treatment room doors. She closed her own door and stretched out on the sofa with Mica's chart balanced on her knees. As she completed her notes, she thought of the tattoo that had meant something to Reese and that Reese had very carefully not explained.

❖

Flynn was drifting, struggling to stay awake as the Percocet kicked in, when someone knocked on the treatment room door and walked in. Hoping Mica had returned, she shifted painfully onto her right side and opened her eyes. "Hi, Reese."

Reese pulled over a stool and sat down next to the treatment table, putting them on the same level. "Doing okay?"

"Not too bad," Flynn said. "Any word on the guy?"

"I was just talking to Bri. She and a couple of the other officers have been canvassing the neighbors and patrolling the general area. Nothing so far."

"He either took off in a car or he's inside somewhere."

"More than likely, but we'll keep looking. Can you give me a description?"

Flashes of those few minutes in the alley ran through Flynn's mind. Mica's shout for her to run, the torrent of blows, the helpless frustration. A wellspring of fury clouded her already cloudy mind. "Give me a second."

"I'm sorry to have to do this now," Reese said.

"No. It's okay. It just happened really fast."

"Take it one thing at a time. Let's start with what was going on before you reached that alley. Where were you?"

"Walking east along Commercial. On our way to Mica's." Flynn smiled at the memory of them rushing down the street, arms around each other, and why they were in such a hurry. She'd been happy and lighthearted, excited to be with Mica, to be connected to her. She'd been thinking about being even closer. "We were half a block from Mica's when it happened."

"Do you remember where he came from? What direction?"

Flynn tensed, reliving the shock of the first blow in the middle of her back. "Someone hit me from behind, pushed me down the alley, away from Mica."

"So he came up behind you? Any indication he might have been following you?"

"I don't know, maybe. I guess he could've been standing in the doorway of one of the buildings when we passed. I remember—" She remembered Mica looking over her shoulder, more than once. As if she was looking for something or some*one* behind them.

"What?" Reese asked.

"Nothing."

"Mica didn't give any indication she was nervous or frightened?"

Flynn's head began to pound. A cascade of flashing lights shot through her eyes, and a thousand needles pierced her brain. "I'm sorry. I'm not sure. I'm a little fuzzy right now."

"I understand," Reese said patiently. "Just give me your impressions. I'll sort things out from there."

"I think Mica looked back a couple times. I can't be sure."

"Okay. She didn't say anything? Didn't warn you in any way?"

"No. We were kind of wrapped up in each other. At least I was. Not paying much attention to anything else."

"The two of you, you're involved?"

"I'm not sure." Flynn flushed. "It was a date. A casual one."

"Uh-huh, okay. So someone came up behind you, shoved you into the alley. Then what?"

Flynn gripped the side of the stretcher, curling her fingers around the cool steel. Surprise, pain, fear, and anger flooded through her in succession. Mica's sharp cry of pain, the sight of the attacker's arm wrapped around Mica's throat, lifting her off the ground, pulling her away. Pulling her into the dark. "He was medium height, heavyset. Maybe three or four inches taller than Mica. There wasn't much light. No beard, close-cut hair. Big arms. No jacket."

"White? Black?"

"Not black. I remember his forearm was bare. There was a mark— some kind of tattoo on his forearm—right forearm."

"Do you remember what it was?"

"No. I only saw it for a second, but it was big, maybe five inches high."

"Did you hear his voice?"

"Yes. He had an accent. Spanish, I think." Flynn's breathing was ragged and she was starting to get light-headed. She settled herself, fighting off the disorienting effect of the drugs and the icy fear of memory. "I'm sorry I don't have more for you."

"That's all right, you did really well." Reese leaned forward and rested one hand on the stretcher next to Flynn's. She didn't touch her, but her presence filled the space. "What can you tell me about Mica?"

"I don't know what you mean," Flynn said almost automatically. Everything always came back to Mica and unanswered questions. And always, her pressing need to protect Mica from everyone, even the people she trusted.

"The usual things people talk about when they first meet—where she's from, what she's doing here. Is she married, seeing anyone, hooked up with friends in the area?"

"Shouldn't she be telling you this?"

"Yes, but I'm not sure she will." Reese held Flynn's gaze. "You know what I'm talking about."

"I'm sorry, I can't tell you anything."

"I can understand that you don't want to. That keeping her confidence is important to you. But one of you could have been killed back there. If there's any chance it's going to happen again, I need to know what's going on."

"I don't know the answer to your questions," Flynn said.

"If you did, would you tell me?"

"I don't know." Flynn struggled to explain what she couldn't even explain to herself. "You'll have to find out from her what you need to know."

"All right. Try to get some sleep." Reese rose. "When we're done talking to Mica, I'll have Allie give you both a ride home."

"Thanks."

Reese paused on the way to the door. "By the way. Is this her priest protecting her or her girlfriend?"

"I'm not her confessor." Flynn took a long breath. "I don't think I'm her girlfriend either, but I'd like to be."

"Word of advice, then—love sometimes makes it hard to see the whole picture, especially when all you see is her. You can get into trouble that way."

"Yeah," Flynn said. "I know."

"Your ID says your name is Mica Butler." Allie motioned to a chair in the small conference room down the hall from the treatment rooms. Mica glanced at the chair and then the door they'd come through, and Allie braced herself to grab her if she tried to run. She looked like she might. "Do you want a soda or something?"

"No," Mica said.

"You might as well sit down. This is going to take a few minutes." Allie pulled out a chair at the small round wooden table and set her hat on the top. She leaned back and waited. It was two a.m. She had all night.

Mica yanked out a chair across from Allie's and flopped into it.

"You want to tell me what happened tonight?" Allie asked.

"We got jumped. He took off when we didn't lay down for it."

"You know him?"

"Nope."

"Know why he went for you?"

"Nope," Mica said.

Allie took out her notebook. "Description?"

"It was dark."

"He almost killed Flynn," Allie said conversationally and looked up from her notes. Mica's bored expression faltered. Her eyes sparked and her lips thinned. Bingo.

"I didn't see him all that well."

"And you don't know him," Allie repeated. *Come on, give me something.*

"I already said no."

"Butler." Allie changed tacks, hoping to catch Mica off guard. "Something tells me that's not your real last name."

"I already told you, I don't know who the guy is. I don't have anything else to say."

"Where are you from?"

"New York City."

"Where did you go to school?"

Mica crossed her arms. "A bunch of places. I quit before I graduated. Can't remember them all."

"And you came all the way here to what, work for minimum wage in a bar?" Allie got up, pushed change into the coffee machine, and waited while steaming liquid the color of muddy water filled a paper cup. She added Splenda from a shelf next to the vending machine and sat back down. She blew on the top, sipped, and wondered why coffee machines couldn't make decent coffee. Ever. "No bars in New York City?"

"Is there some law against me working in a bar?"

"Nope." Allie placed the coffee cup down in front of her. "No law against it at all. There is a law against lying to me, though, and I'm pretty sure you're lying."

Mica stared at some point past Allie's shoulder. The message was clear. She wasn't talking and she knew she didn't have to.

"Whoever this guy was, he's still around. He'll probably be back."

Mica's jaw tightened. She was beautiful, even pissed off and wanting a fight.

"Did you cut him?" Allie asked.

"Yeah, I cut him."

"Stuck him or cut him?"

Mica glanced at Allie with amused respect. "Stuck him, but not as hard as I wished I had. He blocked most of it, caught a shoulder, I think."

"Left shoulder? Right shoulder?"

"Left."

"How'd you get the knife away from him?"

"Asshole held it to my throat, put it right up where I could get it."

"Pretty risky. He could have gotten you first."

Mica shrugged. "He wasn't trying to kill me."

"What was he trying to do?" Mica's face went blank, and Allie took that as a sign she was headed in the right direction. "He wasn't interested in raping you. Men who want to rape women don't jump couples. So if he didn't want to kill you, what does that leave us?"

"You're the cop."

Allie smiled. "That I am. I'm glad you've got that in focus."

"Look, I don't know the dude. It was dark, and he was behind me. Couldn't see him. I got nothing that will help you."

"You shouldn't sell yourself short," Allie said. "You know what he wants, don't you?"

"Got no idea."

"Yet you know he wasn't trying to kill you. Makes me think he wants you. Why would he want you?"

"No idea."

"Let's say I believe you," Allie said, although she let disbelief seep into her tone. "Let's say you're right. This guy comes out of nowhere and goes after you for no good reason. You were lucky to get away. You got a piece of him. Good for you."

Mica narrowed her eyes, looking for the trap.

"Too bad Flynn got in the middle. Maybe next time she won't be so lucky. Maybe he won't just beat her, maybe next time he'll cut her throat quickly."

"Maybe there won't be a next time," Mica said sharply.

She looked like she wanted to dive over the table and get her hands on Allie's throat. Good.

"You better hope there isn't," Allie said. "Because if he comes after you again and Flynn ends up getting hurt, I'm not letting you walk away."

Mica pushed her chair up and stood. "You got nothing. Except maybe the hots for Flynn."

Mica walked out the door and Allie let her go. Mica was partially right. She had nothing, only the same suspicions she'd started with. But she had one thing she hadn't had before—certainty that this wasn't the end of trouble for Mica. And now that Flynn was mixed up in it, she wasn't backing off until she found out exactly what was going on. As to having the hots for Flynn, Mica was wrong. But then, Mica was jealous.

Allie smiled. She could use that.

CHAPTER EIGHTEEN

Allie pulled open the front door of the cruiser parked in front of the clinic. "You'll probably be more comfortable sitting in the front, Flynn."

Flynn took in the backseat—no inside handles, steel mesh and impenetrable plastic between the rear compartment and the front—a cramped prison cell on wheels. Her ribs ached, but the Percocet had helped dull the stabbing pain that accompanied every breath. She could move a little more easily now too. No matter how much it hurt to squeeze into that tight space, she wasn't going to let Mica ride in there alone. "Thanks. I'll be fine in the back."

Allie frowned at her across the roof of the cruiser. The security lights flooded a crescent of the parking lot with harsh light, giving Allie's sensuous features a dangerous edge. Allie glanced from Flynn to Mica, shook her head, and reached inside the cruiser to pop the rear locks. Flynn pulled the door open with her left hand and, seeing Mica hesitate, got in first. Mica finally inched in beside her and pulled the door closed.

When Allie started the cruiser, the locks snapped down. Allie's silhouette was visible through the impregnable barrier, but they were effectively isolated.

Flynn had never been conscious of being a prisoner before, and she quickly discovered she didn't like it. The space was claustrophobic, and just knowing that she couldn't get out if she wanted to brought acid roiling in her stomach. Beside her, Mica sat staring straight ahead, her hands clenched on her thighs. Flynn slid toward her, wincing as the movement tugged at her damaged ribs.

"You should have sat in the front," Mica muttered.

"Yeah, probably." Flynn rested her fingertips on Mica's thigh. Mica's slender muscles were rigid. "This is pretty awful back here."

Mica snorted, her mouth lifting into a smile Flynn guessed held no humor.

"At least nobody's puked back here. Tonight anyhow," Mica said.

"Geez, I hope not."

"You can tell her to take me to my place."

"Is that what you want?"

Slowly, Mica turned on the seat until she faced Flynn, their bodies very close. Her breath gave off the sweet tinge of alcohol and peppermint.

"You're pretty busted up. I don't think you'd be much good tonight."

"Maybe so." Flynn kept her fingers on Mica's thigh and stroked slowly up and down. "Got any more mints?"

Mica sighed, fished a small plastic container out of her front pocket, and shook two into Flynn's hand.

Flynn popped them into her mouth and chewed. "I still want you to come home with me."

"Why?"

"It's been an exceptionally crappy night, but it started out really well. Walking home with you was one of the best evenings I've ever had. I don't want that part to end."

After shooting a quick glance at the front seat, Mica cupped Flynn's jaw and kissed her. "Didn't anybody ever teach you not to say exactly what's on your mind?"

Flynn slid both hands to Mica's waist and leaned in to her until her ribs protested and she had to stop. She rested her forehead against Mica's. "I've sort of been trained to tell the truth, you know? Tough habit to break."

Mica snorted. "Not every priest tells the truth."

"Not everyone does. You're right."

"Sometimes telling the truth can get you hurt."

"Did someone hurt you?"

"We're not talking about me."

"Not right now."

Mica wrapped her fingers around Flynn's upper arms and caressed her. "You're pretty scary the way you never give up."

"I didn't think you scared easily."

"Not usually. If I could figure you out better, I'd be good."

"Nothing to figure out," Flynn said mildly. "I like you. I like everything about you. Plus I think you're beautiful, and I love the way you kiss. Maybe you could do that again."

Mica pressed her palm gently against Flynn's side and Flynn winced. "Like I said. You're not going to be up to doing much tonight."

"More than you think."

Mica kissed her again, easing her tongue between Flynn's lips, teasing her with quick darting caresses and the slow slide of her full warm lips. She kept going, probing and stroking and playing until Flynn moaned. Mica eased back and grinned. "Guess we'll find out."

Flynn nodded, the heavy pall of pain and frustration lifting from her shoulders. "I guess we will."

When Flynn settled back, she caught a reflection of Allie's eyes in the rearview mirror, watching them. Intent, bright, unhappy. Mica shifted closer and Flynn stroked her hair. "Tired?"

Mica nodded silently, rested her head on Flynn's shoulder, and wrapped one arm gently around her waist.

"We'll figure this out in the morning," Flynn said.

"Sure," Mica whispered, not sounding very convincing.

From the front seat, Allie's muffled voice announced, "We're here, Flynn."

"Thanks," Flynn said as the locks popped up. She tried not to rush to get the door open.

The dome light came on, and Allie shifted around to look back at them. "Where do you need to go, Mica?"

Mica shot a glance at Flynn. Flynn pushed the door open, eased one leg out, and gripped Mica's hand. "She's not going anywhere. She's staying with me."

"Do you think that's smart?" Allie asked. "Neither of you is in very good shape, and if you run into any kind of trouble—"

"We're fine," Flynn said gently. "But thanks."

"Yeah, right," Allie muttered as Flynn closed the door.

The cruiser slowly pulled away, and Flynn slid her arm around Mica's waist. "Ready?"

Mica regarded her steadily. "Are you?"

"This is the part where you'll have to trust me." Flynn held her breath. She was talking about a lot more than the two of them maybe sleeping together, and Mica knew it too. This was where Mica would walk away, or take a chance. Flynn's heart thudded in her chest, and with every passing second a cold hard stone grew in the pit of her stomach. She couldn't talk her way into Mica's life. She couldn't talk away Mica's problems. But she could listen to them. And if Mica gave her a chance, she could prove she was worth the risk by staying. No matter what Mica told her.

"I don't want the night to end either." Mica took Flynn's hand.

❖

Allie slowly pulled away, watching Flynn and Mica make their way up the path to Flynn's condo. Four a.m. She'd only had a few hours' sleep after Ash had gotten home, and not much the night before, but she was wired. She set her radio to Bri's channel and tried her. "Adam Charlie one, you copy?"

"Adam Charlie one," Bri came back immediately.

"Anything?"

"Nothing."

"You coming in?"

"Going to make another swing around."

"Roger that. Thanks." Allie switched off and drove back to the sheriff's department where she'd picked up her cruiser earlier. Reese's SUV was in the lot. Allie parked and went inside. The place was empty except for a civilian dispatcher manning the phones. A light shone under Reese's office and the door was ajar, so she knocked.

"Come on in," Reese said.

Allie pushed the door open and stepped inside. "Sorry to bother you, I saw your light."

"No problem." Reese gestured to the chair. "Have a seat."

Allie pulled the straight-backed chair closer to Reese's desk, sat, and leaned her forearms on the edge of the desk. "I didn't get anything from Mica."

"What were your impressions?"

Allie shrugged. "She's been questioned before. Very cool. I think she knows something but she's not talking, either because she doesn't trust us or she's involved in something she doesn't want us to know about."

"What do you know about La Mara?" Reese asked.

Allie frowned. "It's a West Coast gang. I think I saw a documentary on it once."

"It started out as a group whose main purpose was to protect Salvadorans who were being preyed upon by other factions on the West Coast, but it evolved into a gang that took advantage of the very people it was supposed to be protecting," Reese said. "In the late nineties their reach extended through most of California and into some of the surrounding states. In the last few years, offshoots have sprung up all over the East Coast. We've started to see a lot of activity in Boston as well as New York, Philadelphia, Baltimore, Richmond."

"We don't see very much gang activity here, though," Allie said. "Most of the population is seasonal. And there's no local gang culture."

"You're right, but that doesn't mean we won't. This is still a popular place for yachts to harbor, and wherever you have high traffic volume, you have the possibility of drugs and weapons. Easy to come into port, pick up or drop off a shipment that goes out right away by land or water, and then travel on to the next destination. No one's required to register their vessel beyond the most basic information for an overnight berth in the harbor."

"Still, that requires a pretty high level of organization."

Reese nodded. "Ten years ago La Mara wouldn't have been able to pull it off. But times have changed. They're strong, they're organized, and they're violent."

"Why are we talking about this?"

"I'm pretty sure Mica has gang ties. If not now, she has in the past."

Cold dread seeped into Allie's stomach. "I read somewhere that no one gets out once they're in."

"That's true. If she's running, she's in danger."

"And so is anyone with her." Allie wanted to jump up, tear back to Flynn's, and kick Mica's ass around the block for putting Flynn in danger. "You think that's what's going on?"

"I don't know what's going on. I can't get any information until the morning. I've put a few calls in to my contacts in the FBI for background information. They'll get the message first thing in the morning, and we might turn something up. I take it your searches didn't come up with anything?"

"Not yet, but I widened the geographic area and expanded the search parameters earlier today. I was about to fill out my interview report and run down the computer checks again. Nothing popped earlier tonight."

"All right. We still don't have anything concrete, but the pieces I'm starting to see don't look promising."

"What about Flynn?"

Reese leaned back in her chair and rested her arms on the armrests, studying Allie. She knew about Allie and Flynn and knew their involvement was over now, but that didn't mean Allie wasn't still invested. Allie didn't walk away from anything—especially not people she cared about. She was passionate, and passion could be a good thing in a cop. Passion fueled drive, kept a cop looking and searching when it seemed there would never be any answers. But passion sometimes clouded good judgment. "I got the impression Flynn was personally involved. But Flynn is smart. And remember, Mica hasn't done anything illegal."

"That we know of, yet," Allie said.

"That's true. But at this point, she's a victim, and that's how we need to go about running down our leads. As to Flynn, I think you have to trust her judgment."

Allie pushed the chair back and rose. "Yes ma'am. I'll get on those computer checks." She turned and started for the door.

"Tremont," Reese said quietly.

Allie stiffened. "Yes, Sheriff?"

"If you're going to take the lead on this case, you're going to need to have a clear head."

Allie jerked around. "The lead?"

"You're the one who picked up on something being wrong. You've already started the investigation. Stay with it." Reese reached for a stack of papers. "Keep me in the loop at all times. And keep your personal feelings under wraps."

"I'll do that."

Reese watched her go, wondering if she'd be able to keep her feelings for Flynn from interfering with her judgment. She needed to learn how, and there was no better time than now.

❖

Flynn opened the door and flicked the switch just inside. A table lamp came on across the room, next to the faded brown sofa. Allie had been the last woman she'd had in her apartment, and they'd ended up tangled around each other on that sofa. After Mica followed her inside, she closed the door.

"Are you hungry? Need anything to drink?"

"No, I'm good."

"Come on." Flynn took Mica's hand and led her through the living room, past the kitchen alcove, and down the short hall to her bedroom. She flipped another switch and a small lamp next to her bed glowed a warm yellow. "The bathroom is through that door over there. If you check the medicine cabinet, you'll find a couple of new toothbrushes and toothpaste. Do you need a T-shirt or anything?"

Mica glanced down at her dirt-smeared T-shirt and jeans. "Yeah, guess I better."

"I'll get you something. Go ahead and use the bathroom first."

After Mica disappeared into the bathroom and closed the door, Flynn slowly and laboriously undressed. She pulled on an oversized, faded Boston Bruins T-shirt and didn't bother with anything else. By the time she'd accomplished what usually took her ten seconds, Mica was back, still in her soiled clothes. Flynn held out a soft white V-neck T-shirt. "I think this will fit you well enough."

"Thanks."

Flynn took her turn in the bathroom, and after washing up and brushing her teeth, she turned out the bathroom light and crossed to the bed. Mica was already under the covers, the sheet drawn across her chest. Her arms rested on top of the pale blue comforter. Her skin was an even golden brown except for the dark patches of the ink on her right upper arm and left inner forearm. A heart with a knife through it. A crescent moon wreathed in blood-red tears. Mica's tattoos were like her, mysterious and beautiful and kissed with sadness. Flynn pulled back the covers and slid underneath. Six inches separated her from Mica in the double bed. When she turned to shut off the bedside lamp, pain shot through her right side, and she winced.

"I'll get it." Mica leaned up on her elbow and reached over Flynn. Her breasts brushed Flynn's and Flynn's nipples hardened. Mica instantly stilled.

Flynn clasped Mica's waist, her fingers curving around Mica's narrow middle, her thumbs pressed into her firm stomach muscles. Mica looked down at her, her eyes wide dark pools, her full mouth swollen and moist.

"You'll want to be careful, now," Mica warned.

"Why's that?" Flynn's throat was tight with wanting. Mica shifted closer, her naked thighs sliding over Flynn's. Flynn sucked in a breath when Mica's soft, smooth skin pressed against her center. She was wet and Mica had to feel it.

"Because you're hurt and I'm horny," Mica murmured.

Flynn grinned. "If I don't move very much, I don't hurt."

"Then you better not move." Mica carefully shifted, bracing herself above Flynn on her bent arms. Her pelvis settled into Flynn's, heat against heat.

Flynn watched Mica's face come closer and closer. She tilted her head. "I really want you to kiss me."

"You know if we do, there might be no going back."

Flynn tightened her arm around Mica's hips and held her more firmly. Mica remained poised above her, waiting. Waiting for her to decide. Flynn stroked her other hand up the center of Mica's back and buried her fingers in Mica's hair. Mica was absolutely still, her eyes unblinking.

Flynn pulled Mica's head down and kissed her.

CHAPTER NINETEEN

Philadelphia

Sloan punched in a number on speed dial with one hand and alternated scrolling between the three monitors in front of her and tapping keys with the other hand. She hummed a passable version of Springsteen's "Born to Run." Her blood pumped furiously—the thrill of the hunt infusing her with excitement nothing except being with Michael could ever match. Detective Lieutenant Rebecca Frye answered on the second ring.

"Frye."

"Hey," Sloan said, "got something you might be interested in."

"At a quarter after four in the morning?"

Sloan glanced at the time readout in the lower corner of the closest monitor. The last time she'd looked had been when Dell had left a little after midnight. "Sorry. I was chasing some data…"

"Right. Is Michael out of town again?"

"Yeah, she's the keynote at a think-tank summit on cloud communication integration." Sloan laughed. "How'd you know?"

"Because every time she goes away, you don't move out of that chair until she calls and tells you to go to bed."

"Oh. She did. I was going, and then, well. You know."

Frye laughed. "What do you have?"

"I set up keyword tags to send alerts if any query anywhere cross-references to our open cases."

"How you're pulling from other databases is one of the things I don't need to know, right?" Frye sounded wide-awake.

"Technically it's just data sorting—the capture programs, well, they might be a little…specialized."

"Right. Like I said…I don't know how you came by the info. And?"

"Someone in Massachusetts is asking about the identity of a young Hispanic female with ties to La Mara."

"Gotta be thousands of them," Frye said.

"Yeah, you're right, but the various factions have pretty well-defined territories. So if we assume East Coast, that narrows it down. And if they're having trouble identifying her, it means she's either not in the system anywhere at all—and you know how unlikely that is—or she's trying to hide her identity. So why would she do that?"

"I can think of plenty of reasons. Top of the list being she's wanted for something somewhere. What else got you interested?"

"Hector's main squeeze has been noticeably absent on video surveillance for quite a while."

"Whose surveillance would that be?"

"The Gang Control Unit has been watching Hector and crew for over a year, trying to build a RICO case. They've got three or four surveillance units and a wiretap going. Most of the conversations they pull are in code and pretty useless, but every now and then they'll get a good shot of three or four lieutenants and Hector holding a meet somewhere."

"And we have access to the Criminal Intelligence Unit video surveillance tapes how?"

Sloan smiled and tilted her head back, staring at the shadowy patterns in the pressed-tin loft ceiling overhead. Intricate patterns like the information highways she traveled in cyberspace, intertwining in ways that made no sense until suddenly the perfection of the design snapped into view. "Let's just say they left the file cabinet drawer open for anyone passing by to look."

"You hacked their computers."

"That's such a harsh word."

"Okay, I'm not asking," Frye said. "That thread you're pulling is a little bit stronger now. We're missing a girl, someone else has one they can't identify. What did she do?"

"Don't know. Right now it's a missing persons inquiry." Sloan sat forward, switched programs on one computer, and pulled up a reasonably good shot of Hector, two other men, and a young woman climbing into a Hummer. The girl was pretty—dark curly shoulder-length hair; emphatic features; strong, full-bodied build.

"Where?"

"Provincetown."

"That sure is a far cry from the Badlands. What's her name?"

"Mia Gonzales. I know it's a long shot, Frye, but the description fits her. Right age, right distinguishing characteristics."

"Ink?"

"That we don't have."

"What's your theory?"

"If it's her, she's either doing work for Hector up there—muling maybe—or she's running."

Rebecca sighed. "If she skipped out on MS-13, they'll chase her until they find her. And they won't care about leaving a trail of bodies."

"I know. But if it's her, and we get to her first—we've been looking for some way into 13 for a long time. She could be our key."

"Do we have anything on her?"

Sloan tapped keys and another database opened. "I'm looking. Hector is pretty damn arrogant—he takes credit for just about everything that goes down in the region, but no one has any evidence to make anything stick. If she's his girl, she's got to know what he's into. Makes her an accessory at the least."

"Worth working it." Rebecca sounded as if she was getting up. Her muffled voice said, "It's okay. I'm not leaving yet."

Sloan realized she'd probably woken Frye's wife with her phone call. "Sorry about the hour."

"Forget it. I'm up now, and Catherine is used to nighttime calls. I'm going for a run, then I'll reach out to the Massachusetts people when the sun comes up. Text me the name and number of whoever's in charge up there."

"Good enough."

"And, Sloan?"

"Yeah?"

"Go to bed."

"Sure thing." Sloan disconnected, swiveled to face another bank of monitors, and called up another program.

❖

Provincetown

Mica felt as if she was walking through a dark room with her hands out in front of her, trying to identify familiar objects that were no longer where they used to be. She wasn't a virgin. She knew what sex was. She'd thought, before the first time Flynn kissed her, she'd known what desire was. She'd been so wrong. The shape and texture of the landscape she'd thought she understood and knew how to travel had changed. She couldn't recognize the landmarks, couldn't find the guideposts. She was lost.

Her skin burned, her breasts ached, and she was so wet her own body was a foreign country. The pressure between her thighs was unbearable. Unbearable and scarily exciting. She had no idea what she was doing, she only knew she couldn't stop. Flynn lay beneath her, soft and strong and warm. Part of her mind was aware Flynn was hurt, and she kept her weight on her forearms and thighs, but everywhere their bodies touched, Flynn's heat seared through her protective layers and scorched her to the bone.

Mica had never experienced desire so exquisite, or as disorienting, as the brilliant surprise of Flynn's caress. Her touch, gentle and sure, was as mysterious as it was reassuring. Mica knew what it was to be seen as a possession, to be touched with disregard, to be used without consideration. She'd never known the aching tenderness Flynn's fingertips painted over her skin.

"We gotta stop," Mica murmured. "Your side."

"I'm okay." Flynn skimmed her tongue over Mica's lower lip. "You have a beautiful mouth. I think I could be happy kissing you forever."

Mica's hips surged. The look in Flynn's stormy blue eyes melted every wall she'd ever built to keep herself from breaking. Flynn was already too close, already had too much power. "You're gonna hurt when your brain starts working again."

"If you want to stop, we'll stop." Flynn licked Mica's throat from the hollow between her collarbones to the sensitive spot under her jaw. "But my brain is working fine and it's saying I want you. I want your mouth again. Kiss me. Just one more time."

Mica couldn't say no. She couldn't bear to see the light in Flynn's eyes disappear. She wanted to make her burn the way she burned. Flynn's desire for her made her want to cry. The sweetness of Flynn's touch was as sharp as a perfect blade, piercing without pain to her core. "One," she whispered. "You get one more."

Flynn wrapped Mica's thick hair around her wrist and slowly drew her head down until their mouths were a breath apart. "Make it a long one."

Mica brushed her mouth back and forth over Flynn's and teased her tongue over the silky inner surface of Flynn's lower lip. Flynn sucked lightly on her tongue and her clit pulsed rapidly. She couldn't stop at one, she was drunk on the headiness of Flynn's taste. She slipped her tongue inside and played in the recesses of Flynn's mouth, stroking and probing, her kisses becoming harder, more demanding. She wanted her. She wanted her in places she couldn't touch. Groaning, Mica straddled Flynn's thigh and rocked her hips. Her breasts brushed Flynn's and her nipples tingled. Never like this before. Never.

The sounds Flynn made in the back of her throat stabbed through Mica like sweet agony. She couldn't get enough of Flynn's mouth, couldn't get deep enough inside her. She wanted to crawl inside Flynn's skin, but hers felt as if it were going to burst open any second.

Mica yanked her head back. "I can't breathe. *Dios.* I'm going to explode."

"Okay, okay. We'll slow down." Flynn caressed her cheek, the light strokes calming Mica's racing heart. "Better? You good now?"

Mica caught her breath, but her hips pumped of their own accord. She was naked except for the T-shirt and so wet. Every time her clitoris slid against Flynn's hard thigh she wanted to come. She was so close her stomach cramped. She stared at her fingers, gripping Flynn's forearms until her knuckles were white. "I'm sorry."

"For what?" Flynn's hands glided up and down her back, soothing one second, exciting her to the point of screaming the next. "What are you sorry for?"

"Holding you too hard." Mica's sex tightened and she gasped. "Bruising you."

"You feel wonderful. You're not hurting me."

Mica fought back a whimper and tugged her lower lip between her teeth. Spots danced before her eyes. Her throat tightened. She was on the edge of coming, and if she did, if she did…panic swelled in her chest. She'd never felt so vulnerable, so out of control. "I don't know… Flynn. Help me."

Flynn's eyes darkened and her hands tightened on Mica's ass. "Mica. Have you ever—"

"Not like this. Not like this. I can't…" But oh, she wanted to. Wanted to so much.

"You don't have to." Flynn grasped her shoulders. "Mica, stop. Just…lie down beside me. Everything is perfect, just as it is. We don't need to do anything else. We don't—"

"No. Don't go." Mica kissed her again, needing to taste her, needing to breathe her in, anything to give her something to hold on to. She was flying away. Losing herself. She was terrified, amazed. Flynn tasted so good. Flynn's arms tightened around her waist and Mica rocked against Flynn's pelvis. Flynn's fingers came into her hair, holding her, massaging her. Everywhere she burned. The tension in her loins grew harder, brighter, and she felt herself expanding. Electric shocks radiated from someplace deep inside her—down her legs, along her spine. She moaned into Flynn's neck. "Feels so good. Don't stop. Please don't stop."

"I won't," Flynn whispered, trailing her mouth down Mica's throat. She pushed Mica's T-shirt up and kissed her breast.

Mica whimpered, the heat of Flynn's mouth setting her aflame. Her clitoris tightened into a hard knot. "More, do more."

Flynn pulled Mica's nipple into her mouth and Mica felt herself coil inside the way she did before she came. She cupped Flynn's neck, holding Flynn's face to her breast, watched Flynn's eyes glaze with desire. As long as she could see Flynn, see her desire, she wasn't afraid. She pressed her clit hard into Flynn's leg and her control unraveled. "Make me come."

Flynn sucked her nipple, biting lightly.

"Harder." Mica twisted her fingers in Flynn's hair, rode Flynn's thigh faster, soaked her leg. Panting, she pushed her breast harder against Flynn's mouth. Her vision tunneled until all she saw was Flynn's face. Through a haze of unbearable need, she clung to Flynn's fierce bright gaze. Burning for her. Mica's ass clenched. "I'm so so close."

Mica cried out, pleasure tearing through her. Her arms turned to jelly and she sagged against Flynn, quivering, racked with pleasure. She'd never come so hard before. She shuddered and another orgasm rippled through her. She moaned and clung to Flynn. "What's happening to me?"

Flynn cradled Mica's face in the curve of her neck and kissed her throat. "You're all right. Mica, you're all right. I promise."

Mica closed her eyes. For just one minute, she wanted to believe.

CHAPTER TWENTY

Reese pulled into the deserted clinic lot as the first hint of sunrise colored the eastern sky a moody purple. She unlocked the front door and traversed the waiting area with the aid of the faint light coming from the hallway on the far side of the reception desk. She remembered the first time she'd entered the building in the middle of the night after answering a 911 call about a possible break-in. That was the day she'd met Tory. She smiled at the memory of their unexpected meeting in a darkened room and Tory's swift, very effective self-defense move. If she hadn't been in so much pain, she would've realized she was falling in love at that very moment.

Now all the examining room doors were closed, and her footsteps echoed in the silence, but the walk to Tory's office was a familiar one. The door was slightly ajar and the reading lamp on the corner of Tory's overladen desk lit the room with faint yellow light. Tory was asleep on the sofa, partially curled on her side, one arm pillowing her cheek, her legs drawn up. Her right hand rested on her stomach, as if protecting even now what might be growing within. Reese knelt by the sofa and kissed Tory's forehead. "Hi, baby."

"Good, you're back," Tory murmured, sliding her hand up Reese's arm and across her shoulder to the back of her neck. She pulled Reese down for another kiss.

Tory's mouth was warm, her fingers firm and familiar on Reese's neck. The surge of tenderness and desire she always felt on seeing Tory after they'd been apart kindled in her stomach. "Time to go home."

Tory kissed her again. "I didn't know you'd be coming back for me. Thought you'd send Allie or one of the others."

"Allie is still filling out reports and chasing some leads on the computer. The rest are out looking for the assailant."

Tory rose up on her elbow and tugged Reese down so she was sitting on the sofa. Then Tory settled her head in Reese's lap. "Getting anywhere?"

"I'm not sure." Reese stroked Tory's cheek.

"You sound worried."

"I am, a little bit. What you told me about the tattoo—La Mara—it's a gang tattoo. A particularly nasty gang. I don't know if what happened here in town is related to that or not, but it stands to reason it could be."

"And you don't believe in coincidences."

Reese sifted strands of Tory's auburn hair through her fingers, noticing a few new strands of gray. She liked them. Tory got more beautiful every day. "No, I don't. I at least have to consider that what's going on has something to do with her gang affiliation."

"Just how serious might this be?"

"Hard to tell." Reese heard the concern behind Tory's question and tried to deflect it. She wasn't sure how big a problem this might be, and no matter what the situation, she didn't want Tory worrying about it. "Nothing we can't handle."

"You'd say that no matter what you thought." Tory rubbed her cheek against Reese's stomach. "I'm never going to break you of the habit of trying to protect me, am I?"

Reese brushed the backs of her fingers over Tory's cheek. "Probably not. I don't know any other way to love you."

"I know that." Tory caught Reese's hand and kissed her knuckles. "That's why I'm not giving you a harder time."

"You do the same thing, you just hide it better."

Tory laughed. "Probably. Are you ready to take me home?"

"It's still really early. We should probably leave Reggie with the grands."

"You're right. They won't mind keeping her. I'll stop by to see her before I come back to work and make sure everything is all right."

"Sounds good. Maybe if we get lucky, we can even sleep in for a while."

Tory sat up and kissed her. "We can always hope."

❖

Mica rolled onto her side with her back to Flynn and drew her knees up, curling in on herself. Flynn wrapped herself around Mica from behind, bending her legs so her hips fit against Mica's ass. She slipped her arm around Mica's waist and held her breast in one hand, pillowing her face against the back of Mica's shoulder. She kissed the curve of her shoulder. "You're beautiful."

Mica was silent for so long Flynn wondered if she had gone immediately to sleep.

"I don't know how to make you come," Mica finally whispered.

"You don't have to."

"You don't want to?"

Mica was so stiff, Flynn wondered if she was in pain. Maybe the guy had hurt her worse than she'd let on. Flynn instinctively drew her closer. "I never said that. Feeling you get excited, holding you while you came, turned me on really a lot. I'm wet for you. Hard for you."

"Jesus." Mica fumbled for Flynn's hand and gripped Flynn's fingers tight. "I know how it works, I just don't know what you want—not sure where to start."

"Do you want to?"

"Make you come?"

"Yes."

Mica twisted until she was on her back, staring up at Flynn. "Yeah. I do."

"You could start by kissing me again. Pretty much drives me right to the edge."

"Jeez, you're kind of easy." Mica grinned a little unevenly.

"Not so much. You're just mega-sexy."

"Yeah?"

Mica's tone was playful on the surface, but a shadow of uncertainty swept across her face. Flynn's heart twisted. How could she not know how amazing she was? Flynn could barely stand to think of who had touched her before and failed to tell her how special she was. The fury that seethed in her belly gentled her voice. "Like nobody I've ever known before."

"Shut up," Mica ordered, but she was smiling for real when she slid her arm around Flynn's shoulders and tugged her down for another kiss.

The kiss was every bit as sweet and hot as the ones before, only now Flynn couldn't concentrate on the slide of Mica's mouth on hers. She was tied up in knots inside. When Mica had orgasmed, Flynn's clit pounded so hard she thought she might come herself. She was still pounding, so tightly wound inside she wondered if she could come at all. She wanted Mica to touch her, but whatever happened between them needed to be Mica's choice. She doubted Mica had had many choices in her life, especially around sex.

Mica's fingers trailed down her throat and over her chest. When Mica cupped her breast, Flynn jerked.

"No?" Mica breathed against her mouth.

"Yes, please, yes." Flynn groaned.

Mica made a humming sound in her throat and squeezed Flynn's breast gently. Flynn's nipple hardened against Mica's palm, and a small strangled sound escaped her throat.

"You like that," Mica said, no doubt in her voice.

Panting, Flynn nodded. "Yeah, I do. When you do it, I like it."

Mica nibbled on Flynn's lower lip and Flynn's hips started to rock. She needed to come and she didn't want to push Mica. Maybe she should masturbate, maybe that would make things easier for Mica. She kept her hands fisted at her sides. She wanted to wait, she wanted to let Mica decide. But she wanted to come so bad.

"You're vibrating." Mica dragged her teeth down Flynn's throat.

"Can't help it. You're driving me crazy," Flynn confessed.

"Yeah? Excited, huh?"

"So, so bad. You make me so hot."

Mica slid her hand down Flynn's belly. "You're really tight. I like that."

Flynn's arms and legs trembled. Air rushed in and out of her lungs so fast she was light-headed. "Mica, I'm sorry. I want to go slow, but I need you so much."

"You do?"

Flynn moaned. "So much I can't stand it."

Mica drew circles on her stomach with her nails and echoed the movement on Flynn's breast with her tongue. Electricity shot through Flynn's belly and struck her clitoris like a high-voltage current. She jerked, her legs quivering.

"If you keep that up, I'll come."

"Good." Mica kissed her way down Flynn's stomach and nibbled on the taut circle of her belly button. She raked her fingers over Flynn's lower abdomen and confidently cupped her sex. Flynn thrust against her hand, knowing she was getting her wet.

"You're in a bad way," Mica muttered, sounding entirely pleased with herself.

Flynn gasped, circling her hips, desperate to ease the pressure in her clit. "You have no idea."

"I think I do." Mica stroked Flynn's shaft between her fingers. "I think I know what you might be feeling right now." She continued to caress her, steady and firm.

"You'll make me come," Flynn warned. Her eyes were open but she couldn't see a thing. She was blind with pleasure.

"How soon?" Mica sucked Flynn's nipple and circled faster between her legs.

"A minute," Flynn gasped.

Mica tugged on her nipple and sucked it hard into her mouth. The electricity turned into a shock wave and Flynn's clit exploded.

"Now," Flynn exclaimed. "Right now."

And then she was coming all over Mica's hand, groaning and writhing and totally helpless.

Mica threw one leg over Flynn's and rubbed her clit against Flynn's leg while Flynn was coming. Feeling Flynn orgasm, hearing her sobs of relief, made Mica need to come again. The little bit of pressure against her clit was enough to set her off, and she cried out against Flynn's breast, her mouth brushing Flynn's nipple. Flynn's arm came around her, holding her tight, keeping her close.

"Don't stop," Flynn gasped. "Keep going, I'll come again. Oh yeah, just like that. I need you."

Mica lay half on top of Flynn, quivering, still stroking her. She'd never felt so powerful or so out-of-control in her life. "Come. I want you to come again."

"I am. So good. So, so good." Flynn pulled Mica on top of her, settling Mica's thigh between her legs against her still-pulsing clit. The pressure kept her hard just the way she needed it. She stroked Mica's back. "You do amazing things to me."

"You do pretty crazy things to me too."

Flynn closed her eyes. "I'm so glad."

Mica sighed, as if she was suddenly weary, and rested her head on Flynn's shoulder. Flynn wondered how long she had before Mica started to regret what had just happened between them.

❖

Allie got home a little before six a.m. She'd tried to be quiet coming in and undressing, but she knew Ash was awake. She could feel her presence in the dark, waiting for her. She crawled into bed, rolled onto her side, and nestled against Ash. Resting her cheek on Ash's chest, she brought one leg up over Ash's and wrapped her arm around her. Ash's hand came into her hair and Allie sighed. She loved being totally connected like this.

"Flynn okay?" Ash asked.

Allie nodded and kissed Ash's breast. "Pretty banged up, but she's okay."

"Get the guy?"

"No. Probably won't either. At least not right away."

"Random?"

"On the surface, it looks that way. But—I'm not sure."

Ash stroked her back and massaged the tightness between her shoulders and Allie snuggled closer. "How do you always find the spot where the knots are?"

"Because you're mine," Ash murmured lazily.

"Yeah, yeah." Allie melted every time Ash said that. She loved being hers. She loved that Ash belonged to her too. Hers and only hers, in all the world. "Reese thinks there's a gang connection, somehow, with Mica. And I'm pretty sure Flynn is involved with her."

"Really. I wouldn't have called that."

"What? Flynn being involved, or her being involved with that kind of girl?"

"Babe"—Ash tilted Allie's face up with a finger under her chin and kissed her—"I can see Flynn with a girl, no problem—just as long as it's not you. I guess I've been thinking of her as the stereotypical priest—unadventurous, introverted, traditional."

Allie laughed. "That's not Flynn."

"Guess not." Ash tucked Allie's head back under her chin. "So what do you think about Reese's theory?"

"I've been doing some research. If Mica is part of La Mara, it's bad news. I found a couple of reports of members who tried to get away, and they never made it. One girl turned informer and they tracked her down across three states. Killed her. Same thing for a guy."

Ash stiffened. "You think that might be what's going on here?"

"Maybe. I have to talk to Mica again."

"And Flynn is involved with her?"

"Oh yeah. They went home together."

"How are you with that?"

Allie caressed Ash's belly, smiling to herself when Ash sucked in a breath. "That Flynn's seeing a really cute girl?"

Ash's hips lifted into Allie's hand as Allie caressed lower.

"Uh-huh," Ash gasped.

"Mmm. Doesn't bother me." Allie let her fingers drift between Ash's legs. Ash was hot and wet, unbelievably sexy. "Oh yes." Leaning up on one elbow, she kissed Ash, stroking with her tongue in time with stroking between her legs. When she stopped to breathe, she said, "But I'm not real happy about Flynn getting mixed up in things."

"You'll be careful, right?" Ash turned Allie onto her back and fit her hips between Allie's thighs. Allie wrapped her legs around Ash's hips and Ash worked her hand between them and inside her.

"Oh God, baby," Allie moaned.

"You'll be careful, right?"

"God yes, yes. Just fuck me."

Ash pushed deeper and did exactly as Allie demanded. Allie lifted her hips, took her deeper, and forgot about everything except Ash.

CHAPTER TWENTY-ONE

Flynn watched Mica move quietly around the room, gathering her clothes in the gray light of dawn. When she slid her hand across the sheet to where Mica had been a few moments before, the spot was already beginning to cool. She doubted they had dozed for more than an hour.

"Where are you going?"

"Gotta get home. Have to work in an hour or so."

Flynn slowly pushed up on the bed, protecting her still-sore side. "You're going to try to work today?"

"Not like I have any choice," Mica said with her back still turned.

"I think considering what happened, your boss will give you the day off."

Mica, nude, spun around with her T-shirt gripped in her hand and partially covering her breasts. Flynn's heart plummeted at Mica's sudden wariness. They'd been so close, so united, when they'd been making love, the distance now flamed like an open wound.

Mica glared. "When are you going to get that the rules you live by are different than how most of us live? Maybe you never had to worry about losing a job because you had to take your kid to daycare or your grandmother to the doctor and were ten minutes late."

"You're right." Flynn pushed the covers aside and swung her legs over, halting halfway through as another tearing sensation lanced through her side.

"You hurting?" Mica pulled on her jeans, not bothering with panties.

"I'm okay."

"Doesn't look like it. Stay there. You got aspirin or something?"

"There's a bottle of Motrin in the medicine cabinet in the bathroom," Flynn said. "I wouldn't mind having four of them. What about you? You've got to be sore."

"It's not bad." Mica shrugged and pulled on her T-shirt.

"You're a little bit hoarse." Flynn didn't mention the chain of faint red blotches on Mica's neck where their attacker had gripped her. Mica would undoubtedly shrug it off, and reminding her of what had happened just seemed cruel.

When Mica disappeared into the bathroom, Flynn got up, found her jeans, and, bending carefully, pulled them on. Shirtless, she held out her hand for the glass of water Mica brought back, along with four ibuprofen. "Thanks. Did you take some?"

"Yeah, yeah. Jeez." Mica's gaze trailed down over her chest and Flynn's nipples tightened. She couldn't remember ever having been so sensitive to another woman's attention. Maybe because she suspected Mica didn't give her attention easily. She wondered if Mica had a girlfriend. The idea of someone else touching her, pleasuring her, made Flynn agitated and uneasy. There was so much she didn't know about Mica, so much she wanted to know. And after last night, so much she needed to know.

"Okay, so," Mica said, "you ought to go back to bed. Didn't the doctor say you should take it easy?"

Flynn pulled on a cotton shirt and buttoned it halfway up. "Mica, I know last night was crazy," Flynn paused and grinned, "and part of it was amazing, but you told me you would talk to me. I need for us to talk."

"I never said we'd talk." Mica backed up as if Flynn had threatened her.

Flynn stood still, willing to give her space, but not willing to let her put up walls. "I don't want you to go."

Mica took another step back. "I'm gonna be late."

"Maybe you don't remember, but I'm pretty sure you said we'd talk."

"There's nothing to talk about."

"How about us sleeping together?"

"Is there something about it you didn't understand?" Mica slipped into the flip-flops she'd kicked off inside the bedroom door a few hours earlier.

"Oh, I think I understand what happened pretty well," Flynn said.

"Like I said, it was amazing. *You're* amazing. I pretty much lose it the minute you touch me."

Mica went very still, her face hard to read, but her eyes lit up from within. "You mean that."

"I do. If I had any choice at all, I'd want you back in bed with me right now. I'd want to keep going, do a million things we haven't had a chance to do yet. I told you I'd be hungry. I didn't realize I'd be starving."

"I don't know if I can do that for you," Mica said quietly. "Take care of that hunger."

"We won't know, will we, until we try? What about you? Are you hungry at all?" Flynn felt as if she were poised on the edge of a precipice. This wouldn't be the first time she'd been the only one to need, the only one to want. She'd misjudged completely with Evelyn. She'd been so blinded by her own passion she hadn't realized Evelyn was afraid. Afraid of censure, afraid of losing her social status, afraid of losing her position in the church. Evelyn had been willing to sleep with her but not commit to her. She'd chosen the safer route, one that Flynn had never seen coming. Evelyn had chosen her twin, who looked almost exactly like her, except that he was male and therefore acceptable. Her heart hammered wildly, as if she were waiting for judgment. "Mica? If it's only one time, tell me now."

Mica closed the distance she'd created between them, pressed her hands flat against Flynn's chest, and kissed her. Her kiss was open-mouthed, hard and demanding. Her breasts crushed against Flynn's, her pelvis molding to her. Everything about her was hot and possessive. The ache in Flynn's heart vanished. Even the pain in her injured side receded to a distant throb. She wrapped her arms around Mica's waist and lifted until Mica was standing on tiptoe, straddling her thigh, riding her. The movement hurt, but Flynn didn't care. Mica seemed to be the only medicine she needed.

When Mica pulled away, Flynn had lost her train of thought, and that never happened to her. She fought to steady her breathing, her fingertips resting on the outer contours of Mica's hips. "Was that a yes? Please tell me that was a yes."

"Yeah, I'm hungry," Mica said. "I want you to do everything you did to me last night and more. You're so hot when you come—I want to make you do it over and over. I can't stop thinking about it, and I don't know if I'm glad about that or not."

"I'm here," Flynn murmured. "This can be the beginning, not the end. If you let me, I'll stay."

Mica pushed away, the hot light of passion in her eyes turning to a blaze of anger. "Don't say that. You don't know that. You don't know anything."

Flynn caught Mica's hand before she could retreat again. "Then tell me. Help me. Please."

"What do you want to know? What do you think talking will prove?"

"Tell me about the tattoo on your back," Flynn said.

Mica jerked. "What?"

"The tattoo. It's beautiful, but I wonder what it means."

"Forget it." Mica turned and strode out of the room.

For half a second, Flynn contemplated letting her go. She was pushing, maybe pushing too hard. Mica might have a very good reason for keeping her silence. If the attack in the alley wasn't random last night, then Mica was in danger. But if Mica was in danger, Flynn needed to know why. She couldn't help her unless she did.

Flynn went after her. The only way to show Mica she wasn't going to treat her the way everyone else had was not to live up to her expectations. Mica expected her to let her go. And she wasn't going to. Flynn made it to the living room just as Mica reached the front door. "I could use coffee. How about you? I think I might have some bagels or something too."

Mica stopped, paused for seconds that felt like eternity, and finally spun around. "I could do with some coffee. But you are not making it. You sit your ass on one of those stools at the counter over there and tell me where all the stuff is. Then I'll make it."

"Deal." Flynn eased onto one of the stools at the breakfast bar and directed Mica to find coffee, mugs, and the bagels. Despite everything, she was hungry for food, and she suspected Mica was too. It'd been a hell of a night.

"Here you go," Mica said, passing Flynn a mug of coffee.

"Thanks. So are you going to tell me about the tattoo? I've never seen one so big or so elaborate."

"It's the symbol of my crew."

"Your crew?"

"You know, the people I hang with."

"Are we talking about a gang?"

"Yeah," Mica said, thrusting her chin out, preparing for the pain when Flynn walked. She hadn't planned on telling Flynn anything, but she hadn't planned on waking up in bed with her either. Flynn just didn't quit, and every time Mica pulled away, Flynn said something, did something, to reel her back in again. Well, now she knew. Now it was out in the open, and this was when Flynn would quit. At least it would be over quickly, and she wouldn't have to tell Flynn anything that could get her hurt. Better to cut off any connection before they got any tighter. She was already having trouble making it out the door. She never should have let Flynn get over on her the way she had, but Flynn was so freaking beautiful. So amazing. No one had ever made her feel the way Flynn did. No one had ever touched her as if she were special. Flynn turned fucking into something she'd never thought possible. She made it miraculous. If she hung around Flynn much longer, she was going to forget who she was and what mattered.

"Does this gang have something to do with that guy attacking us last night?" Flynn asked.

Mica hadn't expected the question. She'd thought Flynn would pull back, make small talk, and get her out of the apartment as quickly as possible. Now Flynn really seemed to want to know what was going on. Fuck, this was getting way too complicated. "I don't know. Look, Flynn—"

"But it might?"

Mica reached for a bagel, broke it in half, and bit off a piece. If she told Flynn anything else, Flynn could get in trouble. She wasn't going to do that. "Just let it go."

"I want to know, Mica. It matters to me. Whatever is happening, or you think might happen, you don't have to handle it all on your own."

Mica dropped the bagel onto the paper plate she'd found in one of the cupboards. "You don't think so? And just who do you think is going to come to my rescue? I know you're a priest, and for all I know, you can really make miracles. But it'll take more than a miracle, and I don't think you come equipped with what it takes to handle this."

"What does it take?"

"An assault rifle."

Flynn flinched. "Well, you're right. I don't have one of those. If I did, I wouldn't know what to do with it. But I've got friends who probably have something similar. You met one of them last night. Allie. If you're in trouble, why don't we—"

"Your *friend* Allie—if that's what she is, is a cop. She can't help me."

"You're not asking about her"—Flynn took the other half of the bagel Mica had left on the plate, cut it open, and spread some butter on it—"but Allie has a partner she's crazy about. And that's just fine with me—like I said, she's a friend."

"She's still a cop."

"She is. And she's honest. She cares about what happens to people."

Mica shook her head. "I'm not one of her people. I'm the outsider. This doesn't have anything to do with this town or any of you."

"It does now," Flynn said. "It matters now because you're here. And you're one of us now."

Mica stared. One of them? Why—because she worked in a restaurant and slept with one of the townies? Because she was queer, like them?

"I'm not one of you. I'll never be one of you."

"Are you one of them still?"

Mica thought about the tattoo on her back, about the scars on her body, about the memories she'd never get rid of. She thought about Hector's fists lashing out and his cock driving inside her.

"No, I'm not one of them either. I don't belong anywhere."

"Maybe you do, and you just don't know it yet."

"And you think you're going to help me figure that out?"

Flynn took Mica's face in her hands and gently kissed her. "Maybe. Maybe you'll help me figure it out too."

Mica rested her cheek on Flynn's shoulder. "I don't see how. I'm not even sure I can help myself."

"Call in sick," Flynn said. "Then come back to bed and tell me the rest."

"The guy last night in the alley," Mica said quietly. "He's probably just a scout. If I stick around here and anyone else comes, they won't be as friendly."

Flynn suppressed a shudder as ice crystallized in her blood. She wasn't afraid for herself, not physically. But she was terrified of not being able to help Mica. "Why? Tell me why."

"You have to understand what you're getting into. If you get caught in the middle of this, you could get hurt. Do you get that?"

"I understand. I'm not afraid."

Mica gripped a handful of Flynn's shirt. "You should be. You should be fucking terrified. You should let me go right now."

"No."

Mica closed her eyes and pressed her forehead against Flynn's chest. "Why not?"

This was the answer she couldn't get wrong. Flynn stroked Mica's hair and clasped her loosely around the waist. She wouldn't hold her if she didn't want to stay, but she wanted Mica to know beyond doubt that she cared. "Because I love the way you laugh. And I love the way you kiss. And I love how strong you are. You're strong in ways I've never been, but you make me feel I could be. I don't want you to go because I need you to stay."

Mica tilted her head back and studied Flynn's face. She brushed her fingertips over Flynn's mouth and kissed her. "Just for a little while."

"All right," Flynn said softly, taking her hand, "a little while."

CHAPTER TWENTY-TWO

A llie grabbed the phone on the first ring, slipped out of bed, and padded naked into the living room so as not to wake Ash. "Tremont."

"Got a call to route through to you," Smith said.

"What's it about? I just finally got to bed."

"I know, sorry, but I figured you'd want this. You've been running all those checks and something must have popped up somewhere. Got a detective down in Philly wants to talk to the lead investigator, and the file says that's you."

Allie's heart jumped. Finally, something. "Great. Can you connect us?"

"Hold on…" A click and a buzzing came over the line. "Go ahead."

"This is Officer Allie Tremont."

"Detective Lieutenant Rebecca Frye of the Philadelphia PD."

"How can I help you, Lieutenant?" Allie hoped she didn't sound nervous. Ordinarily she wasn't intimidated by brass, but detective lieutenants didn't make callbacks for nothing. All of a sudden, she wasn't certain what she wanted to hear. If Mica was in trouble, then she wanted to know. She wanted to prevent another episode like last night. On the other hand, if Mica *was* trouble, Flynn was going to get hurt. She'd seen the way Flynn had looked at Mica. Flynn was already hooked whether she knew it or not. Mica had been harder for Allie to read. When she'd looked into the rearview mirror and seen Mica with her head on Flynn's shoulder, she'd been surprised. She hadn't expected that kind of vulnerability from the tough street kid Mica obviously was. Now she found herself hoping she wasn't going to hear something that would end up hurting either of them.

"I might be able to help you," the cool, deep voice on the other end of the line said.

"How is that?"

"You sent out a missing persons bulletin—Hispanic female, mid-twenties, using the name Mica Butler."

Allie squeezed the phone so hard the edges made ridge-like indents in her palm. She really was on to something, and she somehow doubted a detective lieutenant was calling back about a missing person. "That's right."

"What has she done?"

"Nothing that I'm aware of. She was involved in a vehicular incident, and then last night, an assault."

"Butler assaulted someone?"

Allie searched for some clue in the detective's voice but could find nothing. She was aware she was providing more information than she was getting, but then again, she was the one asking. "No. She and another woman were assaulted while walking home from the bar where Butler works. Could be random, but I have the feeling Butler was the target."

"What makes you think that?"

"No attempt was made to sexually assault either woman, robbery didn't seem to be the motive, and it didn't have the earmarkings of a hate crime. It appeared the assailant specifically wanted Butler."

"An abduction?"

Allie took a stab in the dark. "Or maybe a retrieval. A jealous husband maybe."

"Do you have a computer handy?"

"I'm at home, but my personal computer is available."

"Let me have your e-mail address and I'll send you a file. You can tell me if your girl is our girl."

Allie strode to the small alcove she used as an office and opened her mail program. She gave the detective her e-mail address. "May I ask what your interest in this is?"

"The file's on its way," Frye said. "If your girl and our girl are one and the same, you've got the girlfriend of the leader of the mid-Atlantic division—Pennsylvania, New Jersey, and Delaware—of MS-13 up there."

Allie's pulse skyrocketed. She knew it. She knew something was off. "Is she wanted for anything?"

"At this point, she's a person of interest. She might be on the run. We're not sure."

"Wait a minute, it's coming through." Allie clicked on the file and a grainy photo appeared. The girl in the image was Mica. She let her breath out and her stomach turned over. She was happy to have been right, but felt no joy in being vindicated. Whatever was going on couldn't be good for either Mica or Flynn. "That's her."

"Her name is Mia Gonzales," Frye said. "She's twenty-three and has been in La Mara since she was fifteen."

"Any arrests?" Allie asked. God, what was she going to tell Flynn?

"Surprisingly, no. Our intelligence is patchy, but reports are she's smart and tough and has managed to avoid routine sweeps."

"Maybe she's clean."

"Maybe. Tell me about the assault."

Allie filled her in. "We don't have much of anything to go on at this point."

"I take it your population is fairly transient—tourist town?"

"The year-round population is small and we know everyone. There's no established gang activity locally, but we've had our share of problems during the height of the season with drugs moving through and even some small-time arms deals."

"I remember there was an offshore shootout a few years back. That was drug related, wasn't it?"

"I wasn't here then, but the acting chief was. Reese Conlon."

"You've got a situation on your hands that could get nasty, Officer. We need to know what she's doing there."

"I can talk to her."

"You could," the detective said. "I'd like to speak to your chief first. Got a problem with that?"

Allie smiled. Like it would make a difference if she did. When a ranking detective wanted to speak to her boss, she didn't have much choice. "Of course not. I can give you her number. Unless you want to wait for her to call you when she comes in."

"I'd like to keep things moving. Let me have her number."

Allie gave her Reese's number.

"Thanks, and nice work, Officer Tremont. Most people would've just let it go."

"Thank you, Detective."

"I have a feeling we'll be speaking again."

"Any time." Allie ended the call, went back into the bedroom, and took a clean uniform out of her closet.

"Going back to work?" Ash asked, coming up behind her.

Allie turned, wrapped her arms around Ash's neck, and kissed her. "That was a police detective from Philadelphia. Mica—the girl with Flynn—is part of a gang there."

"You were right, then, about something going on."

Allie sighed. "Yeah. So why don't I feel better about it?"

"Because you don't want Flynn to get hurt, and something tells me you may even like Mica a little bit."

Allie draped her uniform shirt and pants over the back of a chair and headed for the bathroom. Ash followed. When she turned on the shower and stepped under the spray, Ash came with her. She put her hands on Ash's shoulders and said, "Turn around."

Ash did, and Allie soaped her shoulders and back, running her hands up and down the columns of muscle, her belly heating as Ash's ass flexed with each stroke. "There's something about Mica that's likable." She massaged Ash's neck, pressing along her spine with her thumbs, working out the knots. Ash had spent too many hours behind the wheel lately. "She's tough and strong, but I suppose she'd have to be to survive in that environment."

"Babe, you gotta stop touching me or you're not getting to work for a while."

"Is that right? Well, you were gone longer than usual, so you must be working on a deficit right now."

Ash spun around, grabbed the soap, and tumbled it into the soap dish while backing Allie against the tiled wall and kissing her. "I don't have to be away to build up a powerful need for you. I just have to be breathing."

Allie skimmed her hands over the outer edges of Ash's breasts and rubbed Ash's nipples with her thumbs until they tightened. "You're going to have to hold on to that powerful need a little while longer. Can you do that for me?"

"I can do anything you want." Ash nuzzled Allie's neck and kissed her. "Just be careful."

"I will be, I promise." Allie hoped for Flynn's sake, and Mica's too, that this all turned out to be nothing more than a coincidence. That the assault in the alley had nothing to do with Mica's past. She could hope for that, but she knew it was only wishful thinking.

❖

Flynn lay with her head propped on her elbow facing Mica, who sat cross-legged, her elbows on her knees, her chin in her hands. Mica had pulled off her T-shirt and Flynn had stripped down too. The room was warm, sun coming through the window behind Mica, haloing her body in gold and leaving her face in shadows. She could see Mica's eyes, though, dark and glittering and troubled.

"Why was that guy after you last night?" Flynn asked.

"I'm not sure," Mica said. "He either wanted to take me back, or he wanted to make an example of me."

Flynn couldn't get a deep breath, not because her side hurt, but because the more Mica told her about the gang, the more her stomach tightened with dread. "What does that mean? Make an example of you?"

"When you join La Mara, it's for life," Mica said. "No one leaves."

"But you did."

"I didn't leave. I ran away."

"Why?"

Mica shook her head. Flynn kept catching her off guard with her questions, asking her things she couldn't believe Flynn cared about. Like why she joined, and what her family was like, and if they knew what the gang was like. Asking her what it was like being in the gang, being a woman, being afraid. She answered things she'd never told anyone, because Flynn kept watching her with her calm, gentle expression and eyes so fierce Mica felt Flynn's gaze heat her skin. Flynn was the most amazing combination of steady and strong. Mica reached for Flynn's hand. Warm. Sure. "I don't want to tell you any more. You shouldn't know any of this."

"It doesn't matter what you tell me," Flynn said, "because you're not going back. And no one's going to know what I know."

"But if they find me with you, you need to be able to walk away."

"I'm not doing that."

"Then I hope being a priest doesn't mean you can't lie. Because you'll have to. You have to tell them you don't know anything. That we just hooked up casually and you don't know anything about me."

"Let me worry about what I say and who I say it to."

"I would if you weren't so crazy."

Flynn smiled.

"Now it's your turn," Mica said.

"What do you mean?" Flynn pushed some pillows together against the wall and sat up, her bare leg stretching along Mica's.

Flynn's skin was smooth and hot, and Mica remembered coming with her legs wrapped around Flynn's thigh. Her breasts swelled and her clit started to ache. She wanted to straddle Flynn right then and there, kiss her and rub against her until she made Flynn make those crazy sexy noises, until she got hot and wet and came on her again. That would be the easy thing to do, a lot easier than talking. But Flynn knew things about her now that no one else did. And she wanted to know about her.

"I saw you with that sick guy the other day. I heard you praying for him—and it mattered to him. You're a priest. What are you doing here, why aren't you, you know, being a priest?"

Flynn traced her fingers down Mica's arm, around the edges of the blood-red heart. "I left—not the church. Just the system."

"Why?"

"Because I wasn't very good at it."

Mica narrowed her eyes. "I think that's bullshit. You looked pretty good at it to me. And that man thought so too. Whatever you were saying, it wasn't just words. I could feel it across the hall. You touched him somehow, someway."

Flynn closed her eyes against the piercing pain. She'd always known her calling, always been so sure, until her arrogance cost an unbearable price. When she opened her eyes, Mica was staring at her, demanding an answer. "I was counseling a teenager. Her name was Debbie. She thought she was a lesbian, but she wasn't sure, and she was afraid God would abandon her if she sinned."

"Do you think God cares?"

"No," Flynn said, "I don't. I think love, respect, caring—those are the things that matter. But what I think isn't what's important."

"So what happened?"

"We talked. I urged her to discuss things with her parents, gave her some information on gay and lesbian youth groups where she could connect with other young adults in the same situation. We talked about God."

"You didn't tell her what to do?"

Flynn shook her head. "It's not my place to dictate behavior."

Mica laughed. "You're kind of a strange priest."

"At the end of our last session, Debbie said how much our talks had helped her understand her feelings. That she felt better about who she was."

"So that's good."

"I thought so," Flynn said grimly. "I was very pleased with what we had accomplished. Except the next morning she took a bottle of her mother's prescription medication. By the time anyone realized she wasn't in school, it was too late."

"She didn't tell anybody?"

"No. She didn't call me. She didn't tell anyone. But she left a note. A note that said she knew God wouldn't forgive her for what she'd done, but she didn't believe God would forgive her for who she was either."

"Oh man, that's bad. I'm sorry."

"I didn't see it coming." Flynn rubbed her face. "If I'd suspected, if I'd had the slightest idea what she might do, I could have stopped her. But I let her walk out, pleased that we were making progress. Pleased that I'd helped her. When I had utterly and completely failed her."

"Being a priest," Mica said softly, "that makes you a mind reader too, huh?"

"I should have known, Mica. I should have known and I didn't." Flynn's chest constricted with the agony of her failure. "My arrogance, my pride, blinded me to her need. I failed her."

"You did what you could—if she'd come to you, you would have helped her. It's not all on you." Mica shifted closer and slid her arm around Flynn's shoulders. She tugged and Flynn rested her head on her shoulder. "You can't save everyone, you know."

"Maybe you're right," Flynn murmured. "But if you don't try, what's the point of anything?"

"Do you think you can save me?" Mica asked.

"If you're in need of saving, you'll do it yourself. You're plenty strong enough." Flynn tilted her head and met Mica's gaze. "I don't want to be your savior. I'm no one's savior."

"That's good, because I don't want you to be my priest." Mica kissed Flynn slowly and thoroughly. "Even if you are one, no matter what you say about it. You can walk away from your life if you want to, but you can't change who you are. Didn't they teach you that?"

CHAPTER TWENTY-THREE

What do you think?" Reese asked.

Tory snuggled closer, her cheek pressed to Reese's chest, one of her favorite positions. She loved listening to Reese's heart. The steady, strong, unwavering beat, so much like Reese herself. She pressed a kiss to one of the many scars that were so much a part of Reese too. She might never be able to overlook them, but she understood them. She understood Reese's need to put herself between those she loved and danger. Reese had been raised in a military family to be a soldier, and she lived the concepts that were to so many only theoretical. The words "honor" and "duty" shaped the horizons of Reese's life and guided the actions of every day, in her family, in her job, in her dreams. Tory hadn't expected to find a woman she could count on to be there, physically and emotionally, unendingly. The price she paid for that incredible gift was the ever-present fear that one day Reese wouldn't come home. Joy almost always overshadowed her dread, relegating the agony to the distant recesses of her consciousness, but every morning when Reese left the house, some small part of her worried over what evil Reese would face that day and if she would put herself in the line of fire rather than let even the life of a stranger be at risk. "What do I think about what?"

"The little swimmers." Reese stroked her hair. "Did we hit a home run?"

Tory laughed. "Well, we certainly gave them a good send-off."

"Oh, I know I got my part right." Reese chuckled, a comforting rumble that chased away the whisper of sadness. "A couple of times."

"Your part. Oh really? All on your own?" Tory slapped Reese's stomach, and muscles sang beneath her fingertips. She loved Reese's body, the soft swell of her breasts, the taut stretch of her abdomen and thighs. She skimmed her fingertips in slow circles over the ridges and valleys and lines of past battles, other moments when she could have lost her. But she hadn't lost her. Reese was hers. "In addition to your stellar performance and out-of-the-park winning hits, I have this feeling…"

Reese sucked in a breath. "A feeling? What kind of feeling?"

"There's this thrumming deep inside. A kind of knowing. It feels a lot like coming home to you—comforting, peaceful, exciting."

"That's good, then." Reese kissed her. "That's great. I can't wait until I can feel him."

"Him?"

"Reggie asked for a brother."

"Um, darling? She's not two yet. Are you sure she said that?"

"Positive."

Tory laughed. "You'll need to tell her that's not the kind of thing you can just order up. Even if you do think you can make the world spin just for her."

"I don't—spin, huh? I suppose if she asked me to—"

"You'd find a way." Tory smiled. "I'm a little older this time around. It might be a little harder hitting that home run."

Reese tightened her arms around Tory. "I haven't noticed any difference. You're still just as beautiful, just as hot, and just as sexy as ever. I'm not worried, but the nice thing about all of this is if we have to try again, it'll be a hell of a lot of fun."

Tory pushed up on her elbow and traced the outline of Reese's mouth. Outside the window, the sun had climbed high in the sky. They weren't going to sleep again. She had work waiting in the office. And ever since Reese took over as chief, she went in before the day shift started, no matter how late she'd worked the night before. The day was upon them, but right now, right this moment, she could pretend that time was all theirs. She kissed Reese. "You make me feel like the most cherished woman in the world. I don't think I can tell you what that means to me."

Reese framed Tory's face and ran her thumbs along Tory's jaw. The simple caress set Tory on fire.

"Before you," Reese said, "a huge part of my life was just waiting to happen, and I didn't even know it. I thought I was complete. I thought I was happy. I didn't know there was a difference between satisfaction and happiness. I didn't know what it meant to be fulfilled. You gave me happiness—you gave me a future that was filled with something other than war and death. You gave me Reggie, and soon, you'll give me another gift that I'll never have a way to thank you for."

"You know there's no thank you in love, right? You give, I give. That's how it works."

"I think that might be one of those lessons I'm not gonna be very good at learning."

"We'll work on it." Tory slid on top of her and eased her thigh between Reese's legs. She wanted her. Not to make a baby, but to celebrate who they were together. "I love you."

Reese cupped her ass and pulled her tighter against her leg. The strength in Reese's hands, the ease with which Reese took control, sent pleasure surging through her. Tory moaned, losing focus for a second. "I love—"

Reese's phone rang and Tory closed her eyes, pressing her forehead against Reese's shoulder. "Answer the damn thing."

"Sorry."

Tory chuckled. "Me too. Maybe we'll still have time. If not, later."

"Yeah. That's a good thing about being married." Reese slid her hand under Tory's hair and clasped her neck as she reached for her phone with the other hand. "We'll always have another time."

Tory clung to that thought, needing to believe there would always be another moment when Reese was completely hers.

❖

"Conlon."

"Sorry to call so early, Chief. This is Detective Lieutenant Rebecca Frye—Philadelphia PD. I just spoke with Officer Tremont, and I believe you've got a person of interest up there in a case we're working."

"That would be the Butler girl."

"That's right. We believe her to be Mia Gonzales, the girlfriend of Hector Guzman, the present leader of MS-13 in our region. That would make her the highest-ranking female in the organization."

"That might explain why she doesn't want anyone to know who she is. You have warrants on her?"

"Not presently," Frye said. "The Gang Control Unit doesn't want to move on any of the higher-ups until they've got something solid, and getting something solid isn't easy. This isn't a ragtag street gang that leaves a trail a mile wide every time they pull a job. They're smart, they're organized, and their ranks are leak-proof."

"I've heard that about them. Tough to break into. Tough to turn."

"Pretty much impossible."

"What's your angle in all this? I take it you're not GCU?"

"I head the High Profile Crimes Unit," the lieutenant said. "We interface with most other divisions—a lot of overlap."

"Uh-huh." Reese waited for an answer that actually was one. She had nothing against interdepartmental cooperation, but her first priority, her critical responsibility, was to her community. She needed to have all the information available to her.

"For the past few months," Frye said, "we've suspected La Mara is setting up a cooperative operation with other organized crime families."

"So La Mara's leaders can give you evidence on the players in this other organization," Reese said. "You want them all."

"We want them."

Frye's voice was ice. History there.

"You want to get inside, then."

"Us and just about every other division." Frye paused. "I'd like to send someone who knows the situation up there to get close to Butler, find out what's going on. Hopefully persuade her to help us."

"If she's the leader's girlfriend," Reese said, "she's got to know enough to put him away."

"Probably him and all of his lieutenants. If we can get something on him and squeeze him, we can get to the other players."

"Let me see if I'm reading you," Reese said. "You want to leave her up here as bait and wait to see who comes for her?"

"If she won't cooperate, that's an option," Frye said, "but I'm hoping now that she has some distance we can get her to talk to us. I'm not interested in getting the girl killed."

"Good, because neither am I. She's also a member of our community. I don't want our citizens or my officers getting caught in the middle of a gang war if this all goes south."

"I couldn't agree with you more. Look, it's your turf, and I'm asking to come up and play on your field. I'll send up one of my detectives and you can name one of yours to head the team."

Reese thought about it. Right now, Mica Butler was still in danger from whoever had assaulted her the night before. The attack had to have been a retrieval, because if they'd wanted her dead, there'd been plenty of opportunity and easier ways to do it than a face-to-face physical confrontation. Another attempt was likely, and if that failed, probably another after that. Eventually they'd choose the simpler option and eliminate her. Mica must know they were closing in, and she had only two choices—run again, or stay and hope whoever was after her gave up. If she ran, she'd never be free. If she stayed, she'd have a huge target on her back. She just might opt for a frontal assault of her own. Taking on La Mara alone sounded a lot like suicide. "Are you going to tell her what's going on?"

"How cooperative do you think she would be if we leveled with her?"

"I haven't had a lot of personal interaction with her, but my sense is that she's smart and she probably ran because she wanted a different kind of life." Reese thought about Mica and Flynn. Allie thought they were together. Making ties with people who mattered changed a person. Altered priorities. Falling in love made the future look different. "If you can offer her immunity in return for cooperation, I think she might consider it."

"I'll follow your lead on this, Chief. No one's had any luck turning anyone in La Mara—at least no one who's lived very long. That's why no one leaves. This girl's not only smart, she's brave."

"Send your detective. Then we'll talk to Mica Butler."

"Thanks, I appreciate the cooperation. Detective Mitchell will be on the next plane up there. Ought to get there in a couple of hours."

"We'll be waiting. I'll keep you in the loop."

"Appreciate it, Chief."

"Good talking to you, Lieutenant." Reese disconnected and wrapped her arm around Tory's shoulder. "I have to go in."

"I heard. It sounded pretty serious."

"It could be. Mica Butler is in a lot of trouble."

Tory trailed her fingers back and forth over Reese's chest. "The assault last night, that was no random event, was it?"

"No, and I doubt very much it will be the last."

"What can you do?"

"Wait for the detective from Philadelphia, and then bring Mica in and talk to her."

"Talk to her." Tory shook her head. "Sounded like a lot more was planned. Using her as bait seems dangerous."

"I don't like it much myself."

"Mica could get hurt."

Reese sighed. "Unfortunately, Mica isn't completely innocent in all of this. She's a gang member, and not just a peripheral one at that. She's a high-ranking member of a vicious gang. I don't know what she's done, I don't know what she might be guilty of. I suspect they're going to squeeze her with whatever they have on her to get her to talk."

"She's just a girl, Reese."

"Children are not incapable of violence or criminal behavior. I've seen eleven-year-olds cut down soldiers with IEDs."

"I know. And I know that the streets of some of our inner cities are as violent as the places you fought in over there and just as cruel. But we should be better than those places. You'll look out for her, won't you?"

"I will. Now she's one of ours."

CHAPTER TWENTY-FOUR

Allie paced in the small terminal of the Provincetown airport, waiting for the eleven a.m. Cape Air flight from Boston. When Reese had told her Philadelphia PD was sending up a detective to work Mica's case, she'd had the good sense to say, "Yes ma'am," and nothing else. But she didn't like it. They didn't need a hotshot guy from the big city coming up to tell them how to do their jobs. The sheriff made it clear they would cooperate, and in not quite so many words, she'd also made it plain that Provincetown was their town, and it was their job, no matter what other agencies might be involved, to keep the town safe. Allie took that charge very seriously.

When she'd taken the job in Provincetown, it had been just that, a job. When she'd first enrolled in the academy, she'd thought about going back down south after she graduated, to Charlotte, where the weather was better and the pace was slower and the people had a certain charm. Then she'd met Bri. Back then, Bri's relationship with Caroline had been having some growing pains, and a short stay in Provincetown for a shot at Bri had seemed like a good idea. She'd grown up since then, and the things that mattered to her now were different. She had Ash, for one thing. If she wanted to relocate, Ash would come, she knew that, but this place was home to them both. These people were her people. Reese was the best boss she could ever have—she could learn to be a better cop from her, and she could grow. She belonged here. This was her territory.

She walked to the glass doors that looked out on the single runway as the small twin-engine plane descended and taxied around to stop in front of the outdoor luggage racks. The ten-seater was usually full. She waved to the pilot, who jumped down to open the doors and escort the passengers off. The first few people to climb out she knew, locals. Then the tourists, several looking a little pale and shaky. Probably their first trip in a plane that rattled and shook and appeared to be skimming the tops of the waves. None of them looked like cops.

The last person off was a lean guy in jeans, a black T-shirt, and motorcycle boots. Slicked-back black hair, dark eyebrows, and a swagger that said he knew he was hot. At first glance he looked a little like Bri, but not when you really knew Bri. Sure, Bri looked just as tough, just as sexy, but she still had a little tenderness along her jaw that Allie knew from experience softened when she kissed. Bri's soft side wasn't as well hidden as she liked people to think, but Allie would never tell her that. Everyone needed their armor—young studs like Bri maybe most of all.

Reese had said to pick Detective Dellon Mitchell up in plain clothes, which had seemed odd but she didn't question the chief, not on this detail for sure. She still had the lead, but things were getting complicated fast, and she didn't want to get pushed aside—especially not for bucking the boss's orders.

Detective Mitchell, 'cause that's who this guy had to be, grabbed a canvas duffel and headed to the door. Their eyes met through the glass and Allie smiled. Well now. Detective Mitchell wasn't all he wanted people to think either. He was good, really good, and she doubted anyone who lived anywhere in the world except Provincetown would ever know. Another time, another life, and she would've wanted to peel off Detective Mitchell's armor and find out what was underneath. She knew what was underneath his jeans, and she liked that idea too. Interesting detective the Philadelphia PD had sent up.

Mitchell grabbed the door and pulled it open, and Allie held out her hand. "Allie Tre—"

Mitchell swung an arm around her waist, pulled her against his tight hard body, and kissed her on the mouth. Allie had one second to curb the reflex to plant her knee in his nuts and her fist in his face, and then she went with the kiss. She bet Mitchell could kiss when he wasn't faking it. Even closed-mouthed, his lips were smooth as silk. Allie pressed a palm to his chest and pushed away.

"Easy, boy."

Mitchell grinned. Brilliant blue eyes swept over her. "Long time, Allie."

"Yeah," Allie said, aware of eyes on them. Curiosity was a fact of life in a small town, and there'd be speculation with a greeting like that. She wasn't sure if that was a good thing or not, and she hoped there was a damn good reason for it. "What's it been—three years?"

"More like five."

"You got anything else?" Allie said, tilting her head at the single carry-on.

"Nope. I travel light."

Allie didn't detect a weapon, but she knew there was one. Probably his regulation piece was in his bag. "Okay. Let's go, then." They walked as they talked, and in seconds, they were outside. "Nice entrance. Next time give me a sign before you head off trail."

"Sorry, I guess the bosses were still refining the game plan while I was flying up here. Got a message just as I was leaving Boston that we were supposed to have history."

"History."

"As in exes."

"Great." No warning about that little item. Reese probably tried to call and couldn't get Allie on her cell phone. She wasn't in uniform and didn't have her radio, and the Race Point airport was a dead zone half the time. Well, the plan was in motion now after that kiss. She had driven her own car and pointed to the black Camaro. "That's me."

"Nice ride."

"Uh-huh. Yours?"

"Harley."

Allie snorted. "Figures."

Mitchell slid into the front seat as Allie got behind the wheel. "How so?"

"The boots."

"They could be for show."

Allie started the engine and turned to face him. "It's no show, though, is it?"

"How much do you know about La Mara?"

"I've been briefed."

"Then you know just how tight we have to run this. You can call me Mitch, by the way."

"You always work this way? Undercover?" Allie backed out of the lot and headed toward town.

"Depends on the case, who I'll be talking to, how I'm most likely to get people to talk to me. Mitch is a friendly guy." Mitch smiled. "And legit. I'm a member of the Front Street Kings. I manage backstage stuff for the drag show when I can."

"They tour up here?"

"They'd like to. The Boston guys have it kind of sewn up, but you never know. I'll be asking around about bookings as part of my cover."

"And when we talk to Mica?"

"I thought I'd get your take on that," Mitch said, easing back in the seat, wanting to appear laid back. He stretched his legs out into the wheel well and draped an arm along the window. Officer Tremont wasn't at all sure about him, that was pretty clear. He didn't blame her. All cops were territorial, if they were any good. Right now, he was the lone wolf in more ways than one. Tremont was a few years younger than him, but she had the looks of an alpha female. Smart sharp eyes in a face that wouldn't look out of place on the cover of a magazine. She was in plain clothes, but she was carrying like any good cop would be under the circumstances, and her weapon rode easy on her hip. No doubt she knew how to use it. He wasn't packing anything except his dick at the moment, and as soon as he could get to his duffel, he'd have his weapon on too. But he understood the rules. He was on Tremont's turf, and he needed to show her the appropriate respect. "I'd like to give Mitch a chance to be seen around town with you in a friendly fashion. Establish my cover right away."

"When we talk to Mica, she needs to know you're Philadelphia PD. You ought to meet her that way."

"That works for me. Once Mitch gets settled in a room somewhere, I can call you and meet you at the department more formally."

"I think that will work. Even if Mica bumps into Mitch in town after and makes you, she's not going to blow your cover. Why would she? She doesn't gain anything by putting a cop's life in danger or by even letting anyone know she's talking to one."

"That's what I thought too." He glanced out the window, trying to get his bearings. Bradford Street.

"You ever been here before?"

"A long time ago, when I was…in college." Actually, Dell had come up with another cadet when they'd had a three-day furlough. They'd been looking for a place to have sex where they wouldn't risk being discovered. They hadn't seen much of the town, they'd been too busy discovering each other. In the long run, their caution hadn't helped. But none of that mattered now. She wasn't in the army. She was a cop, she had Sandy, and that was everything she'd ever wanted.

Allie crossed Bradford and turned down Commercial. "A few people just saw me pick you up, though."

Mitch grinned. "We've got that covered. Remember, I'm an ex-lover."

"Huh. I don't know how believable that's gonna be." Tremont smiled, a smile that suggested Mitch would've been lucky to ever have gotten over on her.

He laughed. "If anyone asks, you can always say I didn't measure up."

"I have a feeling you would, but I can work with that." Tremont parked. "That story might just be believable. I guess we'll find out, because I'm taking you to breakfast at Café Heaven. A lot of townies eat there, and trust me, there will be questions. And talk."

"Good. Go ahead and let them know what a jerk I was to let you get away." He didn't doubt for a second she'd left a string of worn-out women behind her. She was too hot not to have broken a lot of hearts. No ring. He wasn't wearing his either. He didn't when he was undercover. He thought about Sandy, how good she looked in uniform. How great she looked out of it. He thought about the send-off she'd given him early that morning after the lieutenant had called and said she had a job for Mitch. Sandy liked to make sure Mitch knew where he belonged, seeing as he often had to get close to women when he was undercover. He didn't mind her staking her claim—he liked knowing the rules, liked knowing where the line was. "Unless you think it would be more credible for me to come crawling back. I'm willing to play if you are."

"Sorry, everybody in town knows I've got a girl. And you know, she's got a temper."

Mitch laughed. The line between him and the beautiful officer Tremont was really clear. Good to know. "I'll be just the ex in town fronting for the Kings, then. Work for you?"

"Fine. Let's go have some breakfast and really give the town something to talk about. Then I'll take you to your room—where are you staying?"

"Nowhere yet."

"I can recommend a place. It's crowded this week, but they'll find you something for me."

"Good enough."

"When you're settled, you can send Detective Mitchell over to meet the rest of the team, and we'll have a talk with Mica Butler."

❖

Bri Parker leaned with her back against the wall in the chief's office listening to Allie lay out the game plan for convincing Mica Butler to provide evidence against Hector Guzman. Dellon Mitchell, in an open-collared white shirt and black jeans, sat relaxed and confident-looking next to Allie in a chair facing Reese, occasionally adding some new intel about Mica or MS-13.

Bri was only half-listening. Allie had run the case by her earlier that morning to make sure she wasn't overlooking anything. She and Allie graduated from the academy at the same time, but she'd had a lot more field experience working with Carter on a big case not long ago. So this was Allie's shot. This case meant a lot to her for a lot of reasons. It was her first lead, and Flynn was mixed up in it to her eyebrows. So Bri didn't mind riding shotgun on this one for Allie, but she wasn't about to take the backseat behind this detective from Philadelphia. Mitchell knew her stuff, that wasn't the problem. Bri didn't even mind that Mitchell was a little cocky and a lot good-looking. She just minded somebody else getting between her and Allie. Until Reese started assigning them different partners to give them more experience, they'd been together, and they were still a good team. She could give Allie all the backup she needed.

"Anything to add, Parker?" the chief asked.

Bri resisted the urge to straighten to attention. She didn't want to look like a rookie in front of the detective. "What do we do if she lawyers up?"

"Good question," Reese said. "If that happens, we have to go with it. Then," she looked at Detective Mitchell, "it may be necessary to bring charges in order to assure her cooperation."

"We could threaten that," Mitchell said, "but I don't think we have anything that would stick in the long run. We know what Hector has done, but we can't prove it. She has to know about his illegal activities, but we can't prove that either."

Allie said, "But if she *thinks* you've got more than you really do, that could be persuasive."

"True," Mitchell said. "But she'll be a better witness if she's not hostile. If she comes over to our side voluntarily."

Bri said, "What about Flynn? Maybe Flynn could talk her into it."

"I don't think—" Allie said.

"Who's Flynn?" Mitchell asked.

"A woman Mica has been seeing."

"Romantically? That's good to know. Definitely something we might be able to use."

"If we have to," Allie said sharply.

"Of course," Mitchell said smoothly. "It's always best to leave civilians out of it if we can."

"Anything else?" Reese asked, looking at Allie.

"No ma'am."

Reese nodded. "Bring her in quietly. We don't want to send up a flag to whoever might be watching her."

Bri said, "Allie and I could pick her up in plain clothes. People around Flynn's place know us both. We're friends of hers. If we bring a cruiser, we might as well take out an ad."

"Good idea. Can we take your SUV, Chief?" Ali asked. Reese nodded and Allie looked at Mitchell. "You'll want to stay here."

"No problem."

Bri pushed away from the wall and Allie joined her.

"Let's go change into street clothes," Allie said, "and then let's go get her."

❖

Mica tensed at the sound of footsteps outside the partially open bedroom window. Two people. Not trying to be real quiet, but not announcing their approach either. She slid away from Flynn and pushed back the covers. That morning she'd collected her clothes and piled them by the bed, as she'd been doing since she'd left North Philadelphia. She couldn't run very far naked. Careful not to wake Flynn, she leaned over and grabbed her jeans. If she could get the window open quickly enough—

A knock sounded on the door. Two sharp raps. She relaxed a fraction but kept dressing. Hector's men would not knock. Beside her, Flynn sat up.

"I'll get it." Flynn scooped up a pair of sweats and stepped into them.

The knock came again.

"Look first." Mica pulled her pants up and yanked her T-shirt over her head. "If you don't know them, don't open the door."

Flynn hesitated, a shirt in her hand. "What will they look like?"

Mica shrugged. "Probably Hispanic, unless he's recruited some associates up here. And they won't necessarily be men. Look, Fly—"

"Stay here," Flynn said quietly, buttoning the shirt. "If I don't know them, you'll hear me say I'm busy and to come back later. Don't go anywhere, okay?"

"Don't worry about me. Just be careful."

Flynn kissed her. "It's probably nothing."

"Sure." Mica waited until Flynn disappeared into the living room to ease up the window. She didn't want to go through. If she did, she knew she'd never come back. If she stayed, Flynn was likely to get hurt. She swung a leg over the sill.

CHAPTER TWENTY-FIVE

Flynn surveyed the empty room and the open window. A cold, sick feeling seeped through her stomach.

Allie said from behind her, "She couldn't have gotten far. We'll pick her up."

"I'll call it in," Bri said.

"No," Flynn said quickly. "She doesn't have anything with her except what's she's wearing. She's got to go back to her room. Let me go after her. Let me talk to her."

"What is it going to take for you to get the picture?" Allie said sharply. "She's running, Flynn. She ran here, she faked her identity, and she's hidden her past. And now she's running again."

"She told me," Flynn said quietly. "She told me who she is and where's she's been. I know what she's been through. She's not who you think."

"Oh, come on." Allie glanced at the bed. "Pillow talk? And you believe her?"

"Yes, I believe her. Please, you can follow me if you want to, but let me go after her. Let me talk to her. Were you planning on arresting her?"

Allie glanced at Bri, who shrugged. "Not at this time. We only want to talk to her."

"Then don't treat her like a criminal."

"She may *be* a criminal," Allie said. "When someone runs, they're usually guilty. We know she's part of a vicious gang. And she's putting you right in the middle of—"

"No," Flynn said quietly, "no, she isn't. I know what I'm doing. You just have to trust me on that. And now I need to go if I'm going to catch her. I'm sure this isn't the first time she's had to leave somewhere in a hurry, and she won't need long to disappear."

"Doesn't that bother you?" Allie shook her head. "God, Flynn. You're worth so much more—"

"Allie, I appreciate how you feel about me. I really do." She touched her bare throat, still not used to being so exposed. "But the collar doesn't make me a saint. And it doesn't make me infallible. I've sinned."

"Only you would see it that way," Allie muttered. "All right. But we're coming with you. We'll wait outside, but if she's there, we can't let her leave. I'm sorry."

"Flynn's right, Allie," Bri said quietly. "We need to soft-pedal this. We don't want to scare her off. We need her."

"What are you talking about?" Flynn asked. Allie avoided her gaze, and that could only mean Allie was bothered by whatever was happening, but she didn't want to admit it. She needed to find Mica now more than ever. "What aren't you telling me? What's going on?"

"Nothing," Allie said. "Let's go." As they walked through the living room, Allie asked, "What about a weapon, Flynn? Do you think she's armed?"

Flynn hesitated. Her instinct was to say no, but she didn't really know. Mica was scared. She'd fought to survive and she would keep on fighting, no matter what it took. "I don't know. She might be. I've never seen her with a weapon." She stopped at the door. "But you have to understand something. She's not the evil you seek. That's what she's running from."

"If that's true," Allie said, "then she'll be all right."

Flynn climbed into the rear seat, wondering what she could say to convince Mica to talk to the law. Mica hadn't trusted her enough to stay. She didn't even care enough about her to say good-bye. Yes, it hurt that Mica had run from her, but she understood why. Too bad understanding never erased the pain.

❖

Mica threw her clothes into the gym bag she'd been living out of for the last six weeks and grabbed the cash she'd stashed in a box of tampons. Dumb to think she could slow down, stay in one place. When Esme hadn't returned her last two calls, she should have known trouble was coming. *Dios*, she hoped they hadn't hurt Esme trying to track her.

Esme hadn't done anything except encourage her to escape and give her the wad of one-dollar bills she kept hidden for emergencies. Maybe for her own escape one day. Mica's hands shook. Someone had tracked her here, to this town, to Flynn's. This was close, way too close. Flynn hadn't sent a warning when she'd gone to the door, but Flynn wasn't street-smart. She thought she could reason with people. Make sense of the world because she was good and saw good everywhere. So naïve. So amazingly beautiful inside.

Mica just couldn't take the chance that Flynn would end up trying to handle Hector's posse. If Hector's men made it through the door and she wasn't there, Flynn would be safe. And sooner or later, it *would* be them, or if Hector really wanted to make a statement, it would be him. And he wouldn't hesitate to cut down whoever stood between him and her. She was as much his territory, as much his property, as the guns he sold and the drugs he smuggled and the girls he traded. She'd always known that, and at first she'd accepted it as the price she paid for his protection. Now she would never be anyone's property again. Whatever she gave of herself would be on her own terms. She thought of how she had given her body to Flynn—not just her body, but a piece of her heart and part of her soul—with complete freedom. Flynn had given her back the freedom to choose. She wondered what it would be like to have a life with a woman like that. To live as she wanted and to share that life with someone who valued her, who cared about her, someone she could love—

Mica yanked the zipper closed on the bag. Someone else's life she was dreaming about.

She grabbed her wallet off the dresser and yanked open the door. Flynn stood on the other side, her hand raised to knock.

"Last night was nice," Mica said, preempting anything Flynn might want to say. "But it's done. You told me to tell you if it was just one night. Well, it was a little more than that, but not much. I've got other places to be." When she tried to shoulder past, Flynn edged in front of her and barred her way. She didn't have much time, and Flynn, for all her gentleness, was unbending. "You don't want to get in my way, Flynn."

Flynn didn't touch her, as if knowing that Mica would not tolerate being restrained. "Allie and another officer were at the door. They wanted to talk to you, Mica. Not arrest you, talk to you. If you go willingly—"

Mica snorted. "Jesus, when are you going to grow up? You believed what they said? That's what they always say. Right before they put you in a room and close the door and leave you there without anything to drink or anything to eat or anyplace to piss. They leave you there until the walls close in, and you'll say anything and do anything just to be treated like a human being again." She shoved Flynn's shoulder and Flynn stepped aside, her hands still by her side.

"They're outside, Mica. They'll pick you up anyway," Flynn called as Mica hit the first stair down.

Mica spun around, fury raging through her. "You brought them here? I trusted you."

"I know. And I trust you. I know you told me the truth. I trust you're here and not in Philadelphia with him because you know what you have to do. You know the right thing."

Mica straightened, considering her options. Flynn was probably telling the truth, inasmuch as she knew it. She couldn't know what being pulled in for "questioning" was like. Maybe they didn't plan on arresting her right now, but if they got her in a box and she couldn't bluff her way out, she might end up behind bars all the same. She had her pay in her pocket—just short of a hundred dollars. She could get a long ways on that if she could make it out of town. But she needed to get up-Cape and had no way to do that without taking the bus. Even the ferry wasn't running anymore. She had no time and no way out. She'd run to the end of the line.

She'd bluffed her way through all those years with Hector, and he'd never known she loathed every touch, every glance, every minute she spent with him. She could bluff her way through a couple of hours, hell, a whole day of interrogation if that's what it took. If they knew anything, they'd be here to charge her, not talk.

She picked up her bag and started down the stairs. Flynn's steps echoed hers.

"Mica—"

She didn't slow, didn't look back. "There's nothing you can say I want to hear. Like I already told you, I don't need a priest."

❖

Looking straight ahead and making sure her face was blank, Mica walked out the front door. Her shoulders tightened when she saw the cops. They weren't hard to make, although they were both in street clothes. She recognized the pretty one, Allie. The one who'd dated

Flynn. She flicked her gaze to the good-looking dude with her—tight jeans, short-sleeved button-up black shirt, black boots. Small breasts, lean hips. She knew plenty of girls who would go for her. They pushed away from the SUV they were leaning against and started toward her. The only way to deal with cops was to surprise them and never let them know you were scared. She crossed directly to them, meeting up a few feet from their vehicle.

"I hear you're looking for me," Mica said.

"That's right," Allie said. "We'd like to talk to you."

"Talk?"

"Just talk," the black-haired one said. "My name is Bri Parker. You remember Allie Tremont?"

Mica smirked. "We keep bumping into each other, so yeah, I know who she is."

"We'd like you to come to the sheriff's department with us," Parker said. "We want to talk to you about Philadelphia."

"And if I don't?" Mica said, thinking fast. Philadelphia. So they knew who she was. If they knew that, then they knew almost everything. But they hadn't come to arrest her. So they didn't have much. "I'm kind of busy right now."

"It's a free country," Allie said. "And you know your rights without us needing to tell you." She spread her hands in a *See? I'm being friendly and reasonable* gesture. "But like I said earlier, someone tried for you once. There's another girl who looks a lot like you lying in intensive care in Hyannis. I think they thought she was you. They almost killed her. Next time, they might not miss."

"If I'm not here, then I don't have to worry about that, do I?"

"Probably not," Allie said. "You can disappear again, for a while. But you know they're going to look for you. And who do you think they're going to ask first?"

Heat scorched through Mica's chest. There was a reason she didn't get close to people. Caring about people made you vulnerable, because they could be used against you. She'd spent years under Hector's thumb, under his goddamn hot, sweaty, cruel body to keep herself and her family alive. He'd promised that her little sister would not get passed around when she came of age and La Mara recruited her, and he'd sworn that her little brother would not have to kill or risk being killed by MS-13. She'd sacrificed more than her pride and her body and her conscience to assure he kept his word. She'd shut herself off from caring about anyone. When you didn't care, you couldn't be hurt.

And now there was Flynn. Flynn, who refused to be frightened when she should be. Flynn, who thought her faith and her crazy-ass ideas of right and wrong were enough to make a difference. And maybe they were. Maybe they were for most people, but not for her. Not in her world. Faith, trust, love, and loyalty weren't part of her world. Letting Flynn get to her had made her forget the lessons she carried in her scars, inside and out. She was probably going to pay in blood for that mistake, but Flynn didn't have to.

"Let's go," Mica said, gesturing to the SUV.

Allie quickly covered her surprise with a brisk nod and opened the back door. "Bri—you drive."

Mica was almost inside when Flynn called, "Wait. I'm coming."

Mica slid into the back as Flynn crossed the street.

Allie blocked the door. "I'm sorry, Flynn, but you can't come."

Flynn leaned around Allie and peered into the backseat. "Mica? Are you all right?"

Mica ignored her and stared at the back of Parker's head. Flynn didn't move even when the cop told her to. Flynn never gave up. And she'd just get herself in deeper if Mica didn't find a way to shut her out. She had to drive Flynn off. She thought of Flynn's story of the girl she couldn't save. Flynn had been wrong to feel guilty, to feel responsible, but she'd probably never believe it. Flynn only knew how to care.

Mica turned on the seat and looked out at Flynn. "You think you know what's best for people, when you don't really see them at all. You think the collar you're still wearing, even if you pretend not to be, gives you the right to interfere in other people's lives. Your arrogance blinds you. I don't want to be the next one to get killed." She grabbed the door and pulled it closed. The heavy thud echoed the heaviness in her heart at the flash of pain and sorrow in Flynn's eyes.

Flynn jerked back from the SUV, pain lancing through her chest. *The next one to get killed. Your arrogance…Your arrogance…*

"Sorry about that," Allie said.

"No," Flynn said. "She's right."

"I don't know what she's talking about," Allie said, "but I know she's wrong." She gripped Flynn's arm. "Look, I need to go. And you need to let her go, Flynn."

"Take care of her, Allie."

"Damn you," Allie muttered. "Damn you for asking that." She stalked around the front of the vehicle. "I will if I can."

Flynn stood in the street as the SUV rolled away.

You need to let her go, Flynn.

Allie was right. Mica didn't trust her. Mica didn't want her. She had made the same mistake with Mica she'd made with Debbie—she'd fooled herself into believing her reality was theirs. Her blindness had cost Debbie her life. Mica was right. They were all right. She needed to let her go.

CHAPTER TWENTY-SIX

The sheriff's department was a lot cozier than the lockups Mica was accustomed to. When they brought her through a side door into a short hallway, she smelled pizza and cleaning solution. Not the usual piss and vomit stench that always seemed to hover in the Philly station. The windowless interrogation room, what *they* called the interview room, was just like the others she'd been in. Gunmetal gray table bolted to the floor in the center of a bare-walled room, plain metal chairs, big O-rings welded to the table for handcuffs. She wasn't wearing handcuffs, but she might as well have been. When Allie'd said, "Have a seat. I'll be back in a minute," and walked out, the snap of the lock slamming shut on the interrogation room door was as sharp as the clang of the steel bars on a jail cell driving home. There was no door handle on the inside. No way out.

Mica glanced up at the surveillance camera in the corner, smiled, and sat back in her chair. Folding her arms over her chest, she stretched out her legs and tilted her head back against the hard metal chair. The ceiling had water stains on it that looked kind of like clouds if she squinted. She tried to let her mind go blank, but she kept seeing Flynn's face—the hurt and sad acceptance. Like Flynn believed what she had said. Mica flinched inside at the idea of hurting Flynn, who had to be one of the only people in her life who'd stood up for her. Stood by her. But she'd had to hurt her to keep her safe. All the same, she hated herself a little for putting that wounded look in Flynn's eyes.

Maybe someday, if she got out of this alive, she'd say she was sorry. Right now she had to get her head in the game and try to piece together what they might have on her. Unlike so many of the other La Mara crew, male and female alike, she hadn't wanted to make her name by pulling some big job, or to gain a reputation by being arrested and doing the time without giving anyone up. As Hector's old lady, she didn't have to participate in anything she didn't want to—unless Hector wanted her with him. Then she couldn't avoid getting pulled into his action.

Thinking back to what they could put on her, she only came up with the night she'd been with Hector after some of his crew had hijacked a truckload of electronics on an exit ramp off the New Jersey Turnpike. She hadn't been in on the heist and didn't know many of the details, only that he'd gone out in the Hummer to oversee the transfer and had picked her up on the way back. He always wanted sex after he'd made a big score. Liked to recount the events while she blew him and, if she didn't get him off right away, while he fucked her. Of course, he wanted sex most of the time—when he was feeling good, when he was feeling frustrated, when he was angry, when he needed to demonstrate his authority. He especially liked having sex with his crew around, so they could watch him dominate her.

That night the police had pulled them over right after he'd picked her up, and took them in for questioning. She didn't know anything except what she'd overheard when Hector was deploying his lieutenants, and that hadn't been much. Hector didn't talk about his business with her, and when he tried, she changed the subject. She didn't want to know. She wasn't naïve, she knew what he did. She knew evil when in its presence, but she was smart enough to know that what she knew could one day get her killed or put her in jail. She hadn't told the cops anything and after twelve hours, they'd let her go.

Now she balanced on the razor's edge between death and being put away. If Hector found out she was talking to the law, or even suspected she had, he would kill her. If she didn't go back to him, he would kill her. And if she talked about what he'd done and the knowledge implicated her, she could go to jail. If she tried for a plea bargain, Hector would kill her before she ever had a chance to testify against him. The only way out was to deny everything. If she didn't cooperate, if she gave them nothing and could keep running until she disappeared, she might live. She'd be living in the shadows, a shadow herself, and might not have much of a life, but breathing was always better than not. Maybe.

A lot of maybes.

So she waited. She figured they'd take at least an hour, maybe two to soften her up, wait until she was anxious, hungry, and thirsty. Maybe wait until her nerves had her bladder on edge and then force her to talk while she was worried she might disgrace herself.

A sharp knock came on the door and Allie walked back in with someone new. Another rangy, dark-haired stud, this one tougher around the edges than the one Allie had been with before—carved cheekbones, blocky jawline, intense sea-blue eyes. Cop's eyes. Harder, more experienced than the ones she'd been looking into recently.

"This is Detective Mitchell," Allie said. "She's got a story for you."

Mitchell pulled out a chair opposite Mica, and Allie took up a post by the door.

So they hadn't made her wait, and now this new one was going to take the lead. Huh. She would've figured Allie to be the one in charge. Maybe this was her boss.

"I'm from Philadelphia," Mitchell said. "I wanted to talk to you about Hector."

"Hector who? Lots of dudes named Hector."

Mitchell smiled. "I guess that's true. But I think we both know who we're talking about. And since I'm not here to run any games on you, I'll lay it out."

And she did. Mitchell told her how they'd been watching Hector and his crew and her. She showed her a picture of her with Hector and a couple of his lieutenants. Mitchell said they knew about Hector's jobs, and they knew she was Hector's girl, and Hector's girl had to know what Hector was doing. They didn't want her, Mitchell said, they wanted Hector. They wanted her to help them get him.

"If you know so much," Mica said, staring at a stain on the ceiling over Mitchell's head that looked a little like roadkill, "why don't you just go get him."

"I think you know the answer, but I'll tell you anyway. Like I said, no games. We know these things, but we don't have the evidence. What we need is someone like you, and a couple of others, to talk."

"To turn, you mean." Mica snorted and shook her head. "What you want is to get a couple of us killed. If you know so much, you know what happens when someone talks about MS-13. Sooner or later, a week, a month, five years, they end up dead."

"We know. We know that's why you're running. You want out. We can help you."

"Oh yeah? And how do you plan to do that?"

"You help us with information on Hector—how the gang is structured, who his lieutenants are, who his contacts in other organizations are, who might be willing to talk if the money is right. You do that and we'll get you a new identity."

"A new identity?"

"WITSEC—the witness protection program. We'll relocate you, get you a job, get you twenty-four-hour protection for the rest of your life."

"And where do you plan to put me? Kansas? Someplace where I'll live in a box wondering when he'll track me down, answering to some cop instead of Hector? How is that any different? At least with La Mara, I'm free."

Allie said softly, "Are you? Then why are you here?"

"I'm here because I choose to be here."

"You're here because you're running for your life," Allie said. "Let us help you."

"You'll help me right into the ground. No deal." Mica shook her head. She'd never live to make it into WITSEC, and if she did, she'd never see Flynn again. Never be able to set things right, if Flynn would even talk to her.

"We *will* get the evidence on Hector," Mitchell said, "and when we do, you'll go down with him. We'll charge you as an accessory. You don't want that to happen. I don't think you're guilty."

"If you wanted to arrest me, you would've done it already." Mica called their bluff, but she believed the detective. Hector had a world of hurt coming his way and didn't know it yet.

"Look," Mitchell said, "there may be a way to work this so you don't have to testify. So Hector doesn't know where the information is coming from."

"How?"

"Help us get the guy who's after you. If we arrest him, with enough evidence to put him away, he's going to be in the same situation you are. He'll know if he goes to jail he's a liability and Hector will kill him. My guess is he'll turn if we offer him protection. And if he's one of Hector's lieutenants, he's got to know what we need to know."

"And what do I get out of this?"

Mitchell looked her right in the eye. "You get freedom. You walk away."

"And if you don't get Hector, he'll know it was me."

"How is that any different than where you are now?" Allie said.

"At least this way, you have a shot at getting Hector out of the picture. With him gone and someone else in his place, you're not going to be so important anymore. At least you won't be at the top of their list."

Mica thought about it. She'd been gone too long now. Even if she wanted to go back, Hector wouldn't be able to let her, not and still save face. He was going to kill her; there was no going back. What they offered was a slim possibility, but it was more than she had right now. "How would it work?"

Mitchell sat forward. "We wire you, we'd watch you, we're pretty sure they know where you are now. These attacks are evidence of that. It won't take very long for them to make another move because they'll expect you to run exactly as you planned on doing. I'll be with you twenty-four seven. We'll pick up whoever comes after you, squeeze him, and you're out of it. We'll have enough evidence from the attack on you to arrest him and charge him. Once that happens, he'll have a big target on his back and he'll know it."

"And I get immunity? Whatever Hector says about me, no accessory charges?"

"That's right. You're out of it."

"And if I say no?"

Mitchell shrugged. "Then we let a few people know that you helped us anyway."

Mica thought she saw Allie stiffen, as if she didn't like what Mitchell said. She didn't think Mitchell was bluffing this time. If Hector or any of his lieutenants thought she'd talked, they'd never stop coming for her, whether Hector was in charge or not. "It doesn't bother you to sign my death warrant?"

"Not a bit," Mitchell said.

❖

Dell closed the door to the interrogation room, leaving Mia Gonzales inside, and followed Allie down the hall to Reese Conlon's office. Bri Parker and Conlon waited inside, Parker in her usual position against the wall and Conlon behind her desk. A video console showing a blank blue screen sat on a triangular platform bolted into one corner of the small room. Conlon and Parker had probably been watching the interview. She sat in the same chair she'd been in that morning, next to Allie, in front of Conlon's desk.

"Nice interview," Conlon said.

"Thanks," Dell said.

"Pretty rough on her there at the end," Parker said.

"La Mara members are used to being interrogated. It's a rite of passage for them to be picked up. I wanted to win her over, but she'd never believe me if I went easy on her. She's going to know if we're selling her a line of goods."

"Are you planning on leaking word that she helped us if she doesn't agree?" Conlon asked.

"That would be up to you and the lieutenant."

"And if it were your call?" Conlon asked quietly.

"Yes, I would," Dell said instantly. "Mia Gonzales may be innocent of any crime—technically. But she's been part of La Mara for years. They'll come after her no matter what we do. We need to make something happen before she disappears. And she will."

Conlon nodded, neither approval nor disapproval showing in her face. The lieutenant had briefed Dell on the sheriff. Conlon was a combat vet and a seasoned law officer. Dell wasn't fooled by the small-town ambience and homey atmosphere in the station. These were sharp officers. She hadn't run an operation by herself before, and she wasn't too proud to learn from everyone. "What would you do?"

"I'd do the same."

Next to her, Allie shifted slightly in her chair. Parker never moved a muscle.

"Butler—Gonzales—is a target," Conlon went on. "Her best chance of getting out of this alive is for us to be all over her. So—whatever it takes, we do."

Parker stirred. "So, Mitchell, you'll be undercover? How is that going to work?"

"You didn't get a chance to meet Mitch," Dell said. "If Mia goes for it, Mitch will hook up with her in the bar tonight and go home with her."

"Girlfriend?" Bri said, looking surprised.

Dell grinned. "No, boyfriend."

Parker shot Allie a glance. "How is that going to play with Flynn?"

"Flynn's out of it." Allie turned to Dell. "What if Mica's been watched and they know about Flynn? Will they believe her hooking up with Mitch?"

"A lot of the La Mara girls fool around with other girls," Dell said. "The guys don't take it seriously—they think it's hot. They'll find Mitch just as believable as Flynn."

"That's going to piss Hector off big-time if he gets wind of it," Allie said.

"Yeah," Dell said. "It'll turn up the heat on her a lot faster and probably make them move on her right away. They might get careless. That will work for us."

A muscle along the edge of Allie's jaw quivered. "You really are likely to get her killed."

"Not going to happen," Dell said. "I don't plan on letting her out of my sight. In a few hours, Mitch is going to be her new main man."

❖

Philadelphia—The Badlands

Hector muted the ballgame and picked up his cell phone. "What?"

"Sorry, boss," Carmen said. "We got a little problem."

"Fuck," Hector muttered. "Who do I have to kill?"

"We sent Ramirez up to look for Mia—"

"Yeah, I know. To that bumfuck place in Massachusetts, right?"

"Right."

"So?"

"He thought he had her a couple days ago, but it turns out it was just some girl that looked like her."

"Dumb motherfucker. Did you pull him off?"

"He said he was sure she was there. Swore he'd seen her working in some dyke bar."

"Dyke bar, huh? I always thought she liked pussy, but she never sampled any I know of."

"He says she got tight with some other girl. He was already there, so I figured he might as well check it out."

"And? Is it her?"

"Ah—probably."

Hector scratched his balls, getting more irritated by the second. "Just spit it out, cocksucker."

"Ramirez tried for the girl he thought was Mia—he didn't get her.

She got away." Carmen coughed. "She got his knife. She stuck him with it."

"You gotta be fucking kidding me! Where the fuck is he?"

"He's holed up somewhere up there. I think he's afraid to come back."

Hector smiled. Maybe Ramirez wasn't as stupid as he thought. "Did the cops make him?"

"He says no. He got away before they showed up, but they took Mia with them. If she talks—"

"She knows better than that." But he wasn't sure. Mia had run away, and he hadn't expected that. She knew way too much to be left alive, and if Ramirez had brought the cops down on her, she might cave. "You head up there—you personally. I want this taken care of right away, and this time for good. You feel me?"

"I hear you," Carmen said.

Hector hung up, turned the game back on, and called out for Angelita, one of the seasoned girls, to get her ass in there. Angelita had a good mouth, but he was going to miss Mia.

CHAPTER TWENTY-SEVEN

Flynn pulled into the lot of the rescue station half an hour after Mica disappeared with Allie and Bri. The sheriff's department was across the street, and she couldn't help but look over, wondering if she shouldn't just walk in and say that she wanted to talk to Mica. If they wouldn't let her see Mica, she could sit there and wait until Mica was finished and they released her. They had to release her. Anything else would be unthinkable. Mica might have lived with crime, might have been part of a criminal social organization, but she wasn't a criminal. There must be some room in the justice system for those who were neither perpetrators nor victims, but casualties of a world in which power and violence ruled above law and humanity. A world where the only currency with which to purchase survival was your soul.

She was amazed that Mica's soul had survived after so many years of subjugation, but Mica's humanity was very much intact. She had experienced Mica's tenderness in every touch. Mica had sacrificed herself for others, and that made her a hero in Flynn's eyes. Mica was so strong, but she wasn't superhuman. She shouldn't be alone now. Flynn couldn't abandon her, no matter what Mica had sa—

"You're a little early, aren't you?" Dave asked, walking out through the open vehicle bay behind her.

Flynn caught herself in mid-step, realizing she'd been halfway across the lot on her way to the sheriff's department. Headed for Mica. "Hi. I didn't think you'd be here. You working a double?"

"Yeah, I need the overtime. Wife's pregnant again."

He said it like it was a problem, but his grin was huge.

"Congratulations."

"Thanks—so what are you doing here? Aren't you on sick leave?"

"I was going to ask you and Wheeler if you wanted some extra shifts—if I need a little more time," Flynn said. She could take a few days off until her ribs were less tender, but she wasn't sure that would be enough time for her to figure out what she was doing with the rest of her life.

"Sure, I could use the hours. Wheeler's inside." Dave put his hands in his pockets and rocked slowly back and forth, his expression one that said he was waiting for her to say something else.

What could she say? That she'd made a mistake, more than one, and she kept repeating them? That she'd gone astray once again, when it mattered more than ever? Mica's words kept running through her mind, tormenting her with their truth. The pain she'd been able to set aside during the moments she was with Mica had come flooding back when Mica turned away. The worst agony, though, came from knowing she had learned nothing from Debbie's death. She knew her weaknesses and still she had not been able to change. She'd tried so hard to give Mica the support she needed, but maybe Mica was right. Maybe all she really wanted was to satisfy her own needs.

"You doing okay?" Dave asked.

Flynn jumped. "What? Oh. Yeah—I'm fine."

"Well, you know, I've got your back."

"Thanks. I appreciate it."

"And Flynn," Dave called as she started into the stationhouse, "I know you've got mine. Never doubted it."

Flynn stopped and turned. "Thanks. That means a lot."

He waved her off, looking uncomfortable. "Yeah, yeah. So take care of business and get back here."

"Will do." Flynn found Wheeler, arranged for coverage, and climbed into her car. She headed west on Route 6, figuring it would take her three hours if traffic was light. As she drove, she thought about telling Dave she'd be back. She wondered if she would. But then if she didn't return, where could she go where once she arrived, she wouldn't still be alone with her memories and her regrets? And if she left, she would never see Mica again. The ache in her chest expanded until she couldn't take a full breath.

Time passed slowly. She kept thinking about Mica, wondering if she was free yet. Wondering if Mica would stay around once Allie let her go. She doubted it. La Mara had found Mica, there was no doubt about that. That morning even she had half expected the knock on her door to be followed by someone shouldering through and demanding to know Mica's whereabouts. Mica had to know she was no longer safe, and she would do what she'd been doing since she'd escaped. She would disappear again.

Flynn rolled down her window. Maybe the cool afternoon air would soothe the aching wound that burned inside her when she thought about never seeing Mica again. Mica's spirit, her strength, and her stubbornness filled Flynn with excitement and awe. She loved being around her, loved watching her work, loved talking with her, touching her. They'd only been apart for a few hours and she missed her. Making love with her had been incredible. Passionate, tender, exquisitely pleasurable. She'd loved stroking her and feeling her body yield, hearing her break with pleasure. She'd loved giving herself, unconditionally, and knowing that the woman who touched her wanted her. She'd never had that with Evelyn, not without the pall of regret tarnishing the joy.

Flynn drove through the small New England town along tree-shrouded streets brilliant with fall color. Students walked in groups, laughing and carefree. On a knoll above town she turned into the wide gravel drive and made her way through the enormous scrolled iron gates up to the stone mansion. She left her car in the turn-around and went through the huge carved double wooden doors into the enormous vaulted foyer, her footsteps tapping along the stone until she reached the alcove where the receptionist waited.

"Reverend Edwards," the sexton exclaimed, rising. His wireless glasses sparkled in the sunlight slanting through the tall narrow window behind him. His meticulously trimmed mustache slanted upward as he smiled in greeting. "It's so good to see you."

"Hello, Mr. Burns. I know it's unexpected, but I'd like to speak to the reverend."

"Certainly. Certainly. I'll call him right away. Would you like to wait in the rectory?"

"That would be fine," Flynn said.

He smiled at her uncertainly and she nodded her thanks before turning away to make the familiar walk through the familiar halls to the rectory adjoining the seminary building. Her brother was waiting for her outside his office. He wore jeans and a plain black shirt and his clerical collar. They looked so similar, except her neck was bare, and she felt the absence even more acutely in his presence.

"Flynn." Matthew kissed her cheek. "It's good to see you. And about time."

"I know. I'm sorry." Flynn saw questions in his eyes, questions that she'd avoided for too long. About Evelyn, and Debbie, and her. "I should have come sooner."

"You're here now." He took her arm as he had so many times when as students they'd strolled and talked for hours. "How are you?"

"I'm afraid I'm lost."

"Your faith or your path to it?"

"Is there a difference?"

"Let's see if we can sort that out. Shall we walk outside?" Matthew said. "It's so beautiful, and you've given me the perfect excuse to avoid the budget I'm supposed to be reviewing."

"I'm sorry to arrive with no warning."

"Don't be. I've missed you. We all have."

She doubted Evelyn missed her. But Matthew didn't know about their relationship. She'd ended it as soon as she'd realized Evelyn was seeing them both, and she saw no reason to tell her brother about the past affair if his wife didn't. "I've missed you too."

The rolling hills of the seminary grounds were still green, although the maples and oaks were dropping their leaves like swatches of blazing confetti. The fall air was crisp, cooler and sharper than on the Cape. She missed the warm scent of the sea already. "I haven't lost my faith, but I can't seem to see past myself to its lessons."

Her brother smiled. "Maybe you just need to see yourself, and the rest will be clear."

"I'm afraid I see myself too well."

"Flynn," he said gently, stopping to sit on a stone bench overlooking the town, "what happened to Debbie was a terrible, terrible tragedy. We all feel it, and in some ways, we are all responsible. You weren't the only person who could have changed her mind. You weren't the only person who might have influenced her, who might have given her support. Yes"—he held up his hand—"I know, you counseled her. That's an enormous responsibility, no matter what the circumstances, but so much more so when we counsel the young, who sometimes are so isolated and feel so alone."

"If I'd been giving her what she needed," Flynn said, "she would have come to me when she thought she had no options. She would have talked to me about what she was going to do."

"You know that isn't usually what happens, not when someone

has truly made up their mind. They almost never tell us. She wasn't making a plea for help. She had already made her choice."

"I can't accept her choice," Flynn said, her throat burning with months of unshed tears.

"Of course you can't. Who could? Maybe the reason you feel so lost is you've forgotten that we are given free will, the opportunity to make our own choices, even when our choices are wrong or self-destructive. As hard as it is to accept, Debbie chose her path."

Flynn looked past her brother to the church and the cross at the top of the belfry, the symbols of their faith. Her belief that every individual had a choice, that nothing in life was completely predetermined, was fundamental to her faith. For if that were not so, there would be no purpose in ministering. Her failure had been in forgetting that ultimately, everyone chose their own path, and all she could do was help them see what those paths might be. She sighed. "Someone told me recently that my arrogance prevented me from seeing others' reality. How can I minister if all I can see is my own belief?"

"This person who told you that, did she know about Debbie?"

"Yes, she did."

"She's hard on you. Why is that?"

Flynn pictured Mica in the back of the police car, imprisoned and alone. Remembered the man in the alley and the knife at Mica's throat. Goose bumps broke out over her flesh. Mica was in danger and she had known it. Mica wanted her gone, and she had said exactly what she knew would drive Flynn away. "She wanted me out of her life."

"The two of you—you have an intimate relationship?"

"Yes." Flynn smiled at an image of an exhausted and sated Mica tumbling into her arms after they'd made love. The tight fist in her chest relaxed. "I'm in love with her."

"How does she feel about you?"

"I don't know." Flynn paused. "No, that's not true. She's talked to me, told me things that I know she's kept hidden from others. I know she cares."

"Then why did she want to drive you away? Why did she deliberately hurt you?"

"Someone is trying to kill her."

His expression never changed as he folded his hands in his lap and crossed his ankle over his opposite knee, as if he were settling in for a long, friendly conversation. "I think you better start at the beginning."

So she did, and the more she told him of Mica, the more she knew what she had to do.

❖

When Mica hurried past Mitch on her way to the ice machine with an empty ice bucket, he leaned across the bar and caught her arm. She pivoted and shot him a glare. She hated being handled by anyone. Stabbing pain shot through her. She didn't mind when Flynn touched her. She liked it. She didn't want to think about Flynn. She didn't want to keep watching the door. She'd accomplished what she'd wanted. Flynn was gone. She yanked her arm out of Mitch's grasp. "What?"

"You've been ignoring me," Mitch said quietly. "And besides that, you're snarling at me. You're supposed to think I'm the hottest thing on the planet."

Mica forced herself to smile, although she thought if anyone looked closely they'd be able to tell she *was* snarling. Mitch did look good, and maybe if she'd been into guys with smoky eyes and sensuous mouths and teasing bulges in their crotches, she'd be smiling at him for real. But when she looked at him, nothing stirred inside her, not the way she'd come alive when she'd looked at Flynn. And now when she thought of Flynn, she just hurt. "I don't fool around when I'm working."

"Just pretend to like me a little bit." Mitch leaned over and caught her hand, tugged her against the bar, and kissed her.

She hadn't expected it, and because she knew him, she hadn't been on guard. His mouth was soft and warm and for an instant, she compared the kiss to Flynn's. When Flynn kissed her, even the very first time, she felt a connection that she didn't feel now. Flynn's lips had been electric against hers. For the sake of the show they were supposed to be putting on, she forced herself not to jerk away, but let him slide his mouth over hers for another minute. When the backs of his fingers glanced over the outer curve of her breast, she figured they'd given everyone enough of a look. She bit his lip and he pulled back, laughing.

"Hey," he complained, loud enough for everyone to know he liked it.

"Save it until later, baby," she said, also making sure she was heard.

He dropped back on his stool, looking pleased. "I've got plenty left for later."

She snorted and spun away. She took one step and stopped, her heart rocketing into her throat.

Flynn stood at the end of the bar, her mouth set in a tight angry line. Mica was so used to Flynn being calm and cool no matter what was happening, the flare of anger in her eyes was as exciting as it was ominous.

"We might have a problem," Mica said softly.

Mitch swiveled and followed her gaze. "I take it that's your girl?"

"Was. Was my girl."

"I don't think she agrees with you."

CHAPTER TWENTY-EIGHT

Flynn's skin flashed hot and cold in dizzying waves. She didn't know the guy who was manhandling Mica, and she didn't care who he was. All she wanted was for him to stop touching her. When Mica kissed him, there was something off in the way she held her body, in the way she kept her hands away from him, even though his were all over her. Mica didn't want to kiss him, and Flynn didn't want her to either. When they broke apart and Mica turned from the stranger, the expression on her face was not one of pleasure. Maybe anyone else who happened to be watching would have thought so, but Flynn knew better. She knew what Mica looked like when she wanted to be touched, when she wanted to be kissed. Right now, Mica's mouth was smiling, but her eyes were hard with suppressed wrath.

Flynn strode toward the dark-haired stranger, who watched her warily without the slightest hint of uneasiness. He was cocky. He didn't look like one of Hector's guys, but then how would she know? Anyone could be one of Hector's guys. It didn't matter. She didn't care. She'd had enough. Time to put a stop to this.

Mica came around the bar so quickly, Flynn had barely made it halfway before Mica blocked her way.

"Flynn," Mica said, intercepting her, "you need to get out of here."

"Who is that?" Flynn didn't recognize her own voice. Low and cold and hard. She wasn't sure she recognized herself. The day had been too long and filled with too many hard memories and too much pain. Too much sorrow. Her existence, her core, was built on forgiveness, on the belief that any wrong could be set right, any soul redeemed, but she didn't feel forgiving right now. She didn't care about understanding. She hurt inside and she had no clue as to how to erase the pain.

Mica grasped her arm, bare skin to bare skin, and the heat of Mica's flesh washed through her. A wave of hope followed, as if redemption were at hand. Flynn looked down at Mica's fingers curled around her forearm, smaller and more fragile seeming than her own, but strong. Mica was trembling, only she was so good at hiding her fear Flynn doubted anyone else would know.

"Who is he?"

"It doesn't matter," Mica said, her voice tight and urgent. "You need to go."

"No."

Mica's grip tightened, and she dragged Flynn away from the bar into the shadows next to the ice machine. She pushed Flynn against the wall and planted both palms against Flynn's shoulders, pinning her there. "You listen to me," Mica said, fury riding every word. "If I'd wanted you here, I would have asked you to come. You're going to get your stupid self killed, and if that happens, you're going to kill me. You understand? If you care at all about me, you'll go away."

Flynn grasped Mica's wrists and raised both hands to her mouth. She kissed Mica's palms and folded Mica's hands inside her own. "I'm not leaving you. I love you."

Mica went as still as a statue, her eyes widening. "Oh my God, Flynn. No. You're crazy."

"I'm not." Flynn smiled as calm suffused her. The terrible unrest and uncertainty that had been eating away at her dissolved. "I'm totally sane. I love you. And I don't want that guy touching you."

Mica leaned against her, fitting into all the waiting places in Flynn's soul. "He's a cop. I'm not in any danger, but you are. Please. I don't want you hurt."

"Why was he kissing you?"

Mica growled and shook her head as if Flynn's head were made of stone. "Are you not hearing me? It doesn't matter. It's not real."

"What are you doing with him, then? Are you waiting for them to come? Is that it?" Flynn cupped Mica's chin and searched her eyes. Mica didn't lie to her, and the truth was plain to see. "I'm not letting you do this."

"Keep your voice down," Mica said.

"Mica—"

"Damn it!" As if she'd totally lost patience, Mica plastered her mouth to Flynn's.

Flynn's anger fractured like mist in the sunlight. Mica's kiss was the softest, warmest, most exciting sensation Flynn had ever known. She wrapped her arms around Mica's waist and pulled her in tight. She needed Mica everywhere, over her and inside her—filling her up. She opened her mouth and drew Mica's kiss inside, making a silent plea for her to stay.

Mica pulled back first. "Now I want you to pretend you're really pissed off at me and storm out of here. And stay out of sight until this is over."

"What will you be doing?"

"Acting normally, if you'd ever let me. Mitch will—"

"Mitch—that's his name?"

"Will you forget about him?" Mica hissed.

"Do you promise you won't disappear?"

Mica tugged at her lower lip with her teeth. She wouldn't lie and she didn't answer.

"If you don't promise me," Flynn said reasonably, thinking it only fair to be open about her intentions, "I'm going to plant my ass on one of those bar stools and stay here until you leave. Mitch or no Mitch."

"All right, all right, I promise. I'll call you. Now go away."

Flynn feathered her fingers through Mica's hair and kissed her, softly, imprinting her spicy taste and the tangy scent of her. She cupped her face. "I don't know if I can pretend to be angry at you."

"Think about Mitch kissing me again—more than once. Does that work for you?"

"I swear," Flynn said dangerously, "if he does that again while I'm watching, I'm going to—"

Mica smiled. "Baby, I love it when you're jealous, but you're no match for him. And he's no competition for you." Mica backed away and said, loudly, "I'm over your attitude, Flynn. I'll date anybody I want."

"Then I'm done. I don't share." Flynn spun around and strode directly to the door and didn't slow until she was outside. If she looked back even once, she wasn't going to be able to leave her. Mica was playing a dangerous game, and the police were taking advantage of her need to be free, even if it was Mica's choice. Mica's choice. Wasn't that what she and Matthew had talked about just that afternoon? The only true freedom was the freedom to choose, and she had to accept that. Accept that she could make a difference, but ultimately, she was not responsible for the choices of others, even those she loved.

Her heart ached. Letting Mica do what she had to do was so hard.

So hard when she had so much to lose. If they hurt Mica, if she lost her, she wouldn't survive, no matter how strong her faith. She slowed when she reached the street, uncertain of where to go. Home? Her apartment was only a set of empty rooms and the bed where Mica had helped her find the way back to herself. The memories of Mica in her arms would drive her crazy. There was only one place she could go. She started walking.

❖

Reese bounced Reggie on her knee, trying to avoid the fallout as Reggie practiced eating SpaghettiO's with a spoon. When Reggie tired of trying to get the slippery circles into her mouth with the utensil, she helped the process along with both hands. The scatter landed on Reese's shirtfront and the leg of her pants. With her free hand, Reese forked the salad her mother had made into her mouth.

"You could put her in the high chair," Jean said.

"I know," Reese said to her mother's partner, "but I don't see her at dinnertime all that much, and I like holding her." She dodged a flying tomato-covered ring and grinned as it landed somewhere behind her on the floor.

"She's getting better at it," Kate observed.

"I think that's a statement only a grandmother could make," Reese said, laughing. Her cell phone rang and she put down her fork to dig it out of her pocket. "Conlon."

"Reese?" Tory said.

"Hi, baby. I'm over at—"

"I've got a Hispanic male in my clinic with an obvious stab wound in his shoulder. He says it happened—"

"Who else is there with you?" Reese signaled her mother to take the baby. Kate scooped Reggie up and carried her around to the other side of the table, watching Reese anxiously.

"Nita is here, and Randy. We've got a full house, Reese."

"Okay. You don't want to alert him that anything is wrong." Reese grabbed her keys and hurried to the hall closet where she'd left her gun belt and weapon. "I'll be there in five minutes. Less. Four minutes, Tor."

"All right—I'll get the patients out—"

"No." Reese raced down the narrow irregular stone walkway from her mother's small harborside bungalow to the street. "Just tell him you're going to get some supplies together. That you'll be right back. Act calmly. If you see Nita, tell her to lock herself in the treatment room with whatever patient she's seeing. Then you do the same in your office."

"What about all the patients in the waiting area?"

"You have to leave them there. If you try to get them outside, you're going to alert him that something is wrong. They'll be in more danger then." She yanked open the door of her SUV. "He ought to be pretty comfortable with a few minutes' wait, and I'll be there soon. What room is he in?"

"Two."

"All right, I'll come in the back." She started the engine and pulled out.

"He'll probably be calmer if I stay in there with him. Just carry on as normal."

"No," Reese said. "Tory, don't go back in there."

"Darling, I've got twenty people in my waiting room. I can't risk him getting spooked and taking them hostage. I'll be fine. Just come and pick him up."

"Damn it, Tory—" Reese swerved around a double-parked car, turned onto a one-way heading the wrong way toward Bradford, and stomped on the gas. The line went dead. She hit speed dial for the station.

"Sheriff's depar—"

"This is Conlon. I need backup at Tory's clinic. No lights, no siren, and no one goes in without my say-so. Have them block the parking lot and set up a perimeter three blocks in every direction." She swung onto a street paralleling the rear of Tory's clinic. "Suspect is inside the building, possibly armed, definitely dangerous. I'm going in. No one enters until I radio all clear. Put a unit on the back door. Have you got this?"

Gladys Martin said calmly, "Yes, Sheriff. One unit on the parking lot, another at the back door, and a three-block perimeter. Calling now."

"Thanks."

"Be careful, Sheriff."

Reese disconnected and careened to the curb. The dashboard clock read a minute to go on her estimate. She parked, jumped out, and cut through several backyards to approach the rear of the clinic through the small stand of trees that ringed the building. Everything looked quiet.

She drew her weapon, eased inside through the back door, and slipped down the hallway that bisected the treatment area. Closed doors on either side led to the equipment room and small pharmacy. Tory's office door was open. The treatment room doors were both shut. Nita was probably still in room one with her patient. Carefully, quietly, Reese sidled along the wall to treatment room two. The door was slightly ajar. Smart, Tory. Very smart. She put her shoulder against the wall and toed the door open another inch so she could see inside.

A youngish male sat on the treatment table, shirtless, his left shoulder partially visible. A two-inch laceration surrounded by beefy red tissue oozed pus. Tory stood a few feet away at the end of the treatment table, arranging instruments on a stainless steel tray. His black hair was matted to his neck with sweat and his face was tomato-red, as if he had a fever. He gripped the edges of the treatment table, his fingers opening and closing convulsively. He seemed to be jittering. She wondered if he was high on drugs, or just high from fever and stress. She raised her weapon, pushed the door the rest of the way open with her foot, and slid into the room.

"Police. Down on the floor. Do it now. On the floor, hands over your head. Do it now." He glanced at her wild-eyed, jumped down from the table, and pivoted toward Tory. Tory jumped back, her eyes registering her fear.

"Take another step," Reese said clearly and calmly, "and I'll drop you where you stand."

"I got no weapon," he said, but he wasn't getting down on the floor. He was facing Tory, partially blocking her from Reese's view.

"I don't care. Get down on the floor or you're dead."

He hesitated, but he must have heard in her voice that she wasn't bluffing. He dropped to his knees, then went face-down and spread his hands out over his head.

"Hands out to your sides. Now." Reese crossed to him, knelt with her knee on his near shoulder, holstered her weapon, and quickly cuffed him. Once she had him secured, she radioed for backup. "Code four here."

"This is Adam Charlie one," Bri answered. "We're at the back door."

"Clear the building."

"Ten-four, Sheriff."

"I'm going to check on the rest of the patients," Tory said.

"Not yet," Reese snapped. At Tory's questioning look, she tamped down the adrenaline surge that kept her temper burning hot. Tory was fine. Safe. "Wait until Bri clears the place. In case he's not alone."

"All right." Tory hesitated as if she were about to say something else but left the room and the question unasked. Her eyes held worry she couldn't hide. Reese thought she knew why, but there was nothing she could do about Tory's concern. She wasn't sorry. She'd do what she had to do. She wasn't going to let anyone hurt her family. Ever.

CHAPTER TWENTY-NINE

I'm about finished here," Mica told Mitch as she stacked the last case of beer in the cooler.

"Good." Mitch tossed down the tequila he'd been nursing all night, stood, and stretched. He gave her a lazy smile as he dragged his hand through his hair and cocked his hips. His message was clear—*I know you want in my pants.* "I'm ready."

"Like, when aren't you?" Mica grabbed her denim jacket and came around the bar to join him. More than a few girls had eyed him with interest the last few hours. His sexiness wasn't an act—he was hot. He wouldn't have survived long around Hector—like all the guys, Hector liked watching girls get it on, as long as the girls looked like girls. The butch ones, they got the shit kicked out of them—and dudes like Mitch? They better learn to fight or they were dead. The memories chilled her, and she wondered if Mitch knew what he was risking by playing this game with her. She grabbed his hand. "Let's go."

"You okay?" Mitch murmured as he wrapped an arm around her waist.

"Yeah," Mica said flatly. "Just great."

At least Flynn was out of it. Mica still couldn't believe Flynn had come after her. Come after her and called her out over Mitch. Just remembering the blaze in Flynn's eyes when she'd said she didn't want Mitch touching her sent a current of excitement right to her clit. She'd been a possession all her life, but for the very first time, she liked the feeling of belonging to someone. As long as that someone was Flynn. Flynn on fire melted her.

Everything in her life had come with a price tag, but Flynn asked nothing of her, other than the truth. Funny, she'd spent her life with people who wanted part of her, but no one had ever wanted that from her before. Hector had been happy with her lies. Even her family, in some ways, had been too. She didn't blame them for looking the other way, for pretending they didn't know what she did, or why—but deep down inside she wondered if anyone would ever really see her. And then along came Flynn, gently and unyieldingly demanding she talk to her, reveal her secrets, share her pain. Now that she'd been touched with tenderness, held with desire, she couldn't imagine living without it. Couldn't imagine living without Flynn.

"Oh fuck," Mica whispered. Flynn. *Dios*, she wanted her. She… "Oh no. No, no."

Mitch stopped under the awning of a darkened storefront and nuzzled her neck. "Something wrong?"

"No."

Mitch kissed her and murmured teasing suggestions of what he planned to do when they reached Mica's apartment. His delivery was smooth and practiced, with just enough humor in his tone for Mica to know it was part of the act.

"I bet you get a lot of action this way," Mica whispered in Mitch's ear.

"You'd be surprised," Mitch whispered back, pressing his lips to a spot below Mica's ear.

She let him hit on her, but she wasn't giving anything back. "What are you—about five-ten?"

"Mmm. Yeah." Mitch kissed the corner of her mouth. "See anyone on the streets you recognize?"

"No." Mica looked past his shoulder. No one behind them but tourists. "My couch is about five feet long. You're going to be really uncomfortable tonight."

"I'm heartbroken."

She bit the underside of his jaw. "You should be happy I'm not really into this. You'd have more than a *heart* ache to worry about."

He laughed. "I'll suffer silently."

She pulled away, shoved her hand in his back pocket, and tugged him along the street. "You have a girlfriend?"

He snugged her close with an arm around her shoulders. "More like a wife."

"She good with this?"

"If she thought I was seriously trying to make it with you, she'd cut off my nuts."

Mica laughed and rested her head against Mitch's shoulder. "I like her."

"You would, I think."

"What does she do?"

"She's a cop."

"Huh. I guess she'd have to be."

"She wasn't always."

"Yeah?" Mica pointed up the street. "That's my place. So what was she? Your girl."

Mitch didn't usually talk about Sandy when he was on the job, even though she'd been undercover with him a time or two. Maybe hearing about Sandy would settle Mica down. She'd been jumpy and wired since they'd left the Piper. Not that he could blame her, but he needed her thinking. They'd both need to be sharp if they were going to pull this off. "When I met her, she was working the streets."

"Really."

"Yeah." He didn't tell many people that, but he thought Mica would get it. Where you came from didn't define who you were. "She's tough. Strong. A lot like you."

"Sounds like she might be smarter than me. Was some pimp running her?"

Mitch tightened inside but he didn't let anything show. "No. She was independent."

"That's hard to do. I couldn't manage it."

"The two of you came from different places, but you both survived, right? She got out. So did you."

"I'm not out yet." Mica stopped, turned into him, and kissed him. She said against his mouth, "This is my place. Are you going to get me out, cop?"

"Yeah," Mitch said. "I am."

"Then I guess you better come up and sleep on my couch."

She took his hand and pulled him up the walk. Once inside, she led him up a couple of flights of stairs and down a hall. She slowed and pointed to a door with chipped brown paint, a tarnished number 4 hanging askew, and a sliver of light edging out underneath. "That's it, and I didn't leave a light on."

"Get behind me." Mitch pulled Mica against the wall and inched up to the door. "Sounds quiet. Unlock it, but don't open it."

Mica nodded, slid her key silently into the lock, and slowly turned the tumblers. After Mica unlocked the door, Mitch motioned for her to back up, slid his weapon from the holster at his back, and turned the knob. He went in low, weapon first.

Flynn Edwards sat on the sofa across the room, a bottle of beer in her hand and her feet up on the coffee table. She didn't look surprised.

"Damn it, Flynn," Mica snapped, crowding into the small apartment behind Mitch. "What the fuck are you doing here?"

"This is where I belong. You're here." Flynn stood and held out her hand. "I'm Mica's girlfriend. She tells me you're a cop."

Mitch checked the windows and noted the shades were pulled. Flynn was smart, for someone who didn't know much about what she was up against. She returned the handshake. "I'm Mitch. I don't know if you know about what's going on here, but—"

Flynn moved over next to Mica. "I gather you're waiting for whoever is after Mica to come back. You think you can keep her safe?"

"I know I can," Mitch said. "But you're kind of a complicating factor."

"I'm not going to get in the way," Flynn said, "but I'm not going to wait on the sidelines while you put Mica's life in danger either."

Mica jammed her hands on her hips. "Did you think maybe you should ask me about any of this, Flynn?"

"Like you asked me?" Flynn's eyes sparked. "Did you consider I might have a stake in this? What it would do to me if something happened to you?"

For the first time since Mitch had met her, Mica looked as if she didn't quite know how to play things. She touched Flynn's face with incredible tenderness.

"I never know what to do about you," Mica whispered.

Flynn smiled and kissed her as if she were spun from glass. "Haven't you figured out I need you yet?"

Mica stepped into her, wrapped her arms around Flynn's waist, and rested her head against Flynn's chest. "I don't think so. But that's okay. I'm working on it."

Mitch turned away, giving them privacy. Some things were too personal to witness. He said, "Okay. Well, if you're staying, here are the rules—" His cell rang and he fished it out of his back pocket. No one had that number except the other officers. "Mitchell."

"This is Conlon. Where are you?"

"At Mica's."

"We just picked up the suspect who attacked Mica and Flynn the other night. I ran his prints. His name is José Ramirez. You know him?"

"Yeah. He's one of Hector's musclemen. Works out of Jersey."

"We'll need Flynn and Mica to ID him as the assailant, but looks like we may have what you need."

"Definitely," Mitch said. "He must have stayed around to finish the job. Dumb of him. Where did you pick him up?"

Reese laughed, a sharp, dangerous laugh. "The idiot was stupid enough to go to my wife's clinic. Tory called me."

"Any trouble?"

"Nope." Reese sounded hard as stone.

"He's lucky he gave in quietly."

"Very lucky."

"When do you want to run the lineup?"

"Let us interrogate him for a few hours, soften him up overnight. Come morning we can have Flynn and Mica ID him. That will give us more ammunition to go another round when we've worn him down some."

"Are you pulling off the detail on Mica?"

"What do you think?"

"I'd feel better if we keep up the surveillance. Maybe Ramirez isn't alone."

"Then whoever is with him will know we've picked him up," Reese said. "If they see us pull off, they may get overconfident."

"Anybody who's watching knows I'm up here," Mitch said.

"If they see you leave, that could work for us."

"I'll go out the front, head to my place, and circle back."

"Sounds good," Reese said.

"Where do you want me?"

"Bri is in the cruiser and Smith is outside across the street. Take the back. Check in with Smith when you're in position."

"Okay." Mitch glanced at Flynn's protective, possessive expression as she kept Mica tucked against her. "I'll fill them in."

"Them?"

"Flynn is here with Mica."

Reese laughed. "Read her in on the plan, then."

"I don't think I have much choice about that."

❖

Reese hung up and observed the rest of Allie's interview of José Ramirez on the video feed. Allie hinted they had enough to put him away and hadn't offered him any deals, although he clearly had expected one. He hadn't lawyered up, which was good, but he probably would once they began to squeeze him for information about Hector. The plan was to keep him in the dark as long as they could before pushing him to roll on Hector in exchange for a safe place beyond Hector's reach.

"Good job," Reese said when Allie came into her office. "You've got him wondering what we have on him, but he's not running scared. He thinks he can wait us out and we'll let him go."

"Thanks," Allie said, rolling the kinks out of her shoulders. "It's a lot harder than I thought. I really wanted to jump to the chase."

"I know. But I think you're pacing things well."

"Should we get him dinner, do you think?"

Reese looked at her watch. Ten thirty. "It's not that late. Give it another hour or so."

"Should I go another round tonight?"

"What's your take?"

"I was thinking it would be better not to."

"I agree. Let him sit." Reese rose. "I'm heading home. You should too."

"Okay." Allie went to the door, then turned. "Thanks for letting me handle the questioning."

"You did a good job."

"You sure you don't need me on surveillance—"

"No, we're covered. Mitchell is outside now."

"I thought Mitch was staying with Mica tonight."

Reese nodded. "Now that we have Ramirez, we're pretending to back off in case anyone else is watching her. Flynn is with Mica."

"Oh."

"You okay with the way things are playing out with Flynn?"

Allie stiffened. "You mean with Mica?"

Reese nodded.

"Yeah," Allie said. "Mica really stepped up. The rest is Flynn's business."

"Okay, then. See you in the morning."

"Thanks, Sheriff. I'll be ready."

Reese left a few minutes later, stopped to get pizza, and got home a little before eleven. Tory reclined on the couch, her feet up and a medical journal propped open on her chest.

"Is the baby asleep?" Reese stowed her gun belt on the top shelf in the closet and put the pizza on the counter separating the kitchen from the dining area.

"I just heard her talking to her rabbit a few minutes ago. If you want to see her, she's probably still awake."

Reese edged the journal out of the way with one finger and kissed Tory. "Hi."

Tory slid her hand around Reese's neck and kissed her back. "Hi. Are you all right?"

Reese sat on the coffee table. "Yeah. You?"

Tory sat up, dropped the journal on the floor, and eased her legs across Reese's lap. Reese automatically cupped the ball of her foot and rubbed her arch.

"Mmm, that feels so good." Tory sighed. "Are you very angry with me about this afternoon?"

"You mean about you completely disregarding the instructions of a law officer in the performance of her duty?" Reese switched to massaging Tory's heel.

"Yes. That."

"I'm enormously pissed off," Reese said.

"Why are you so calm?"

"I'm angry at my wife for putting herself in danger. I understand why the doctor wanted to protect an office full of patients. I'm between a rock and a hard place and I don't know what to do about it." Reese took Tory's hand and rubbed Tory's knuckles against her cheek. "If he'd so much as blinked in your direction, I would have killed him."

"I know, and I'm so sorry. I didn't want to put you in that position, darling, but I didn't have any choice."

Reese couldn't argue. "I guess that's how you feel when I do things that put me at risk. I don't think I ever really appreciated how that must make you feel."

"Scared."

"Yeah." Reese remembered the icy flood of terror that gripped her before her training kicked in and everything went cold and silent and she just did what she had to do.

"Would you have really killed him?"

"Without a second's hesitation."

"I understand that too. I'd do the same to anyone who threatened you."

Reese stood and pulled Tory up into her arms. She kissed her, harder than usual, a little deeper, a little rougher. "Don't do anything like that again."

Tory clenched her hand in Reese's hair. "I can't promise—not if you're in danger. You're mine to protect."

"I love you."

"I love everything about the way you love me." Tory crushed her mouth to Reese's. Her kiss was a claiming that banished the fear from Reese's soul. "I want you to make love to me. I want to feel you everywhere. I want to know you're safe."

Reese lifted Tory into her arms. "Remember the first time I carried you? I was shaking so much I was afraid I was going to drop you."

"I remember you made me wet the second you picked me up."

Reese skimmed her mouth over Tory's and headed for the stairs. "Are you wet now?"

"Enormously." Tory wrapped her arms around Reese's neck. "This is better than the first time. Now take me to bed."

CHAPTER THIRTY

The door closed behind Mitch, and Mica turned to Flynn. "You know, José Ramirez might not be the only one."

Flynn rose and took Mica's hand. "Let's go to bed."

Mica sighed but followed Flynn into the tiny bedroom that barely fit a double bed and the boxes where she kept her clothes. Standing at the foot of the bed, she had trouble concentrating on anything other than Flynn, just inches away. Her brain said she needed to prepare for Hector's next move, but all she wanted, all she needed, was Flynn. She wanted to kiss her, more and more with every passing second. When she tried to step back so she could think, Flynn gripped her hand more firmly. Exasperated with herself for being so easily distracted by Flynn's smile and the teasing glint in her eyes, she said, "Ignoring what's going on isn't going to change anything."

"I'm not ignoring anything." Flynn framed Mica's face and kissed her. "I know you're right. Someone else might come looking for you. Maybe tonight. Maybe next week. Maybe a year from now."

"Then you know this is crazy, right?"

"You've been saying that to me since the first day we met." Flynn rubbed her thumb over a faint bruise on Mica's jaw. "This is the best crazy I've ever known. I know something else too. We can't predict the future. We can only live the life we have, and the only life I want is the one with you in it. I love you."

I love you. The words sounded like a foreign language. Mica remembered her mother saying them when she was small. Then the men. Sometime before she was grown she'd stopped believing the words meant anything more than *I want something from you* or *I own you.* With Flynn, the words promised something completely different. Something selfless and wonderful and terrifying. The first time Flynn had said the words, she'd scarcely dared believe them. Now she wanted to hear them again and again. What was happening to her? Where had this gut-deep need for Flynn come from, and how would she ever live without her?

Flynn waited, watching her, calm as always, but now Mica recognized the fire beneath Flynn's steady surface. Flynn burned, but her fire ran deep. Flynn didn't hide her need, and Mica couldn't let her burn alone. "I want you. I want you to love me, and I don't even know if that's right."

Flynn exhaled hard and fast, as if she'd been holding her breath underwater. "How could it be wrong?"

"Because your loving me puts you in danger." Mica leaned into her, helpless not to touch her. She loved the way Flynn never yielded but stood firm, absorbing all her uncertainty and fear. Guilt ate at her joy, a searing pain in her middle. "It's not fair, bringing my troubles down on you. You could get hurt."

"I'll hurt a lot more if I lose you."

Flynn's honesty always stopped her heart. She could give her nothing less. "What I said that night—about you hurting people— that's not true. I was afraid next time he'd hurt you. I wanted you to go away."

"I know," Flynn said. "But I couldn't. I was dying inside without you."

Mica brushed the shadows under Flynn's eyes, hating how worn she looked. "I don't want you to hurt."

"Then let me love you."

"You haven't even asked me how I feel about you," Mica said.

"My loving you doesn't come with an escape clause, and there are no contingencies. I'm not going to stop loving you even if you tell me you don't care about me."

"Dios," Mica muttered, wrapping her arms around Flynn's waist. "I'll never say that."

"Then I figure you'll tell me what you need to when you want to." Flynn cupped Mica's cheek. "But even if you never say a word, I'll know how you feel when you let me touch you, when you let me inside you, when you let me see your heart." Flynn kissed her again, lingeringly, caressing her slowly, feathering her fingers over her breasts until her skin was molten.

"Flynn," Mica groaned, "I want you so much." She slid both hands into Flynn's hair and pressed against her, needing to be closer than she'd ever been with anyone before. "This thing I have for you inside, it's so huge, sometimes I can't breathe." She pressed her mouth hard to Flynn's, opening to her, slipping her tongue into the soft furnace of Flynn's mouth. She whimpered, trembling in Flynn's arms.

"It's okay, sweetheart." Flynn eased Mica's T-shirt from her jeans. She worked the shirt up over Mica's head and off, dropping it along with her bra beside them on the floor. She fused her mouth to Mica's and began unbuttoning her own shirt, until they were both naked except for their jeans, their breasts and stomachs gliding with the faint mist of desire. Flynn wrapped her arms around Mica's waist, her fingers laced over the tattoo covering the base of Mica's spine. "I need you, Mica. You've given me something I've never had before."

"What? What can I possibly give you?" Mica brushed her lips over Flynn's chest and kissed her breasts. Her tongue tingled as if a fine electrical current ran beneath Flynn's skin, and she sucked the salty sweetness. The tangy taste of her stirred her hunger. She wanted to devour her.

"Can't think," Flynn moaned and lifted Mica's mouth from her breast. She smiled shakily. "You gave me hope, Mica, when I had none. Your will, your strength, your bravery restored my faith when I was faltering." Flynn slowly kissed her way down Mica's body until she knelt in front of her and opened her jeans with trembling fingers. She kissed the base of Mica's belly and pressed her cheek to Mica's stomach. "I was so lost until I found you."

"Baby," Mica whispered, holding Flynn's face to her body. She stroked Flynn's cheek and her heart seized at the wetness on her fingertips. "I love you, Flynn. I love you."

"Then don't make me leave you." Flynn gazed up at Mica, her face streaked with tears, her eyes completely undefended. "No matter what comes, let me be with you."

Mica grasped Flynn's shoulders and dropped down in front of her. "I'll stay with you as long as you want me."

"I'll want you forever."

"Then that's how long I'll stay," Mica whispered against Flynn's mouth.

Flynn shuddered under a wave of helpless longing. She needed something beyond words, beyond even promises. She needed Mica— heart, mind, and soul. She grasped Mica's wrist and pressed Mica's fingers to her bare abdomen. "Please. I need to be yours, Mica."

Mica gasped, and hunger consumed her fears. She pushed Flynn against the bed and straddled her. Pushing one hand between them, she worked Flynn's jeans open while she kissed her. She watched Flynn's eyes glaze and her mouth tremble with need as she filled her. With her mouth on Flynn's, her heart to Flynn's, she took her in long, deep strokes. "You are mine. Always."

❖

Carmen approached Commercial Street from the beach and made his way up the darkened alley one cautious step at a time. He'd waited until midnight, when the people hurrying through the streets or lingering on the water's edge were not likely to take notice of a lone man strolling on the shore. He hadn't had much trouble convincing the bouncer at the dyke bar that Mia was his cousin. After he'd told her he was totally bummed that he'd just missed her and he'd lost the number she'd e-mailed him, she'd given him Mia's address. The twenty he'd offered for her troubles probably helped her decide he was harmless. She hadn't even questioned why he didn't call Mia "Mica," the name she used when telling him where Mia lived. Stupid cunt probably thought Mia was Spanish for the fake name Mia was hiding behind. The counterman in the pizza shop across the street from the bar had set him in the right direction, and now he was looking at her apartment building across the street.

He stopped abruptly in midstep. A shadowy figure materialized just inside the mouth of the alley. Might be some guy taking a leak on his way home, or he might be there for another reason. Carmen checked his watch and waited five minutes. Whoever was standing there never moved. He was watching Mia's building too.

Ever so slowly, checking each footstep to be sure he didn't step on a discarded soda can or kick a loose stone and give himself away, he made his way closer. Street noises from people walking by and the occasional passing car camouflaged his approach. When the moon came out from behind a bank of clouds, he detected the unmistakable outline of a weapon on the guy's hip. The law. Why was the law watching Mia? He hoped the *puta* hadn't gotten herself into some kind of trouble, bringing the attention of the law down on all of them.

Hector should have tracked her down weeks ago and cut her to pieces in front of the rest of the whores to remind them where they belonged, and who they belonged to, and just what happened if they forgot. As soon as he got past this cop, he'd take care of the problem, and Hector would owe him for saving his rep. When the time came for Hector to split the territory in the next expansion, he would be next in line and no would question his promotion. Not even Hector. Slipping the sap from his back pocket, he took the last two steps quickly and swung the leather-covered weight at the back of the cop's head. The cop went down without a sound. Carmen kept moving, shoving the sap into his pocket as he strode across the street, climbed the few steps to the porch, and pushed inside. Four mailboxes, three with names. The one without a name would be hers. Amateurs always made that mistake. Better a fake name than nothing at all. He touched the grip of the Saturday Night Special he'd picked up before leaving the city. Disposable, untraceable. One quick shot and his future was assured. He walked down the narrow hall and started up the stairs to number four.

CHAPTER THIRTY-ONE

Allie rolled over and looked at the clock for the third time in an hour.

"What's the matter?" Ash asked.

"I guess I'm just wound up. Can't sleep."

"Come here." Ash pulled Allie down into the crook of her arm, nestled Allie's head against her shoulder, and slowly stroked her back. "Big day, long night. Takes a while to come down."

Allie pillowed her cheek against Ash's breast and closed her eyes. Her mind wouldn't shut off. She kept thinking about José Ramirez and his genuine confusion over some of the questions she had asked him. "I don't think the guy we picked up tonight was hanging around to go after Mica again. I think he was trying to figure out how to get out of town and got sicker before he could manage to leave. Why else would he risk going to the clinic?"

"Because he's a dumb fuck?"

"Oh, that's him, but still. He's street-smart. He had to know he was taking a big risk seeking medical attention."

"What did Tory say about his condition?"

"He's not quite sick enough to need hospitalization, but he was headed there without the antibiotics she pumped into him. She said he would've felt pretty bad and probably wouldn't have been able to drive even if he'd had a car. So far there's no sign of one. The only other way off-Cape would be the bus, unless he was really dumb and tried the airport." Allie snuggled closer, sliding her thigh over Ash's. "He might have been afraid someone would realize there was something wrong with him if he had to spend hours cooped up with a lot of people."

"That all makes sense. So what's bothering you?"

"I think us picking him up tonight was a lucky break. We were looking for someone after Mica, and we know he was the one who assaulted her in the alley. Feels too easy."

"And?"

Allie shifted, the uneasy feeling prickling up her spine again. "Maybe he's not alone."

"It's been a few days since he tried for Mica, and you haven't seen any sign of a partner, have you?"

"No, but that doesn't mean he doesn't have one."

"Agreed. You haven't aborted the plan, right? You're still watching her, still on the lookout for someone making a move against her?"

"Yeah," Allie said. "We're still watching her."

Ash tugged Allie on top of her and cradled her ass in both hands. "So what do you want to do differently?"

"Nothing, really." Allie sighed and braced her arms on the bed. "You think I'm obsessing, don't you?"

Ash kissed her. "No, babe, you're a good cop and your instincts are telling you something's off. I say listen to your gut."

"Let me just run a quick status check." Allie rolled away, switched on the bedside lamp, and gripped her cell phone. "Sorry, I won't be long."

She hit the speed dial for Smith and waited out ten rings, the prickly feeling getting sharper with each ring. Smith always answered by the third ring, and when she got voice mail she hung up. She punched in Mitchell's number.

"Mitchell," Dell said instantly.

"What's going on there?"

"I'm still on Bradford, covering the back. Everything appears quiet. Why?"

"I can't raise Smith."

"I just talked to him ten minutes ago. He's due for another check-in in twenty."

"He wouldn't leave his post."

"Maybe his cell isn't working. The reception up here sucks, I have to tell you."

"Maybe, but I don't like it. I'm coming over."

"All right. I'll try Smith again. If I don't get him, I'll notify the sheriff and go check on him."

"I'll be there in three minutes." Allie jumped out of bed and threw on clothes. She hated coincidences.

❖

Mica sat up in bed, rousing Flynn from a light doze.

"What is it?" Flynn asked.

"I don't know, probably nothing. I just thought I heard…" Mica pressed her hand to the center of Flynn's chest. "Stay here. You have your phone?"

"Yes, but—"

"I'll be right back."

Mica, her figure illuminated by the glow of moonlight, jumped out of bed and yanked on sweatpants. She slowly slid open the bedside drawer and removed a long, thin object. The switchblade snapped open like a shard of lightning cleaving the night sky. "Someone's outside."

Flynn followed, grabbed her shirt and pants off the floor, and threw them on. Her cell was in her pants pocket. "I'm calling nine-one-one."

Mica disappeared into the other room, and Flynn's stomach lurched. Mica had lived with the expectation of death so long she was fearless. Flynn went after her, sliding around the corner into a room lit nearly as bright as day by a blood moon. Flynn thumbed the digits on her phone. "Mica?"

The front door swung open and a shadowy figure filled the doorway.

"Flynn, get dow—"

Lightning flared. Thunder cracked. The air burned with the acrid scent of fire and blood. Mica was gone.

"Mica!" Flynn rushed forward, tripped, and went down on her knees. Lightning flashed again, red and hot this time, like a meteor shooting in the dark. Flynn's head rang with the roar of thunder.

A tinny voice said *What is your emergency? What is your emergency? Where is your location? What is…*

Flynn couldn't see Mica. She fumbled for a lamp. If she made herself a target, she didn't care. She needed to see Mica. Shouts came from somewhere close by, then a bright light struck her in the face, making her blink. Mica lay on her back, her lips parted slightly, her eyes calm. Blood trickled in delicate lacey patterns from a dime-sized hole just under her left breast. Not very much blood at all. Why was she so pale, then?

"Flynn," Mica gasped.

Flynn's brain threatened to shut down. Agonizing fear ripped through her. Mica shivered, her eyes starting to close.

"Mica!" Flynn's shout rang hollowly, a solitary note echoing inside a glass chamber.

"I'm sorry," Mica breathed, her voice so faint it was as if she spoke in a dream.

"No. You're fine. You did fine." Flynn saw herself moving like a player on a ghostly stage. Her hand came down over the hole in Mica's chest. Warm, thick crimson liquid seeped between her fingers. Mica looked so calm. So pale. The shouts grew louder, the words a tangle of indecipherable syllables. "Help will be here soon. Baby, you're going to be all right."

"Hurt?" A sliver of blood trickled from the corner of Mica's mouth.

"No. Mica, please. Please. Don't talk. Just rest. You'll be all right."

"Sorry." Mica smiled. "I love you."

"I love you." Flynn choked. Her throat was so tight. "Sweetheart, I love you."

"Flynn," Mica whispered, her lids fluttering.

"Yes, baby, I'm here."

Figures raced by them. A voice yelled *Clear*. All Flynn saw was Mica. Mica was everything.

"Think I need"—Mica's smile faltered and she grasped Flynn's arm—"a priest."

"I'm here," Flynn murmured. "I'm here, baby."

Flynn kept one palm pressed to the hole in Mica's chest where Mica's blood pumped out with each heartbeat, crossed herself, and signed the cross on Mica's forehead. Mica's eyes were all she saw, open and trusting and beautiful. She put her faith in Mica's eyes and prayed.

"Almighty God, look on this your servant, lying in great weakness…"

"EMTs are on their way." Allie's voice.

"…and comfort her with the promise of life everlasting…"

Dave said, "Got no pulse."

"From all evil, from all sin, from all tribulation…"

"Move over." Allie pressed both hands to the center of Mica's chest.

"…by the Coming of the Holy Spirit…"

"We need more help."

"That it may please you to deliver the soul of your servant..."

Reese said, "Bri's bringing Tory."

"...mercifully to pardon all her sins."

"We need her STAT," Dave shouted.

"Our Father, who art..."

"One...two...three..."

"...forgive us our trespasses..."

"Dave? Where are we?" Tory's voice.

"...as we forgive those who trespass against us..."

"She's bleeding out."

"...lead us not into temptation..."

"We need blood."

"...deliver us from evil..."

"I'm O-neg. Take mine."

"...for Thine is the Kingdom, and the Power..."

"I've never done a battlefield transfusion."

"...and the Glory, forever and ever..."

"I have."

"Amen." Flynn closed her eyes and held Mica's hand to her lips. *Please, baby. Please don't leave me.*

CHAPTER THIRTY-TWO

The chapel held four wooden pews on either side of a narrow central aisle. A plain wooden cross hung on the wall behind the unadorned altar. The beige walls were muted in the dim glow of the recessed lights in the arched ceiling.

Flynn knelt alone at the rail. Her solitude enclosed her so deeply, she was only distantly aware of the passage of time. She didn't turn when she sensed a presence beside her.

"It's Allie. I'll go if you want."

"No." Flynn crossed herself and rose slowly. Her body seemed foreign, a hollow shell that belonged to someone else. She sat in the first pew. "You're welcome to stay as long as you like."

"I didn't want to disturb you," Allie said, sitting next to Flynn, "but I wasn't sure if you should be alone."

Flynn smiled softly, wondering if she would ever not be alone again. "I'm glad you came. I didn't have a chance to thank you."

Allie's eyes welled with tears. "God, Flynn, don't. If I could have done more…"

"You gave her your blood. That's a tremendous gift."

"I wish Tory had let me give another—"

Flynn took Allie's hand. "You gave enough. Thank you."

"Are you all right?" Allie laughed shakily. "Stupid question. Of course you aren't. Did you eat?"

"No. I'm not hungry." Flynn looked around for a window. "Is it morning?"

"Not yet. Can I do anything? I feel so useless."

"Did you get him? Everything happened so fast and then…I never thought about him."

"We got him."

"Is he alive?" She probably ought to be jubilant at the news, but she was too cold and numb to feel anything at all.

"He didn't put up much of a fight once he saw he was outgunned. We apprehended him right outside Mica's building." Allie sounded almost apologetic.

"Just a minute too late."

"Yes," Allie said. "I'm so sorry."

Flynn squeezed Allie's hand. "I didn't mean it that way. You're not responsible. He is—do you know his name?"

"Carmen Alvarez. According to Dell, he's one of La Mara's top lieutenants and Hector's right hand. Hector is—"

"I know who he is. He's the man Mica was with."

"No," Allie said. "He's the man Mia Gonzales was with. Mica has only ever been with you."

"You're right. I...she—" Flynn's throat tightened and her eyes burned. She hadn't thought there were any tears left. "Sorry. I... sorry."

"It's okay." Allie slid her arm around Flynn's shoulders and pulled her close. "Sometimes tears are all we have."

❖

"I thought you might want some coffee," Dell said, handing Flynn a paper cup from the vending machine.

"Thanks." Steam rose from the surface of the muddy-looking liquid, but Flynn's fingers were cold.

Dell dropped into one of the nearby plastic chairs. "I let you down. I let Mia—sorry, Mica down. I know sorry doesn't help, but I am."

"He was coming, him or someone else, whether you were here or not." Flynn put the coffee aside. "I'd like you to do something for me."

"Anything, if I can do it, it's yours."

"Make this worth it. Make him tell you the things you need to know to put an end to this, so there is never another Mica."

"My lieutenant's making arrangements with the sheriff for transport right now. With what we have on him, he's not getting out and he knows it. He'll talk to save his own skin."

"That's enough, then."

"No, it isn't. You asked me if I could keep her safe." Dell's voice was rough with sleeplessness and remorse. "I told you I could, and I let him get by us. I let him get to her."

"You know," Flynn said, replaying those moments for the hundredth, for the thousandth, time, "another thirty seconds—a minute, and you might have gotten him before he got to her." Flynn kept wondering if she'd reached out, if she'd pulled Mica back down onto the bed, if she'd kept her from going into the other room—maybe she could have kept her safe. "I was there and I didn't stop her from meeting him head-on. Mica never expected to be rescued. Not by you, not by me. She wouldn't let anyone fight for her."

"Brave of her," Dell said.

"Yes, brave. And selfless."

"Maybe if she'd waited, I would've got there in time," Dell said, "but maybe he would've gotten both of you. She had to have been thinking about that."

"Oh, I know she was." Flynn studied her hands. She'd washed them, many times, but the blood was still just as visible to her as if it still covered them. Mica's blood. "It's hard, isn't it, when the ones we love won't let us protect them."

"It's hell," Dell said.

❖

Flynn's eyes flew open at a touch on her shoulder. "Mica?"

"It's Tory, Flynn." Tory leaned down, her eyes liquid with tenderness. "It's time."

Flynn pushed to her feet, her body stiff and protesting. Her chest ached, her head throbbed with sleeplessness and pain. She followed Tory through the eerily silent halls, where only the drone of the machines broke the stillness. Outside the windows, the sky was black and starless. Shadows followed them as they walked.

"Is there anything I can do?" Tory asked.

Flynn shook her head. "I never had a chance to thank you for what you did."

"I can't take very much credit for it," Tory said. "Allie took all the risk, and without Reese's directions, I doubt I would have been able to do it. We all did it."

"Mica told me once that she didn't belong anywhere," Flynn said. "She was wrong."

Tory gently took Flynn's hand. "Yes, she was."

CHAPTER THIRTY-THREE

The cubicle was dark, lit only by the glowing faces of the monitors and a single flat ceiling light set to low. The sheets were very, very white. Mica's dark hair stood out against the covers like cinders on snow. Her eyes were closed, her arms extended, palms up by her sides. Tubes ran from her arms, from underneath the sheets, from the corner of her mouth. Not even the barest flicker of movement rippled beneath her alabaster lids. She wasn't asleep, she wasn't dreaming. Her body, her mind, perhaps her spirit, had drawn in on itself, a protective reflex as she gathered her strength for the ultimate battle.

"I can get you a chair," the nurse said.

"No, thank you," Flynn said. "I'll be fine."

"You can stay as long as you like."

Flynn nodded and took Mica's hand. Her fingers were cool, dry, motionless. Flynn knelt, and prayed for clarity.

❖

She'd only ever been swimming once, when she was five, and her mother and her mother's then-boyfriend took her and her brother and her baby sister to the beach in Atlantic City. The sand was too hot and too stony and hurt her feet. The ocean was so big, the waves so high, she'd been afraid to go into the water. Her mother's boyfriend had carried her on his shoulders, and she'd felt safe until he'd swung her down and into the water, laughing, telling her she'd like it. The salty water flooded her nose and her throat. She couldn't breathe, she couldn't see, and the world became a frightening place. She'd reached out for someone to save her and she'd found only more blackness. She couldn't hear, couldn't move her arms and legs, couldn't break free of the crushing weight of the waves. Like now. She reached out for something to hold on to, and warm, strong fingers closed around hers, calming her, anchoring her. She held on tight and the fear swept away with the tide.

❖

Pulse racing, Flynn searched for any sign that Mica was aware. She'd felt Mica's fingers twitch, she was certain of it. Tory had explained that the bullet had lacerated the left pulmonary artery and Mica had nearly exsanguinated. Even the blood Allie had given her right there on the floor of Mica's apartment hadn't been enough to keep her blood pressure in a safe range. The surgery to repair her artery had gone well, the surgeon had said, obviously pleased with himself. The bullet had passed through her body from front to back and, other than that one lethal laceration, had done no significant damage. Now that the tear in the artery was repaired, he had said, she should recover very quickly. If the rest of her recovered, that is. If the blood loss and the hypotension hadn't caused irreversible brain damage. The initial EEG had been inconclusive, according to Tory. There was brain activity, but disorganized and erratic. The abnormal function could have been due to any number of things—the stress, the anesthesia, the shock to her system. Or it might mean that Mica was gone. Flynn should prepare herself for that, Tory had said.

Flynn told them they were wrong. Mica would never give up so easily. Tory had nodded and said from what she knew of Mica, she agreed. Tory had said Mica needed to know Flynn believed in her too.

"I'm here, baby," Flynn said quietly. "You're safe. Just concentrate on getting better. I'll be here when you wake up."

❖

Somewhere in the center of her chest, a fire burned. Every breath scorched her lungs, and she wanted to flee from the pain. She'd been running forever, it seemed. First from the life she seemed destined to inherit, then from Hector, then from the men Hector sent. She was tired of running. So very tired. She didn't fear the water as much as she had when she was small. She could let the cool comfort engulf her, carry her away, put out the fire. If she just let go, stopped fighting. Went under.

Mica struggled against the seductive undertow that pulled her farther and farther from shore. Without fire, there was no heat, without heat, there was no life. She knew how to fight for what she wanted. She knew how to fight for what she needed. She remembered soft lips, strong hands, the protective curve of a warm body holding her, keeping her safe. There was the fire. There was the passion. She held on to her anchor and swam against the currents. Swam toward the flame.

❖

"Mica," Flynn said urgently. "Mica, I'm here, baby. Everything is all right."

Mica's eyelids fluttered. Flynn leaned over and brushed her fingers through Mica's hair. "It's all right. You're in the hospital. You have a breathing tube in and you can't talk. I'm right here, everything is all right."

Mica started to thrash, and all the bells and whistles and alarms started blaring.

"You're in the hospital, Mica," Flynn said steadily, calmly. "You are all right. I promise, I'm right here."

Mica's eyes flew open and her gaze fixed on Flynn. Flynn's breath caught, fearing to hope. Recognition flared in Mica's eyes, and Flynn smiled.

"Hello, baby. Welcome back."

CHAPTER THIRTY-FOUR

Tory, weary from only a few hours' sleep for the past several nights, arrived home from her daily trip to the hospital in Hyannis a little before seven p.m. Her spirits lightened at the sight of Reese's SUV in the drive. She parked and hurried inside. Reese, still in uniform, sprawled on the sofa. Reggie played with Jedi on the floor amidst a mountain of plastic blocks.

"Hi." Tory kissed Reese and curled up next to her.

Reese wrapped an arm around her shoulders. "How are things?"

"No big changes, which is good at this stage. Any news?"

"I talked to Rebecca Frye this afternoon," Reese said. "Alvarez is looking at hard time in a maximum-security federal prison, and he's starting to see the big picture. Hector and the other La Mara leaders are going to view him as a liability, and that does not say good things about his life expectancy."

"I thought one of La Mara's honor badges was to do time without giving anyone up."

"That's true," Reese said, "but that mostly pertains to low-level members who don't know enough to be a threat to the leaders if they talk. If someone like Alvarez, who knows a lot about the organization, cuts a deal to shorten his time or to get moved out of the general prison population, he could take down some important gang members."

"Wouldn't it make the La Mara members uneasy if one of them was arrested and then ended up being killed in prison?"

Reese rubbed Tory's back. "As long as nothing ties Hector or any of La Mara's leaders to the execution, a death in prison is just business as usual. Rival gang members square off against each other all the time. Being shivved in the shower is a routine occurrence."

"So he's got to think cutting a deal now is his best option." Tory edged closer on the sofa and wrapped her arm around Reese's middle. "If he doesn't talk, he'll never be able to prove that he hasn't, and the threat to the organization will be there as long as he's in prison."

"Which is going to be a damn long time," Reese said grimly. "Remember, he shot Mica and put Smith in the hospital."

"I talked to the neurosurgeons today," Tory said. "Smith's edema is subsiding and they don't think there'll be any need for surgery. He may be out of work for a while, but he's going to be fine."

"That's one message I'll be happy to take to his wife," Reese said.

"Do you think they'll be able to shut Hector down?" Tory unbuttoned the middle button on Reese's shirt and slid her hand inside.

"Put his crew out of business completely? Doubtful. But while the local gang is reorganizing and the leadership is chaotic, Rebecca's team will have a better chance of putting someone undercover."

"It really is a long-term plan, isn't it?"

Reese covered Tory's hand and pressed Tory's fingers to her abdomen. "It's a lot like a war. You know the endgame, but not how long it will take to get there or how many battles you have to wage before the last one."

"What about Mica?"

"That's going to be up to her," Reese said. "There are not going to be any easy choices, if and when she's ready to make them."

"She's showing signs of improvement. Her scans are clear. She's got youth on her side."

"Good," Reese said. "She deserves a shot at freedom."

"How about you, Sheriff? Are you going to be able to take a break soon? You've been in the office or filling in on patrol for the better part of a week."

"Soon. I've recruited some officers from up-Cape for temporary duty."

"Good," Tory said, tracing the curve of Reese's ribs with her fingertips. "You'd better start storing up on sleep as soon as you can."

Reese's eyes darkened and she tilted Tory's chin with a finger beneath her jaw. "And why would that be?"

"Because I'm feeling decidedly pink these days."

Reese grinned. "Are you sure?"

Tory nodded. "I told you it was a home run."

"I love you." Reese stroked Tory's abdomen and kissed her. "Both."

Tory relaxed against her, knowing whatever was coming, she'd have Reese to lean on and a lifetime to celebrate.

❖

The face bending over her was familiar—wheat-blond hair, sharp cheekbones, strong jaw. Compassion in the deep blue eyes. Something was missing, something she needed. Mica blinked, tried to sit up, and someone said, "Everything is all right. You're going to be fine."

The voice was wrong. She thrashed, trying to sit up.

"Mica, baby, it's okay."

Mica turned her head and the swirling anxiety in the center of her chest subsided. This face she knew, deep down inside. These blue eyes held love and tenderness. The voice was soothing and reassuring. She swallowed, her throat burning. "Flynn?"

She knew this smile too, playful and sure.

"Hi." Flynn folded Mica's hand between hers and kissed each knuckle. "I love you."

"I love you too." Mica slowly swiveled her head until the other face came into focus. Flynn, but not. "Who are you?"

"I'm Matthew, Flynn's brother. Hello."

He was handsome, but not as handsome as Flynn. The collar around his throat was different too, but she had no trouble envisioning that on Flynn. "Thanks for coming."

"I'm happy to," he said.

She hadn't thanked him for herself, but he probably knew that. If he was anything like Flynn, he understood the meaning behind the words. She wasn't sure of all that had happened, but she knew where she was, and what Carmen had done. Flynn would have needed someone.

"Did he hurt you?"Mica said, returning her gaze to Flynn.

"No." Flynn sounded rusty and worn. "Just you. You surprised him and after he…shot you, he took off."

Mica swallowed. The nightmare wasn't over. "He got away?"

"Oh no," Flynn said quickly, and Mica's dread evaporated. "They got him."

"Dead?"

"No, arrested."

That might be better. Mica felt around her body—tape on her

chest, plastic tubes sticking out of her side and her arm and her leg. Breathing hurt and her throat was raw. "How long have I been here?"

"Almost three days," Flynn said. "You had surgery. They took the breathing tube out last night, and you've been sleeping on and off since then."

"How about you?"

Flynn stroked Mica's hair. "I'm just fine, now."

"You should go home, rest."

"I will. In a little while."

Mica squeezed Flynn's hand. "Remember, you're not supposed to lie."

Flynn grinned. "*A little while* is open to interpretation, so technically, I'm not lying."

On the other side of the bed, Matthew laughed. "I hope to talk to you again, Mica, when you're feeling better." He waved to Flynn. "Good luck with the new position."

Mica's stomach dropped. "What new position?"

"My brother spoke to the bishop. The church in town needs an assistant priest. The job's mine if I want it. I'd still keep my EMT post too."

"Do you want to?"

Flynn rubbed her throat. "Yes, I do."

"And do you get to wear that sexy collar?"

Flynn laughed. "Yes."

"Then I'm all for it." Mica loved the shy excitement in Flynn's face. Heat raced along her spine and her mind wandered to an image of lying with Flynn, limbs entangled and supple flesh beneath her palms. She wanted her, in her heart and in her body. "When can I get out of here?"

Flynn laughed quietly and stroked her arm. "A few days. A week. You had a lot of surgery. The doctors tell me you're going to be fine. A hundred percent."

"Good—can I...can I stay with you a while?"

"A while? How about forever?" Flynn kissed her hand. "Remember the *I love you* part? That means we're together, all the way...if you want."

Mica's breath stopped. A swell of expectation, so foreign, so wonderful, flooded her. "What's happening with Carmen?"

"Last I heard, he's ninety-plus certain to testify against Hector. That will put Hector and the others away. Dell—Detective Mitchell—

feels pretty certain once they start arresting the leaders, getting some of the other members to turn informant will be easier. You're going to break that gang, Mica."

"Until then," Mica said, "I might not be so safe to be around."

"I don't want us to put our life on hold waiting for anything."

"I don't want you hurt," Mica whispered.

"I won't be." Flynn leaned down and kissed her. "I just need you."

"I need you too," Mica whispered. "But what if—"

"Baby," Flynn murmured, "we can figure it out when you're feeling a little stronger. Sheriff Conlon—Reese—has some ideas about how to protect you."

"Like what?"

"No one knows the name you've been using here," Flynn said slowly. "As far as Carmen, or Hector, knows, Mia Gonzales is dead."

Mica's chest tightened and she winced.

"What is it?" Flynn asked. "Does something hurt?"

Mica shook her head. "I can get behind letting everyone think I'm dead, even my family—at least for now. They'll be safer if Hector thinks I'm dead. But I'm not going into that program."

Flynn's brows drew down. "What program? You mean witness protection?"

"No way," Mica said. She wasn't leaving, not unless Flynn wanted her to. Flynn was all that mattered.

Flynn rubbed Mica's fingers against her cheek. "Damn right you're not going into witness protection. You're not going anywhere at all. You're staying here with me, where you belong."

The tightness in Mica's chest eased. Flynn wanted her. Flynn loved her, and she loved Flynn. She did belong somewhere, finally. "If you're here, that's where I belong."

About the Author

Radclyffe has written over thirty-five romance and romantic intrigue novels, dozens of short stories, and, writing as L.L. Raand, has authored a paranormal romance series, The Midnight Hunters.

She is an eight-time Lambda Literary Award finalist in romance, mystery, and erotica—winning in both romance (*Distant Shores, Silent Thunder*) and erotica (*Erotic Interludes 2: Stolen Moments* edited with Stacia Seaman and *In Deep Waters 2: Cruising the Strip* written with Karin Kallmaker). A member of the Saints and Sinners Literary Hall of Fame, she is also a 2010 RWA/FF&P Prism award winner for *Secrets in the Stone*. Her 2010 titles were finalists for the Benjamin Franklin award (*Desire by Starlight*), the ForeWord Review Book of the Year award (*Trauma Alert* and writing as LL Raand, *The Midnight Hunt*), and the RWA Passionate Plume award (*The Midnight Hunt*). She is also the president of Bold Strokes Books, one of the world's largest independent LGBT publishing companies.

Coming in March 2012: NIGHT HUNT,
Book Three in L.L. Raand's Midnight Hunters series.

Lara, a dominant wolf Were and one of the elite centuri guards, has only one mission—to protect the wolf Alpha, Sylvan Mir. When Lara makes the ultimate sacrifice to save Sylvan, a Vampire detective saves her life only to change it forever in ways no one can anticipate.

Sylvan, driven by primal instincts to protect her pregnant mate, grows more powerful, and more deadly, than any Alpha Were in centuries. While Sylvan rallies her allies, Vampire and human, to fight extremists, radical groups, and members of their own Praetern coalition in a war to preserve the autonomy of all Praetern species, Lara fights a private battle with her own dark urges—a battle which, if lost, will make her a more dangerous adversary than any Sylvan has ever faced.

Books Available From Bold Strokes Books

Sheltering Dunes by Radclyffe. The seventh in the award-winning Provincetown Tales. The pasts, presents, and futures of three women collide in a single moment that will alter all their lives forever. (978-1-60282-573-4)

Holy Rollers by Rob Byrnes. Partners in life and crime Grant Lambert and Chase LaMarca assemble a team of gay and lesbian criminals to steal millions from a right-wing mega-church, but the gang's plans are complicated by an "ex-gay" conference, the FBI, and a corrupt reverend with his own plans for the cash. (978-1-60282-578-9)

History's Passion: Stories of Sex Before Stonewall, edited by Richard Labonté. Four acclaimed erotic authors re-imagine the past…Welcome to the hidden queer history of men loving men not so very long—and centuries—ago. (978-1-60282-576-5)

Lucky Loser by Yolanda Wallace. Top tennis pros Sinjin Smythe and Laure Fortescue reach Wimbledon desperate to claim tennis's crown jewel, but will their feelings for each other get in the way? (978-1-60282-575-8)

Mystery of The Tempest: A Fisher Key Adventure by Sam Cameron. Twin brothers Denny and Steven Anderson love helping people and fighting crime alongside their sheriff dad on sun-drenched Fisher Key, Florida, but Denny doesn't dare tell anyone he's gay, and Steven has secrets of his own to keep. (978-1-60282-579-6)

Better Off Red: Vampire Sorority Sisters Book 1 by Rebekah Weatherspoon. Every sorority has its secrets, and college freshman Ginger Carmichael soon discovers that her pledge is more than a bond of sisterhood—it's a lifelong pact to serve six bloodthirsty demons with a lot more than nutritional needs. (978-1-60282-574-1)

Detours by Jeffrey Ricker. Joel Patterson is heading to Maine for his mother's funeral, and his high school friend Lincoln has invited himself along on the ride—and into Joel's bed—but when the ghost of Joel's mother joins the trip, the route is likely to be anything but straight. (978-1-60282-577-2)

Three Days by L.T. Marie. In a town like Vegas where anything can happen, Shawn and Dakota find that the stakes are love at all costs, and it's a gamble neither can afford to lose. (978-1-60282-569-7)

Swimming to Chicago by David-Matthew Barnes. As the lives of the adults around them unravel, high school students Alex and Robby form an unbreakable bond, vowing to do anything to stay together—even if it means leaving everything behind. (978-1-60282-572-7)

Hostage Moon by AJ Quinn. Hunter Roswell thought she had left her past behind, until a serial killer begins stalking her. Can FBI profiler Sara Wilder help her find her connection to the killer before he strikes on blood moon? (978-1-60282-568-0)

Erotica Exotica: Tales of Magic, Sex, and the Supernatural, edited by Richard Labonté. Today's top gay erotica authors offer sexual thrills and perverse arousal, spooky chills, and magical orgasms in these stories exploring arcane mystery, supernatural seduction, and sex that haunts in a manner both weird and wondrous. (978-1-60282-570-3)

Blue by Russ Gregory. Matt and Thatcher find themselves in the crosshairs of a psychotic killer stalking gay men in the streets of Austin, and only a 103-year-old nursing home resident holds the key to solving the murders—but can she give up her secrets in time to save them? (978-1-60282-571-0)

Balance of Forces: Toujours Ici by Ali Vali. Immortal Kendal Richoux's life began during the reign of Egypt's only female pharaoh, and history has taught her the dangers of getting too close to anyone who hasn't harnessed the power of time, but as she prepares for the most important battle of her long life, can she resist her attraction to Piper Marmande? (978-1-60282-567-3)

Wings: Subversive Gay Angel Erotica, edited by Todd Gregory. A collection of powerfully written tales of passion and desire centered on the aching beauty of angels. (978-1-60282-565-9)

Contemporary Gay Romances by Felice Picano. This collection of short fiction from legendary novelist and memoirist Felice Picano are as different from any standard "romances" as you can get, but they will linger in the mind and memory. (978-1-60282-639-7)

Pirate's Fortune: Supreme Constellations Book Four by Gun Brooke. Set against the backdrop of war, captured mercenary Weiss Kyakh is persuaded to work undercover with bio-android Madisyn Pimm, which foils her plans to escape, but kindles unexpected love. (978-1-60282-563-5)

Sex and Skateboards by Ashley Bartlett. Sex and skateboards and surfing on the California coast. What more could anyone want? Alden McKenna thinks that's all she needs, until she meets Weston Duvall. (978-1-60282-562-8)

Waiting in the Wings by Melissa Brayden. Jenna has spent her whole life training for the stage, but the one thing she didn't prepare for was Adrienne. Is she ready to sacrifice what she's worked so hard for in exchange for a shot at something much deeper? (978-1-60282-561-1)

Suite Nineteen by Mel Bossa. Psychic Ben Lebeau moves into Shilts Manor, where he meets seductive Lennox Van Kemp and his clan of Métis—guardians of a spiritual conspiracy dating back to Christ. But are Ben's psychic abilities strong enough to save him? (978-1-60282-564-2)

Speaking Out: LGBTQ Youth Stand Up, edited by Steve Berman. Inspiring stories written for and about LGBTQ teens of overcoming adversity (against intolerance and homophobia) and experiencing life after "coming out." (978-1-60282-566-6)

Forbidden Passions by MJ Williamz. Passion burns hotter when it's forbidden, and the fire between Katie Prentiss and Corrine Staples in antebellum Louisiana is raging out of control. (978-1-60282-641-0)

Harmony by Karis Walsh. When Brook Stanton meets a beautiful musician who threatens the security of her conventional, predetermined future, will she take a chance on finding the harmony only love creates? (978-1-60282-237-5)

nightrise by Nell Stark and Trinity Tam. In the third book in the everafter series, when Valentine Darrow loses her soul, Alexa must cross continents to find a way to save her. (978-1-60282-238-2)

Men of the Mean Streets, edited by Greg Herren and J.M. Redmann. Dark tales of amorality and criminality by some of the top authors of gay mysteries. (978-1-60282-240-5)

Women of the Mean Streets, edited by J.M. Redmann and Greg Herren. Murder, mayhem, sex, and danger—these are the stories of the women who dare to tackle the mean streets. (978-1-60282-241-2)

Firestorm by Radclyffe. Firefighter paramedic Mallory "Ice" James isn't happy when the undisciplined Jac Russo joins her command, but lust isn't something either can control—and they soon discover ice burns as fiercely as flame. (978-1-60282-232-0)

The Best Defense by Carsen Taite. When socialite Aimee Howard hires former homicide detective Skye Keaton to find her missing niece, she vows not to mix business with pleasure, but she soon finds Skye hard to resist. (978-1-60282-233-7)

After the Fall by Robin Summers. When the plague destroys most of humanity, Taylor Stone thinks there's nothing left to live for, until she meets Kate, a woman who makes her realize love is still alive and makes her dream of a future she thought was no longer possible. (978-1-60282-234-4)

Accidents Never Happen by David-Matthew Barnes. From the moment Albert and Joey meet by chance beneath a train track on a street in Chicago, a domino effect is triggered, setting off a chain reaction of murder and tragedy. (978-1-60282-235-1)

In Plain View, edited by Shane Allison. Best-selling gay erotica authors create the stories of sex and desire modern readers crave. (978-1-60282-236-8)